THE WATCHER

NETTA NEWBOUND

Junction Publishing

Junction Publishing

United Kingdom - New Zealand

Junctionpublishing@outlook.com

www.junction-publishing.com

Publisher's Note: This is a work of fiction. Names, characters, places, and incidents are a product of the author's imagination. Locales and public names are sometimes used for atmospheric purposes. Any resemblance to actual people, living or dead, or to businesses, companies, events, institutions, or locales is completely coincidental.

Ordering Information:

Quantity sales. Special discounts are available on quantity purchases by corporations, associations, and others. For details, contact the "Special Sales Department" at the email address above.

The Watcher/Netta Newbound -- 2nd ed.

To Paul - my very own stalker.

PROLOGUE

Germany - 17 years ago

Donald stepped out of the darkness, and tensed, as his eyes darted across the crowd of drunken revellers. It took a moment for him to spot his target. When he did, he breathed deeply, and struggled to calm his pulse.

Pulling himself together, he forced himself forward, keeping the woman's bright red jacket in his sights at all times. All his senses were on high alert, yet, on the surface, he fought to appear nonchalant.

He stood behind her in the queue leading to the nightclub, and inhaled her scent. Fruity conditioner was the overriding smell coming from her luscious red curls, but he'd watched her dab *Dune*, her favourite Christian Dior perfume, behind her ears, before she left the bathroom less than an hour ago.

The line shuffled forward, and he bumped into her.

"I beg your pardon." He smiled, running his fingers through his short, prematurely grey hair.

Clair nodded, but several people spluttered with laughter, followed by a tirade of German piss-taking.

Donald gritted his teeth, as the fingers on his other hand

found, gripped, and slowly lifted the phone from Clair's jacket pocket.

Once inside the club, he kept his distance, watching as Clair spotted her friend at the bar. They hugged and squealed at each other for several minutes. He could pick out the odd word here and there, but he hadn't been interested in learning the lingo—he never intended being in the country this long.

They took a seat, and he slid into the vacant booth backing onto theirs, and waited.

Within moments, more squealing followed the start of a popular song, and the girls dashed onto the dance floor.

Donald didn't waste any time. He opened the small paper square, leaned over the table, and slipped the crushed sleeping tablet into Clair's glass. Then, once he was sure he hadn't been spotted, he returned to his seat to begin his wait.

An hour later, Clair made a move towards the exit. Her voice couldn't be heard above the music, so she hand-signalled she would call her extremely irritated friend soon.

Donald scooted around her, and left the building first. He was already leaning against the outer wall by the time Clair appeared, looking flustered, as she rummaged in her jacket pocket.

"Are you okay?" he asked, knowing she could speak good English.

"Somebody stole my phone."

"Bloody scoundrels. Do you want one of these?" He offered her a pack of the cigarettes he knew she'd been struggling to give up all week.

She hesitated, before taking one.

He lit a match, and, after lighting his own cigarette, he leaned in to light hers.

"Thank you."

"You're welcome. I'm sorry I don't have a phone to lend you. I left it at home, otherwise my sister would be calling me every two minutes."

"Your sister?" A smirk played at the corners of her mouth.

Donald shrugged. "My wife died recently. I'm staying with my sister, but she keeps thinking I'm going to top myself."

"Top yourself?"

"You know?" He made a shape of a gun with his fingers, and popped it into his mouth. "Pow! Top myself."

"Ah, kill yourself?"

He smiled sadly. "But, I won't."

"How did your wife die?"

"Cancer."

Clair nodded. "My mother also."

"That's shit. Hey, can I give you a lift home? My heart isn't in this place, after all."

"I should call my man. He will come for me."

Donald shrugged one shoulder, and smiled. "You don't have a phone, remember?"

She grinned, and nodded.

"No skin off my nose. I can have you home in ten minutes."

"You do not know my address." She leaned against the wall, and her beautiful green eyes appeared heavy.

Donald could've kicked himself. "Can't be too far, if your man was going to come over."

"True. Okay." She nodded. "I will accept. Thank you."

They walked through the passageway to the backstreet.

He'd parked his scruffy white van less than a five minutes' walk away, but Clair couldn't make the last few steps, without his support.

"That drink has affected my legs." She chuckled.

He opened the passenger door of the van, and carefully placed her inside, before running around to the driver's seat.

He turned the key, and drove out of town.

Clair was snoring softly, and he smiled, thrilled with himself for pulling it off. He knew his meek and mild appearance fooled everyone. It always had, but playing the cancer card was a stroke of genius.

Her phone rang from his pocket.

Startled, he reached for it, but he wasn't fast enough.

Clair sat upright, and stared at him questioningly.

He glanced at her, and then, back at the road ahead, his thoughts in a whirl.

"Let me out!" she said, her voice high-pitched.

"Shh, Clair. Calm down."

"Let me out. Fucking let me out," she screamed.

With one fluid movement, Donald smashed his fist into the side of her head. "Less of the language," he growled, as the woman slumped unconscious into her seat.

CHAPTER 1

"You need to tell your mother to make more stock," Denise said from the market stall beside Hannah's. "You're selling out earlier and earlier every week."

Hannah nodded, smiling good-naturedly. "You can tell her yourself next week. I won't be here."

"Going anywhere nice?"

"I've been called to a meeting in Manchester on Friday, and decided to make a weekend of it. To tell the truth, I'm thinking of checking if there are any job vacancies while I'm there."

Denise feigned shock, her jaw dropping exaggeratedly. She threw a handful of potatoes into the basket she was refilling. "What do you want to go there for? Aren't you happy where you are?"

Hannah ran a hand through her long, auburn curls, and shrugged. "I'm happy. But, you know what it's like around here; nothing much happens from one week to the next. I fancy a change—a little excitement."

"Your mother will be lost without you."

"She'll be fine. But, I haven't told her yet, so if you don't mind…?"

Using her fingers, Denise pretended to zip her lips, turn the lock, and throw away the key.

"Don't tell me you've sold out already?" The booming voice of her father came from behind Hannah.

She twirled around, delighted to see him. Although she still lived at home, she worked long hours, and didn't get to see him very often. Hannah worked the stall every second Saturday morning to give her mother a break, but her dad was always out tending the land, fixing something or other, by the time she got out of bed.

"I'm afraid so, Daddy. They were queuing up before I arrived this morning."

Her mother, Agnes, had a regular stall at several local farmers' markets around Shropshire, selling a selection of homemade jams, chutneys, biscuits, cakes, and a few organic vegetables. The produce was grown and made on their property, which comprised of five acres just outside of Bishop's Castle. For years, Hannah helped her mother after school, and at weekends, she would design flyers, and walk around the markets handing them out. Her mother was very proud of her little marketing helper.

"I knew it—taken long enough, mind you." Her dad beamed. "But, I knew once word got out about your mother's curried potato chutney, she'd make her millions."

"Got a few jars to sell before she makes that much, Daddy." She gasped, and held her hand to her mouth. "Oh, no! Your chutney!"

"Hannah—? Are you trying to tell me you didn't save me a jar?"

A smile peeked out from behind her hand. "You know I'd never forget you?" She bent, and pulled out a large glass jar from under the stall. It was filled with mustard-coloured chutney, and proudly displayed her mother's green and white *Little Shamrock Preserves* emblem.

"I knew you were teasing me—I don't go a day without having this stuff on my sandwiches."

"I don't know why you don't ask Mammy to put a jar aside, after she's made it."

"What? And break with tradition? I've always said this is the food of Mother Nature—made by an angel, and delivered by my own little cherub."

"Things change." Hannah sighed, and glanced at Denise, who had begun packing up her remaining produce.

Denise raised her eyebrows, and, with tight lips, she shook her head slowly to confirm she'd heard every word.

"Your brother's arrived at the house. I've been sent to hurry you up. You know what your mammy gets like. She wants everything perfect."

"Everything's always perfect, Daddy."

"I know that, you know that, but your mammy...? Well... best we get a move on. That's all I'll say."

"What's Shaun here for, anyway? Seems a long way to travel, with two little kids, for just one day."

He shrugged. "I don't know. They left at the crack of dawn, and drove almost six hours straight. Shaun looked dead on his feet when he dragged himself from the car."

"Didn't Miranda share the drive?"

He shook his head, taking a deep breath of disapproval.

Shaun lived on the far side of London, with his snooty wife, Miranda, and their beautiful children, two-year-old Chloe and six-month-old Sebastian. None of them understood his choice of wife. They found her uppity, and could tell she thought they were beneath her, especially her parents-in-law, with their lovely Irish lilt. But, Shaun loved her, and they had no choice but to welcome her into their family with open arms.

It stuck in their daddy's craw why he'd moved so far away. He didn't understand the appeal of living in the city, and he'd given his son a wonderful life, as far as he was concerned.

Shaun had spent his childhood fishing and catching rabbits. He'd helped with all the manual jobs on the property after school and weekends, and when he was old enough, their daddy taught him all about the workings of machinery, and got his son started as an apprentice mechanic in the company's small plant service department when Shaun turned fifteen.

He broke their daddy's heart when he left, but Hannah understood her brother's need to spread his wings. She'd been putting off her own test flight for a while now.

Hannah left high school at eighteen, having gained a diploma with honours. Time spent on the school paper served her well, and she soon began working at the *Daily Post*, the local newspaper, assisting in the advertising and marketing department.

She'd worked hard in her eight years there. It was an area-wide newspaper which relied mostly on advertising revenue to keep afloat. AdCor, the *Post*'s parent company, was based in Manchester. It had always been part of Hannah's plan to work toward a promotion, and head off to corporate office, one day. She loved country life, but deeply longed for some excitement.

After arriving home, Hannah unloaded her mother's van, and stacked the empty trays in the garage, before following the sound of a child's laughter through to the large family kitchen.

"Here she is," Shaun said, clambering to his feet, much to the outrage of the little madam in his arms. He kissed Hannah on the forehead. "So, what's new, sis?"

Shaun put Chloe on the floor, and Hannah crouched down to speak to her beautiful niece.

"Hello, cutie. You've grown!"

Chloe's eyebrows knitted together, and she scowled, her shoulder turned toward Hannah.

Affronted, Hannah stood upright, shaking her head at her brother.

Shaun barked out a laugh, and ruffled the child's golden-brown curls. "Hey, squirt. Don't you remember Auntie Hannah?"

Chloe ran from the room, calling for her mother.

"Where *is* Miranda?"

"She's feeding Sebby in the bedroom."

"Hasn't she got used to breastfeeding in public by now?"

"Don't start sniping already. I need you onside this weekend."

"Why? What's going on?" she said.

"I've got a new job."

"Why do I sense a *but* coming on?"

"It's in Ireland."

CHAPTER 2

"You've got to be kidding me!" Hannah hissed.

"Shhh!" He nodded at the door.

"What're you two fighting about already?" their mother said, suddenly behind them at the kitchen door.

Hannah glared at her brother. "Oh, nothing, Mammy." She turned to kiss her mother's cheek. "Shaun was trying to wind me up, as usual."

"Can we all be on our best behaviour until *after* dinner, at least?"

"Mammy tells me you struck gold with that tip-off I gave you," Shaun said.

He'd called her a few weeks ago to tell her about a large satellite television and mail order company planned to set up in the new business park built near Market Drayton.

Market Drayton was in a prime location, and had good transport links. It was ideal for the national company's expansion plans.

The European Distribution Director happened to be a close friend of Shaun's, and had told him, after several beers, about the intended move.

Hannah nodded. "Yes. Sorry, I meant to call you back, but it's been hectic at work ever since."

"Tell me all about it."

"Well, I did what you suggested," she said. "And within the week, I'd managed to arrange a meeting with the head of advertising and marketing, David Ludlum."

"Nice."

"I didn't know if I could pull it off. I had only two weeks to prepare the proposal, before pitching it to him. In fact, I almost handed it over to Karl Monroe at the last minute."

"I would've boxed your ears, if you'd done that."

"I know. That's the only reason I didn't."

"She didn't even go to bed the night before her appointment," their mother said, shaking her head.

"So, you got the contract?" Shaun rolled his eyes at their mother's comments.

Hannah nodded, unable to stop the grin spreading across her face. "David Ludlum said he was so impressed with my presentation he agreed to give the *Daily Post*, and its subsidiaries, the total advertising contract. That includes the regional newspaper ads, as well as all the poster and magazine ads for the next three years."

Miranda came into the room, with the baby on her hip, and Chloe hugging her leg. "Hi, Hannah." She smiled.

Hannah jumped to her feet, and held her arms out for the cute, bald child. "Where's his hair?"

Miranda laughed. "He *has* got hair—it's just very fine and fair."

"Hannah was just telling me about the new contract she won. Carry on, sis."

"Hold your horses, bossy britches." Hannah hugged the baby, and kissed his pudgy cheek, before handing him back to his mother.

Miranda chuckled, seeming much happier than she had been all the other times they'd met.

Hannah sat back on the dining chair. "Well, old Mr Turnbull, my department manager, almost keeled over when I got back to the office. He couldn't believe his eyes when I handed him the estimated £1.9 million contract, which would span three years!"

"Oww!" Shaun jumped from his chair, and slam-dunked thin air. "Way to go, sis!"

Miranda shook her head in amazement. "Well done, Hannah."

"Thank you." She smiled.

"Tell them the rest, sweetheart," their mother said, her eyes glowing with pride.

"Well, this single contract has more than doubled the department's current annual turnover, and I've only been called to head office for a meeting with Maxwell Myers, the CEO, on Friday."

"Ka-ching!" Shaun high-fived his sister. "You'll be able to name your price I imagine. Who would've thought it? My sister— a bloody superstar."

It wasn't until they'd finished dinner and cleared the dishes away that Shaun dropped his bombshell.

The silence was deafening, and, after an awkward few minutes, Miranda jumped to her feet, saying something about getting the children ready for bed.

Neither of her parents said anything, so, in the end, Hannah felt she had no choice but to help her sibling out.

"Oh, you lucky thing. I've always wanted to visit Ireland after all the lovely stories Mammy and Daddy have told us over the years."

"But, he's not just going for a visit, Hannah," their dad finally said. "He's going there indefinitely."

Their mother removed a hairgrip from the back of her head, and refastened a tendril of red hair that had sprung loose. Then, she picked up a couple of dirty dishes left behind from the kids' dessert, and placed the bowls in the sink, before excusing herself, and heading upstairs.

"I'm sorry, Dad, but it's too good an opportunity to turn down. It's not as if we're going away forever!"

"I just don't understand why you'd want to go back at all. We brought you here for a better life, and now, you plan on taking our grandchildren away. Who knows how long you'll stay for? If you settle down, we may never see you again!"

"That's preposterous, Dad. It's a couple of hours max on a plane. You could even come for a visit."

"If I'd wanted to go back there for a visit, don't you think I'd have done it by now?"

Shaun shook his head impatiently. "Whatever. We'll be back before Chloe starts school, anyway. We want her to have an English education."

"I'll bet that wasn't you who said that!" their dad spat.

"And what's that supposed to mean?" Shaun said defensively.

"Well, seeing as you ask—we all know Miranda thinks we're beneath her. I'm surprised she's agreed to go at all, because one thing I *can* say about Ireland is it's full of us Irish!"

Hannah sat dumbstruck. She'd never witnessed such a heated discussion between her family members before.

"Miranda doesn't have a problem with you being Irish." Shaun got to his feet, and roughly shoved the chair back underneath the table. "She has a problem with the way you treat her. It's clear as day you blame her for me moving to the city." With that, he stormed from the room.

CHAPTER 3

Max Myers made a habit of keeping his ear to the ground when it came to company gossip, news, and announcements—preferring to promote from within whenever possible. During last month's performance meeting, he'd noticed a spike in the revenue analysis report, and asked the department heads for more information.

That's when he learned about the new contract in Market Drayton, and the role Hannah McLaughlin, a loyal, hardworking employee, had played in securing it.

Max was in no doubt anyone with that sort of initiative, confidence, and foresight deserved a more senior position. After all, she'd scouted out the deal and clinched it, without any help from anyone, and all in her own time. She made the deal purely for the future of the business, with no apparent personal gain.

The very next day, he asked Angela, his PA, to contact Hannah personally, and arrange for her to come for a meeting. He would listen to what she wanted, and ensure her dreams came into fruition. There was no way he wanted to lose this girl.

Hannah felt like a terrified kitten as she walked into the foyer of AdCor's head office. Although she'd worked for the company for eight years, this was the first time she'd been summoned, and, even though she knew she wasn't in any trouble, she couldn't calm her jitters.

Angela Beanie, an attractive—if a little bony, thirty-something woman, welcomed her warmly. She wore a black suit, regardless of the ninety-degree heat outside, and a lacy white blouse. Angela explained that, although Maxwell Myers had called the meeting, he had been held up, and would join them as soon as he could.

Hannah relaxed a little. She'd heard all about Max Myers over the years. Nothing bad. In fact, old Mr Turnbull wouldn't have a bad word said about him. But, she knew there had been a lot of speculation regarding his love life. He'd never been married, which was strange in itself for a man in his thirties, but considering his wealth, he was sure to have women throwing themselves at him. She'd seen his photograph, and he was incredibly handsome and, no doubt, an awful bighead. Stephanie Dwight, a journalist for the *Daily Post*, was certain he was gay, but Hannah assumed he'd probably rebuffed her advances when they'd met one time at a conference.

Angela Beanie led her into a lift, and swiped her card before pressing the button to the top floor.

Hannah's mind was racing. She felt like a child on her first trip to Disney World—in awe of everything. Even the lifts were something special. All glass!

"This is the executive floor," Angela said. "We'll go into my office for a chat, while we wait for Mr Myers."

They passed a small reception desk, and the beautiful, exotic-looking receptionist smiled and nodded at Hannah.

Angela led her along a bright hallway filled with artwork and foliage, to a large glass-fronted office and the most breath-taking view of the city.

"Can I get you a hot drink?" Angela asked.

"I'm fine, thank you."

They settled in the ergonomically designed office chairs in a room with an ornate oak desk. Once again, Hannah marvelled at the stunning views of Manchester from another plate-glass window.

"I'll cut to the chase. I'm sure you're itching to know why you've been asked here?"

Hannah bobbed her head, nervously.

"Mr Myers heard about the deal you secured. I must say, Hannah—can I call you Hannah?"

"Of course." She nodded again.

"I must say, that deal was terribly impressive, especially when we discovered you were solely responsible."

Hannah gulped, her mouth suddenly parched.

"At AdCor, we believe in rewarding loyalty, initiative, and hard work. Mr Myers is interested in your aspirations. Have you thought about your future?"

"Kind of. I'd certainly like to work my way into a higher position, but the *Daily Post* doesn't have any vacancies—hasn't for ages."

Angela glanced inside a file on her desk. "Neil Turnbull isn't far off retirement, surely?"

"Oh, I wasn't meaning…" She shook her head. "…Mr Turnbull has been there forever. He has the place running like a well-oiled machine, and has years in him yet."

"If that's the case, where do you see yourself in five years' time?"

Hannah looked down at her fingers. "I don't really know."

"How about coming to work for us here, in the marketing department? I'm sure we can shuffle things around."

Hannah gasped. "Really?"

Angela smiled, nodding.

The desk phone rang.

"Excuse me a minute." She reached to answer it. "Yes, Max?…

That's okay... yes, I've told her about the proposal, and she seems thrilled... No problem, I'll let her know. Safe trip." She hung up, and gave Hannah an apologetic smile. "Mr Myers has been called away. He won't be able to make it, I'm afraid."

"That's okay. I understand."

Angela got to her feet. "I could get somebody to show you around the marketing floor, if you like? But, I've got another meeting booked."

"There's no need. I just need to know when you'd want me to start?"

"I'll get HR onto it right away. With it being a transfer, it will be a lot easier, and you shouldn't need to give a lot of notice where you are. But, it will all be negotiable—let them do their bit first, and somebody will be in touch early next week."

Angela walked her to the small desk beside the lift, and asked the receptionist to arrange for somebody to escort Hannah downstairs. Then, with a smile, she was gone.

Since being medically discharged from the British Army seventeen years ago, diagnosed with post-traumatic stress disorder, Donald Henry had worked as a security officer. That was the official reason, anyway. In reality, the specialists had found him to be totally sadistic and on the edge of murderous tendencies, but to be dishonourably discharged and imprisoned would make it into the European newspapers—something the Army couldn't afford to have happen.

Don hadn't agreed with their findings, however. He'd made it this far without attacking or murdering anybody. He'd just enjoyed being a soldier a bit too much.

During his fifteen-year stint, he'd discovered there were two types of ex-combatants. Those who did what they were asked for the period they were contracted, out of a sense of duty, and those full of anger and hate. The first type was able to leave the army and slot right back into society, whereas the second type never liked being a soldier in the first place, but enjoyed the killing parts. He was the latter.

Don was ready to leave for home, when the call came in to escort somebody from the nineteenth floor. As the night-shift supervisor, he would normally have left long before now, but one of the day guards had been late when his car wouldn't start, and had only just arrived.

"I'll do it, and then I'm off," Don said, tight-lipped, as his colleague shrugged out of his leather jacket and into his uniform.

He swiped his security pass, and rode up to the top floor. As he stepped out of the lift, his heart skipped a beat. Before him stood the loveliest vision he'd seen in years.

Her red curls cascaded down her back and framed the milky white skin of her face, and he knew, before he got close enough to see for himself, she had incredible green eyes. He wasn't disappointed.

Don escorted the woman into the lift, and forced his voice to be calm as he attempted small talk.

She seemed in awe of the new sights and sounds.

"Your first time here?" he asked.

"Is it that obvious?" She smiled shyly.

"A little." He chuckled.

"This place is amazing."

"Yeah, I suppose it is. You get used to it when you see it every day."

"I won't. I can't wait."

"So, are you joining us, then?"

She grinned. "I think so. I'm still pinching myself, if I'm honest."

"Congratulations. When do you start?"

"Thanks. I'm not sure. You're the first person I've told. I still need to break the news to my family."

The doors opened up into the foyer.

"Here we are. Good luck, miss…"

He held out his hand, and she shook it with gusto.

"McLaughlin, but call me Hannah."

Don walked her to the main doors, and, after hanging back slightly, followed her to the train station.

Something about the young woman had awoken a need in him. She was so like Clair Dietrich, his last girlfriend. She even smelled the same. Once he'd watched her train leave the station, he headed back to AdCor with a newfound spring in his step. He looked forward to Hannah McLaughlin joining them.

The following Tuesday, Hannah received an email from Human Resources with an offer to join Corporate Services. She was blown away, and sat with her mouth agape while she read the offer over and over again.

After her initial meeting with Angela Beanie, Hannah had made her mind up not to accept the position. Her parents would hit the roof if she were to tell them she was moving away so soon after Shaun. But, reading the offer now, she felt torn in two.

She'd dreamt of this moment—in fact, the package they were offering her was phenomenal, and exceeded any of her wildest dreams.

After the hundredth read through, she contemplated calling her parents, but how could she? Her mother hadn't even stopped crying over Shaun yet. Her fucking brother had given her this opportunity with one hand, and viciously snatched it away with the other.

She pinched the top of her nose between her eyes, and knew she had a doozy of a headache coming on.

She closed her laptop and headed to Mr Turnbull's office.

"Knock, knock," she said, peering in through the open door.

Her aging boss eased himself to his feet and shuffled toward her. "Ah, I was just about to come and find you. I can't say I'm surprised, especially after the deal you pulled off. But, you'll be missed, Hannah."

"Sorry?" She shook her head, trying to process what the heck he was talking about.

"I just received the email informing me of your promotion. They've offered me a number of potential candidates to fill your position, but it won't be *that* easy to replace you."

"Replace me?" she asked, still confused.

"When you move to the city! You have checked your emails, haven't you? Tell me I haven't put my big foot in it."

"I need to go home, Mr Turnbull. I have a terrible migraine coming on."

"Hannah? Is that you, sweetheart?" her mother called from the conservatory.

The glass room ran along the back of the house. Agnes grew a lot of her vegetables in there, using it more like a greenhouse.

"Yes, Mammy. I'm not feeling too well. I'll go and have a lie down."

Agnes charged through the door, her eyebrows furrowed. "That's not like you, sweetheart. Do you have a temperature?" She pressed the flat of her palm against her daughter's forehead.

"I'm fine, Mammy. Don't fuss."

"You're not fine. You're as white as a sheet. Go on up. I'll bring you a glass of water and a nip of my homemade tonic—that'll see any nasties off before they get a strong hold."

Hannah nodded, and headed for the stairs, knowing there was no point arguing.

Feeling totally drained, she climbed onto the bed, fully clothed, and closed her heavy eyes. Uncertain what was wrong with her, she presumed it must be stress related, as she'd felt perfectly fine before reading the email.

Her mother, suddenly standing over her, shook her by the shoulder. "Take this, sweetheart. You'll feel right as rain in a jiffy."

Hannah opened her mouth, allowing her mother to ply her with one of her many herbal potions—they often joked she would have been hung as a witch, if she'd lived a few hundred years ago.

It felt late when she woke. The house was in silence, and, although still light outside, the sun had shifted away from her window.

She reached for her phone—7.55pm. She'd been out for the count for hours.

Padding downstairs on bare feet, she found her parents snuggled on the sofa. Her mother was engrossed in a book and her father was watching the history channel on the TV.

"Oh, there you are, sweetheart. I was beginning to fret," her mother said, discarding the book, and jumping to her feet. "Can I get you something to eat? I made a plate up for you."

"I'll do it, Mammy. You stay there."

Her father paused the TV program, and watched the exchange in silence.

"Nonsense. It won't take a minute. How are you feeling?"

"Okay, I think. I'm shocked I slept so long though."

"You clearly needed it," her father said. "You've been pushing yourself for weeks."

Her mother got to her feet, and steered Hannah to the lounge chair. "I told you, didn't I, sweetheart? You've had a mini crash." She nodded, before rushing out to the kitchen.

"Everything should settle down now," Hannah called after her. She sat down, and curled her feet underneath her.

"Why? Have you heard from head office?" her father asked.

Hannah hesitated, contemplating a lie, then nodded. "They offered me a huge promotion. But, I'm going to turn it down."

"Whatever for?" He gaped.

"I would need to move to Manchester. That's why."

Her father closed his mouth, and turned to stare at the still screen showing the back of someone's head. He sat in silence for a few minutes.

"I understand you love living at home—we love having you. But, this is a terrific opportunity. You at least need to consider it."

"Consider what?" her mother said, breezing in with a plateful of stewed steak, mashed potatoes, and cabbage.

Her father cocked a thumb towards Hannah. "She's been offered a promotion, but it would mean moving away. She's not taking it."

"Don't force her. If she doesn't want to go, she doesn't have to."

"Of course I won't force her. But, I'm just questioning why she won't accept it." Her father peered at her face intently.

"Why are you looking at me like that?" Hannah dropped her head, and began stuffing her face full of food.

"I asked you a question. Why do you intend to decline the promotion?"

Hannah shrugged.

Her mother returned to her seat, and also stared at her daughter.

Finishing her mouthful, Hannah sighed. "You need me here. It's fine—I'm fine with it."

"Oh, no, you don't, young lady. We're not going to be responsible for holding you back," her mother said.

Shocked, Hannah looked from her to her father.

He nodded.

"But, you've been so upset about our Shaun moving away. I didn't want to add to that."

"Of course I'm upset. What kind of mother would I be, if I wasn't?"

Hannah shook her head.

"But, that doesn't mean I'd allow you to throw an opportunity like this away. I'm hoping you won't be leaving the country, like Shaun, however."

Hannah laughed. "Just Manchester, I swear."

"That settles it. You're taking the job—deal?"

Hannah scrambled to her feet. "Oh, come here. I'm going to miss you guys so much."

Later that night, as Hannah lay in bed, she had to pinch herself several times. She'd needed no further persuading from her parents, and, after the initial excitement, the nerves had set in.

She opened her laptop and re-read the finer details of the contract.

As it was basically a transfer, she had no reason to work her notice. But, there was so much to organise.

Firstly, she needed to find somewhere to live.

CHAPTER 4

The following week passed by in a flash. And on Friday afternoon, Hannah handed her portfolio over for the rest of the team to share out amongst each other—she felt that was the fair thing to do.

On Saturday morning, she loaded up her multi-coloured, 1996 Volvo estate. After a teary farewell, Hannah left for Manchester.

The flat she'd found through an agency was in Cheadle, a suburb of Greater Manchester, and was around eight miles outside the city. It would take her twenty minutes to the office by car or fifteen minutes by train. There had been quite a lot of flats to choose from, but the one she settled on had been newly decorated, and came fully furnished.

She'd taken a week off work to organise the flat, and acclimatise herself to the area.

Pulling up outside the 1900s style four-storey converted building, she knew it had been the perfect choice.

There were three flats on each floor. Hers, 4b, the middle one on the top floor, had a lovely view of the garden and an open outlook.

The décor and furnishings were top quality and neutral

colours, which would make it easy for her to later add a little of her own personality. But, the best part, in her opinion, was the dinky steel balcony, filled with two chairs, a table, and four lavender-laden planter boxes.

By Sunday lunchtime, she'd unpacked her car, and everything she possessed had a new home.

Wanting to be neighbourly, she baked two batches of cookies, using her mammy's fool-proof recipe.

She called at 4c first. She'd heard shuffling through the wall all morning, so she knew the occupants were home.

The door swung inwards as soon as she knocked, startling her. She squealed and jumped backwards, almost throwing the cookies in the air.

An attractive man, who appeared to be in his late twenties-early thirties, stepped towards her, his arm held out as though to catch the container, if she did indeed let it go. "Sorry, I was just behind the door when you knocked," he said, in an American accent.

She laughed. "I'm Hannah. I moved in next door yesterday, and to say 'hi,' I brought you some cookies."

"Oh my God! You've only been here five minutes, and you're already baking. It took me at least two weeks to find the stove when I moved in."

"Well, I didn't cook myself a meal last night, and I probably won't tonight, if that makes you feel any better." She grinned. "But, I figured making cookies was the neighbourly thing to do."

"Hey! You won't find me complaining." He took the offered plastic tub, covered with an ill-fitting lid, and peered inside. "Beautiful and a wiz in the kitchen to boot!" He fluttered his eyelashes at her.

She laughed, delighted to have such a fun and down-to-earth neighbour.

"Do you want to come in?"

"Actually, I just planned to introduce myself, and then pop to the flat on the other side, too."

"Diane works nights as an ER doctor at Cheadle Royal Infirmary. I'd leave it an hour or two, before you go knocking on *her* door."

Hannah winced. "Gosh, I'm glad I came here first, then—that wouldn't have been a good way to meet the neighbour."

"Tell you what. How about I ask you and Diane to come over here for a drink this afternoon? That way, we can all get to know each other at the same time."

"That sounds like fun. What time?" Hannah asked.

"Shall we say around three? Then, if Diane's working tonight, it shouldn't interfere with that."

She nodded. "Fine by me. I'll bring the wine."

"Something tells me I'm going to enjoy having you as a neighbour. I'm Simon, by the way. Simon Fowler."

Hannah went back to her flat, and, after cleaning the kitchen, she took her Kindle out onto the balcony.

The June sun peeked out from the clouds, and she lifted her face to bask in the rays. Manchester was also known as 'the rainy city,' but she'd heard the summers were, on average, warm and pleasant. But, this was the first time the elusive sun had made an appearance since her arrival.

Startled by a sound to the side of her, she opened her eyes and watched her neighbour, Simon, come out onto his balcony.

He stretched and scratched his balls, clearly oblivious of her presence.

Hannah stifled a giggle, as she watched him through the bamboo partition between their balconies.

He bobbed back inside briefly, returning with a newspaper and a large bag of peanut M&Ms.

She coughed as he reappeared, letting him know she was there.

"Hi, again," he said.

She dipped her Kindle down and peered over the top of it. "Hello."

"I left a message for Diane. She's not got back to me yet. I'm sure she will though. Want one?" He tipped the bag of M&Ms towards her.

She laughed. "No, thanks."

They spent the rest of the afternoon chatting, and, just before three, she excused herself, and knocked at his front door a couple of minutes later, with a bottle of wine under each arm.

Simon barked out a laugh and ushered her inside.

After an hour passed, they presumed Diane couldn't make it. But, that didn't make any difference to them. They got on like old friends, and seemed to have the same warped sense of humour.

Hannah told him all about her new job, and moving away from her family.

Simon could relate to her being homesick. He'd left his home-town of Seattle, USA four years ago, with his *then* girlfriend.

"Once we'd actually moved in together, this woman I'd left my whole life for turned into a psychotic shrew. I couldn't get away from her fast enough."

She giggled. "How come you didn't go back home?"

"I'd got a decent job by then. I'm an Operations Manager for Texaco, but I'm working out a month's notice, then I'll go home for a few months."

"Oh, that's a shame. And just when I thought I'd found my first friend in the area."

"I'll still be your friend." He grinned, and looked her up and down suggestively.

She laughed, and flicked her hand his way.

"I'm teasing. No, I'm sure you'll have plenty more friends by the time I leave."

"What will you do with this place?" She glanced about the neat and tidy flat.

"I don't know if I'm coming back yet, so I'll leave it empty until I decide. Maybe my new best friend will keep an eye on it for me?"

A knock sounded at the door.

Simon glanced at the wall clock. It was 5.30pm. "Be back in a sec."

Moments later, he returned with a short, dark-haired woman, who was chattering nonstop.

Hannah didn't catch a word.

"Diane, this is Hannah—she's our lovely new neighbour," Simon said.

Diane took Hannah's hand and pumped it enthusiastically. "I'd heard the place had been let, but I wasn't sure when you were moving in."

"It was a rush job, I'm afraid. I got a transfer from work, and there was no point wasting time."

"Hannah's never lived away from home before," Simon volunteered.

"What? Never?" Diane said, her mouth agape.

Hannah chuckled. "There was never any reason to move out. I worked close by, and Mammy's a terrific cook."

"I don't blame you," Diane said. "I couldn't wait to get a place of my own, and ended up running home to my parents several times before I left for good. I still wish I lived at home sometimes when I get home from work and have to cook and clean for myself."

"Hear, hear," Simon said. "Glass of wine?"

Diane shook her head. "I only have ten minutes, then I'll need to get ready. We're short-staffed at the hospital, and I'm doing a double shift."

"When will you sleep?" Hannah asked, shocked.

"Sleep? What's that?" Diane laughed, rolling her eyes. "Hopefully, if it's not too busy, I'll be able to snatch forty winks."

Soon after, they all parted ways, promising to meet up again soon.

Hannah returned to her flat, suddenly feeling less homesick and alone.

Hannah spent the week exploring the immediate area, and was thrilled to discover a shopping centre within walking distance of the flat. She also found several second-hand shops, and managed to buy the rest of the things she needed, without blowing her budget.

On Wednesday, Diane invited her in for a coffee. They got on famously, and Hannah prayed she would be as fortunate in her new job.

By Sunday evening, the place looked like home. Hannah opened a bottle of wine and sat on the balcony, watching the sun go down.

Her parents called to wish her luck for the following day. They seemed much happier once she told them about her new friends, and she promised to call them with a blow-by-blow account when she arrived home tomorrow.

Her stomach did a funny jiggle every time she thought about her new job. She'd had a trial run on the train a few days ago, and knew exactly where to go. In fact, the station was on the very next block to the company, so she had no concerns on that score.

She hoped she would get on with the rest of the staff. Coming from the slow environment she was used to, she was worried she'd be out of her depth.

Hannah hardly slept a wink, and got out of bed well before dawn. She spent the early hours soaking in the bath and preparing her outfit. She left far too early, and sat outside the offices on a bench for a while.

As she watched the people go in and out, Hannah wondered if she would be working with any of them. They all appeared cheerful, which was a good sign—but she would soon find out.

CHAPTER 5

Just before 8.30am, Hannah made her way to reception, and asked the pretty receptionist to let Angela Beanie know she had arrived.

She took a seat on one of the beige leather sofas to the right of the desk area. After browsing for a few minutes through one of the company's promotional magazines, she noticed a shadowy figure approach her. She turned to see a security guard.

"Hello again, Ms McLaughlin," he said, extending his hand to her. "Angela's caught in traffic, and has asked me to escort you up to your office, and get you settled."

Don had screwed up the security roster on purpose to ensure he'd still be there to greet Hannah. After his night shift, he showered and doused himself with aftershave, before changing into a freshly laundered shirt.

His racing heart turned to stone the instant he realised she didn't recognise him. He'd thought of nothing else but her since their last meeting, yet she could barely offer him a smile. He wanted to punch something.

For the second time in as many weeks, he was reminded of Clair Dietrich. All he'd needed from *her* had been loyalty. He'd watched her for months, set up several state-of-the-art cameras around her flat, and he would've been happy with that, if she'd stayed true to him—but she couldn't. Clair was weak, like every other woman he'd known, and she'd fallen for her drug-addicted colleague. If that wasn't bad enough, the druggie had been trying to convince *her* to try cannabis. He'd had no choice but to rescue poor Clair from such a dangerous situation.

The lift door opened, and the bell startled him.

Once again, he escorted Hannah up to the fifteenth floor.

He tried to make small talk, but she remained monosyllabic in her responses, seeming miles away, as she gazed through the glass taking in all the new sights.

As the lift stopped, Don's earpiece crackled to life. *"Ms. Beanie has entered the garage level two."*

He led Hannah to the staff room, and offered to make her a drink, but she declined with a shake of her head. He knew he should make allowances for her—she was clearly terrified, but he'd never been able to tolerate bad manners.

"Ms. Beanie will be with you shortly, miss," he said, before heading back down to the ground floor.

Inside the lift, he pressed the emergency stop button and roared, punching the console three times. He paced the small distance, and tore at his hair. *Why did it always happen to him? One thing was certain—if he couldn't have her—no other fucker would.*

He began snapping at the thick elastic band at his wrist—a technique he used to keep his temper under some kind of control.

After a few minutes, he pressed the lift button again, straightened his tie, and brushed down his jacket, stepping into the foyer, smiling broadly.

Angela appeared moments after the security guard left. She seemed flustered, and couldn't apologise enough.

"No problem. I've only just arrived myself."

"Did Don show you to your desk?"

Hannah shook her head.

"Introduce you to the team?" She raised her eyebrows in question.

"No."

Angela exhaled noisily. "If you want a job doing..." she grumbled. "Come on. Let's show you around."

Hannah tried to memorise all the names of the people she would be working alongside, but she knew it was pointless. She shook hands with each of them, but all the other information Angela volunteered went in one ear and straight out the other.

After Angela showed her the staff gym on the basement level, and canteen on the fourth, they headed back to the fifteenth floor.

"Ah, there you are," a male voice said from behind them, as they exited the lift.

They stopped, and spun around.

A tall, broad man, dressed in an immaculate grey suit, sauntered towards them.

Hannah gasped. She barely recognised Maxwell Myers from the grainy image she'd seen. He was even more ruggedly handsome in the flesh. His mid-length, brown hair was fashionably messy, and his dark brooding eyes had a mischievous glint, but it was his easy smile and full, luscious lips which caused Hannah's stomach to twirl.

"Sorry, Max. Have you been looking for me?" Angela said. "I was just showing Hannah around."

"Yes, I can't find the Steadman file. I've searched everywhere."

"Did you check my desk?"

"No. Why would I check your desk?"

"Probably for the same reason you're looking for it, I imagine.

The deadline is tomorrow. I'll get it for you shortly. Anyway, Max meet Hannah McLaughlin. It's her first day today."

He did a double-take, as though he'd only just noticed her standing there.

"Hannah. Welcome. I'm sorry I missed our meeting last week, but I was unavoidably detained, I'm afraid."

Hannah cleared her throat—suddenly feeling self-conscious. "No problem, Mr Myers." Her heart thundered in her chest.

She'd convinced herself he would be a flash and cocky bighead, not as charming and remarkably likeable as he appeared to be.

"I'll get off, and leave you to it. Lovely to meet you, Hannah." He took her hand, and held onto it a fraction longer than was necessary.

"And you, sir."

Hannah needn't have worried. She settled into her new role, no trouble. The initial feedback from her clients was she seemed professional, and was doing an excellent job.

On the home front, she'd seen more and more of Diane, often meeting in either of their flats for coffee as Hannah arrived home and before Diane left for work.

Simon had been working away since the first weekend they'd met, but he was due back that weekend. This coincided with Diane's days off, so they planned a get-together, where they could all let their hair down.

She'd seen Max a couple of times in passing, and each time he asked how she was faring. She turned into a gormless mute when he spoke to her, smiling and nodding like a dimwit.

She still felt an all-encompassing attraction to him, but she knew, by the reaction of every other woman in her office, she wasn't the only one. She needed to put him out of her mind.

Easier said than done. She'd never felt such a strong attraction to a man before. She'd had plenty of boyfriends, but never anyone who made her feel light-headed and breathless just by being in the same room. This was the type of thing she'd read about. However, she wasn't gullible enough to think this situation could get any better for her. She was lucky in her career—she didn't expect to be lucky in love as well.

On Saturday morning, Hannah and Diane got a train into Manchester city. After a leisurely breakfast in a café, they hit the shops.

While Diane had gone into the changing room of her favourite boutique with her arms laden, Hannah browsed the racks. She noticed a beautiful, close-fitting black dress, which would be impossible to wear any undies with. Hannah didn't go for a lot of clothing—so long as she had the basics, she was fine. But, she loved that particular dress. She glanced at the price tag, and her hand shot away as though burned. £389—*for a dress!* And *that* was the sale price.

She spun away from the racks, and stood beside the counter, waiting for Diane to come out.

"Can I get you anything?" The salesperson smiled.

Hannah shook her head. "I couldn't even afford a paper bag from here."

"Me neither," she whispered.

Just then, a toffee-nosed woman stormed in, and slammed a bag on the counter. "Excuse me," she said to the salesperson. "I bought this yesterday, and I noticed the bone is missing from the bust area." Out of the bag, she pulled the exact same dress Hannah had just been drooling over.

"Really? Let me see." After fiddling with the corset part of the dress, the girl agreed. "I'm so sorry about that, madam. Let me replace it for you."

Hannah watched as the girl found another dress, and handed it to the woman for inspection.

With a tight-lipped nod, the woman accepted the exchange, and flounced from the shop.

"What will you do with that now?" Hannah asked the girl, and nodded at the dress.

"I don't know. Hang on." She walked to a woman, who was standing on a stepladder fiddling with a display. "Francine. This dress has been returned, because it has a bone missing. What shall I do with it?"

Francine examined the dress. "So it does. Mark it down."

"What to? It looks as though it's been worn."

"Just put fifty quid on it. Somebody will want it for that."

Hannah already had her purse out when the girl arrived back at the counter. "I'll take it."

"Don't you want to try it on first?"

"No, thanks. I'll make it fit, at that price."

The girl chuckled, and placed the dress in a bag.

Diane appeared a few minutes later, but put most of the items back. She settled on a plain navy blouse and a cerise pink vest top.

Hannah was walking on air for the rest of the day. She loved getting bargains—she put it down to her Irish blood. She wasn't stingy by any means, but she wasn't frivolous, either. Now, she just needed to arrange a night out to show it off.

They were in great spirits by the time they arrived home, laden with bags. They'd bought several bottles of wine and a selection of pre-made finger food to take to Simon's flat later.

Hannah was looking forward to seeing Simon again. She'd actually missed him, considering she'd only known him for a day.

She unpacked her bags, and freshened up, before going next door.

Diane's chatter greeted her, as she pushed the door open. "It's only me."

Simon met her in the hall, and pulled her into his arms for a bear hug.

Hannah squealed, and held the supermarket bags out to her sides, unable to hug him back.

He ushered her through to the lounge where Diane sat, an almost empty glass of wine in her hand. "Hello, you. Long-time no see!"

"You didn't waste much time." Hannah nodded at her glass.

"We considered waiting for you, didn't we, Si? But, the wine had begun to evaporate—you were taking so long."

"A likely story." She smiled. "I brought some nibbles, Simon. Shall I grab a couple of plates?"

The evening began with much laughter and frivolity. Hannah, once again, found herself marvelling at how close they'd all become in such a short space of time.

Simon got his acoustic guitar out after a few drinks, and they all sang along to the limited number of songs he had in his repertoire. One of the songs he insisted they sang was the most annoying song Hannah had ever heard called *Agadoo*. He even insisted they do an equally silly dance to go with it, and had them laughing hysterically when Hannah and Simon discovered Diane didn't know her left from her right. She blamed the booze, of course.

At the end of the night, Simon escorted them back to their flats. They kissed Diane goodnight, and when they reached Hannah's door, Simon surprised her by going in for a proper kiss.

She hesitated at first, but he tasted so nice, she found herself kissing him back. She drew a halt to any more shenanigans, when his hand began snaking up her top.

"Oh, no, you don't, mister." She ducked out of his embrace, and quickly put the key in the door.

"Come on, Hannah. We're both adults."

"That doesn't mean we should jump into bed with each other." She laughed. "And besides, I like you too much."

He raised his eyebrows comically. "Don't you go falling in love with me, lady."

"Be quiet, silly. I mean we get on well as friends. I'd prefer to keep it that way."

He shrugged. "Well, you know where I am, if you change your mind."

"I do, indeed."

She entered the flat, and closed the door, leaning against it for a moment. She had been tempted to allow him in. It had been ages since she'd had a boyfriend, but she knew Simon wasn't boyfriend material. Plus, he was heading back to the States in a few weeks.

CHAPTER 6

On Monday morning, Hannah bumped into Max Myers in the lift. There were just the two of them, and no distractions. She nodded at him, and looked down at her feet.

"Hello, Hannah," he said.

"Hi." Her voice sounded croaky, so she cleared her throat. "Hi." She tried again, giving him an embarrassed smile.

"I was meaning to seek you out today."

Her breath caught in her throat, as she hesitantly gazed up at him.

He grinned. "Don't look so frightened. I only wanted to ask how you're settling in."

"Oh, I thought I was in trouble."

"Not at all. I've heard nothing but high praise about you." He raised his eyebrows expectantly.

Hannah panicked, confused about what he was waiting for.

"So? How's it going?"

"Oh." She sighed heavily, and nodded. "Great actually. Everybody's been so kind to me, and the systems are the same as at the *Daily Post*, so it hasn't taken me long to get into the swing of things."

"I'm pleased to hear it."

The doors opened at her floor, and she rushed towards them at the same moment he did. They crashed into each other, sending her bag and phone clattering to the floor.

"I'm sorry," he said, reaching down to retrieve the phone at his feet. "I hope it's not broken."

She pressed the on button, and nothing happened. Then, suddenly, the screen lit up. "It's okay," she said. As she looked up at him, she realised he'd moved closer to her so he could also see the phone, and their faces were almost touching.

He sprang back, seeming flustered, then followed her onto the marketing floor. "We have the weekly meeting. Are you coming?"

"I wasn't aware," she stammered.

"That's okay. You missed last week's, as you were with Angela for your induction. It's quite informal. Nothing to worry about."

She bobbed her head, feeling like a dork. "I'll just…" She indicated to her bag and phone.

"Of course."

She dropped her things off on her desk and ran to the bathroom. She couldn't believe the way he made her feel. She should've just taken the plunge with Simon on Saturday. At least she had a shot with him.

Checking her reflection in the mirror, she took a couple of bracing breaths, before heading back to the open-plan area, where everyone had begun to congregate.

At lunchtime, she decided a session in the gym was what she needed to occupy her mind. She'd signed up the previous week and had been forcing herself to attend daily.

Down in the basement, she opened her locker. It was empty.

Confused, she double-checked the number on the key matched the number on the locker. It did. She knew it would anyway. She was always one to keep things symmetrical wherever possible, and she'd chosen this particular locker, from the choices presented to her, because it was third from the left, third from the bottom, and third from the top. *Where the hell were her things?*

The gym instructor was busy showing several people how to use a weight machine, so she gave up on the idea of the gym and headed to the staff cafeteria.

After ordering a coffee, she chose a seat at the back of the room, and took out her phone. She'd downloaded the Kindle app, and would often read a book on the train, or if she had any spare time on her hands.

"Still working, then?" A man's voice infiltrated her thoughts.

She glanced up, startled to see Max standing beside her table, a tray in his hands.

"I—I'm sorry?"

"The phone—it's still working?"

"It is," she said.

"Mind if I join you?" He nodded at the table.

She screamed internally, all the time smiling at him. "Of course not. Take a seat."

He sat opposite her.

Hannah was so glad she hadn't ordered any food. There was no way she'd be able to eat a bite with his beautiful brown eyes staring at her.

He had no such issue. He chowed down on a cheese sandwich hungrily, and followed it with a strawberry slice.

"You not eating?" He pointed at her cup.

"Not hungry."

"I don't know how anybody can go all day without eating."

She shrugged. "I always eat breakfast."

"You should try one of these slices. They're the best in the country."

She smirked. "In the country? That's a bold statement."

"One I am willing to stake my life on, if I must."

"Maybe I'll try one sometime." She smiled.

"I should warn you—as soon as you've eaten one, you'll be hooked."

She laughed. "Thanks for your concern, but I'm willing to take the risk."

"A woman after my own heart—weigh up the pitfalls, and do it anyway."

She glanced at her watch and gasped, scrambling to her feet. "I've got to go. Thanks for the chat."

She sped towards the lift, but inside, she felt as giddy as a pup. There had been at least twenty empty tables, yet he'd chosen hers. Maybe he felt the attraction after all.

As she reached her office, she noticed Angela Beanie at her desk.

"Hi. Sorry I'm late. Do we have a meeting arranged?" Hannah asked.

Angela got to her feet and shook her head. "No, but you're not making a good impression, are you? Just one week in and already you're displaying shoddy timekeeping."

Hannah was dumbstruck. She'd never seen the other woman act like this before. "I-I'm sorry. It won't happen again. I assure you." She felt the blood rush to her face.

"See that it doesn't." With that, Angela stomped from the office.

"What have you done to upset her?" Dawn, the girl on the desk in front of her, whispered.

"I have no idea." Hannah stared at the doorway Angela had recently vacated, shaking her head.

After work, Hannah returned to the gym, and checked her locker one final time, before seeking out the gym assistant.

"Excuse me. I think somebody's been in my locker."

The muscular woman in her twenties seemed surprised. "Really? What makes you think that?"

"Because my gym bag is missing." Hannah shrugged.

"Yes. That would do it." The woman smiled. "But, I'm sure there must be some perfectly simple explanation. We've never had anything like this happen before."

"Well, it seems it's happened now." Hannah got the feeling she didn't believe her.

The assistant held her hand out for the key.

Hannah handed it over, and followed the woman to the lockers, then stood by, while she opened the door and flung it wide open.

"See. What did I tell you?"

"It's certainly empty. Are you sure you didn't take the bag home by mistake?"

"No. I left it here, so I'd have a change of clothes and a towel for the gym. There'd be no point taking it home."

"I guess not. We'll need to report it to security. Like I said, we've never had any problems before."

Hannah didn't like the woman's lackadaisical attitude. "Don't worry. I'll report it to security myself."

Don was thrilled to see Hannah step from the lift. He pulled down his jacket and stood up straight.

She approached him with a smile.

"Good evening, miss. What can I do for you?"

"I seem to have lost my gym bag."

"Oh, that won't do. Where did you last have it?"

"That's just the thing. I left it in my locker."

"In your locker? Was there any sign the lock's been tampered with?"

She shook her head. "Not that I could see."

"Let's get some information, and I'll look into it for you." He reached behind his desk, and pulled out a piece of paper and a pen. "So, what's missing?"

"Nothing fancy. Just my gym kit. An Adidas sports bag, white cropped T-shirt and shorts set, sports bra and undies, a pair of socks, and a pair of Reebok trainers with pink trim."

"Okay, leave it with me. I'm sure they'll turn up. You may have left the locker open, and the cleaners could have put your belongings away for safekeeping."

Hannah nodded. "I hope so. Thank you."

"My pleasure. I'll be in touch in the next day or two."

She turned to leave. "I appreciate it. Have a good evening."

"Sweet dreams, Hannah," he whispered, once she was out of earshot.

The next morning, Hannah arrived at her workstation to find a message to contact security. She picked up the phone and pressed number nine on the internal system.

"Steven Miller."

"Hello, Mr Miller. My name is Hannah McLaughlin. I've received a message to contact you regarding my missing gym bag."

"Ah, thanks for getting back to me, Ms McLaughlin. I'm pleased to inform you we've located your bag."

"Have you? Great! Where was it?"

"It was discovered in the unused locker next to your own. We can only assume you put it in that one by mistake, and then locked *your* locker without realising."

"Really? Oh, I feel such a fool. I'm sorry to have caused you any trouble."

"No trouble at all, miss. Mistakes happen. We've placed your belongings back into the correct locker using the master key."

"I can't thank you enough."

Hannah was confused—she was *certain* she'd put her clothes into the correct locker.

The lift swished open, and Max stepped out. All thoughts of her gym bag were instantly forgotten.

Steve Miller had been Head of Security for sixteen years. Back then, AdCor was part of the HGT Newspaper group. He'd begun his career as a 19-year-old police cadet, and served twenty-five years in the police force. He was pleased he'd got out when he had —life on the streets of Manchester was getting tougher by the day.

His son, Kyle, had been the General Manager for HGT in Birmingham at the time, and had asked him if he would set up the security at the company's new head office. Steve hadn't looked back. He enjoyed his role, and had every faith in his staff.

However, his job had changed over the years. After 9/11, security across the world had been up-scaled, and AdCor was no exception. But, he was fortunate to be part of a reliable and loyal team. Mostly.

He had ten staff under him, and the only one he didn't get along with was Don Henry. Don was the one who gave him headaches, and always seemed to be in the wrong place at the wrong time. He'd been made night supervisor purely on a time served basis, not on his skills. Don wasn't a team player. He couldn't wait to point out other people's mistakes. He'd never cover for his colleagues, and instead, would try to drop them in the shit at any opportunity. If management called looking for Steve, Don would say he didn't know where he was—even insinuate he was never around, and the rest of the team had to pick up the slack. When confronted, he'd deny it, of course.

Another thing, which drove Steve to distraction, was the way Don would try to undermine him. Steve guessed it was because Don was the next longest serving member of the team. He was the second-in-command, and perhaps, in his mind, next in line for the Head of Security. But, since Don had been put on permanent nights, his and Steve's paths rarely crossed.

Steve had considered hanging up his uniform for an easier life. He wanted to be off fishing, or spending quality time with his seven grandchildren. But, if Steve was to put anyone forward for his position, it certainly wouldn't be Don Henry.

At morning break, Hannah was sitting alone on the comfy lime-green leather sofa in the communal coffee area. She had made herself a strawberry and rhubarb tea, and was munching on a croissant left over from one of her colleague's birthday breakfast. For once, the floor was peaceful as she sat in a daydream.

Her thoughts returned to her gym bag. She was certain she'd put it in her own locker. *Why would somebody swap the lockers over?* It didn't make sense. She felt frustrated. Not because it wasn't like her to do such a thing, but because she'd also kicked up a stink, making her appear stupid.

"Good morning, Hannah."

It took a moment for the voice to jolt her from her daydream. She opened her eyes to see Max standing beside her. "Oh! Sorry, I was a world away."

"That's okay. Is everything all right?" He brushed his floppy fringe out of his face.

"Yes, fine, thanks. I've just got a few things on my mind. Nothing serious."

"Good. I came to see you this morning, but I got distracted." He sat beside her.

She could smell his citrusy aftershave and it was making her feel heady. "Okay."

"I've had an email from Danny Leno. Do you remember him? You met him last week."

"Yes, of course. He's the scary man—the underwear king."

"That's the one. He's a pussycat, really."

She loved the way Max's eyes twinkled when something amused him.

"Well, I don't know what you said to him, but he's requested you work on his campaign."

"Really?"

He nodded slowly. "Do you feel ready? Obviously you won't be on your own."

"I suppose."

"He wants to meet with you on Friday evening. For dinner."

"Oh. Is that usual?" She didn't like the thought of meeting the fiery man out of office hours.

"Yes, and no. With somebody as important as him, we bend the rules a little. But, don't worry. I'll come along, too."

She pressed her lips together. "Okay. I'd feel better if you did."

He got to his feet. "Great. I'll send a car for you at 7pm."

And with that, he was gone.

Although petrified at the thought of being summoned for a meeting with Danny Leno, the bombastic owner of a string of lingerie stores, Hannah was thrilled to be able to spend a little more time in the company of Max. She was under no illusions—it was purely a business meeting. Nothing else. But, dreams were free.

Suddenly, the realisation struck her. Not only was she going to be spending time with Max, a man she struggled to string a complete sentence together with, but Mr Leno would want to grill her as well. All of this was to take place over dinner. *How would she be able to eat a thing?* And she didn't have a clue where they would be taking her. Or, more importantly, what the heck she was going to wear!

Panic was beginning to set in; she couldn't wait to get home and talk it over with Diane.

CHAPTER 7

"What's so urgent?" Diane said, as Hannah opened the door. "Your text sounded so desperate I didn't even dry my hair."

"Oh, I'm sorry, Diane. I managed to catch the earlier train, and forgot you'd be getting ready for work." Hannah stepped backwards, allowing her friend to enter.

"What's that smell?" Diane covered her nose with her forearm.

"What smell?"

Diane headed for the kitchen. "I think you've got a gas leak. Open the front door, Hannah."

She opened the door, and then followed Diane into the kitchen. "Oh, yeah. I can smell it now. What is it?"

"You've got a faulty knob on your cooker."

"Do I? Wow! Lucky you came in, as I hadn't noticed it."

"It's ok. I've turned it off now, but if you lean up against it in future, be careful. They're supposed to have a safety cut-off fitted, but I'm guessing this cooker is ancient."

"Okay, thanks, Diane. Fancy a coffee?"

"I'd love one. So, come on. Spit it out. What's got you all het up?"

Hannah quickly told her of her predicament while she made a pot of coffee.

"Oooh! So, the man himself will be picking you up, and escorting you home?" Diane said, wiggling her eyebrows suggestively.

"I wish. He's sending a car for me—whatever that means."

"It means... silly lady, he's interested in you."

Hannah blew a raspberry. "I don't know how you come up with that."

"He's the CEO, Hannah. Think about it. He has plenty of people he could send to accompany you and this client. But, no. He's going himself, instead. For a clever person, you can be pretty stupid at times."

"Hey! Who are you calling stupid?" Hannah laughed.

"What are you going to wear?"

"I have no idea."

"How about that dress you bought from Luscious?"

Hannah shook her head. "I haven't even tried it on. It probably needs altering, and definitely dry-cleaning—it had been worn remember? It stinks of cheap perfume."

"Drop it into Chang's at the bottom of the hill. His wife will do any alterations, and he'll dry-clean it for you."

"How long will that take? We're talking Friday, you know."

"So, go and try it on, and see if it needs anything altered."

Hannah headed to her bedroom and pulled the dress out from her wardrobe. She threw her skirt and blouse onto the bed, and stepped into the satin and chiffon garment. She pulled it up, then glanced in the mirror.

Her breath caught. The hem finished just above the knee and the fine spaghetti straps crisscrossed deeply at the back.

Holding the back of the dress together, she walked through to the kitchen. "Can you fasten the zip for me?"

Diane gasped and jumped to her feet. "How much did you pay for that? Fifty quid?"

Hannah nodded, turning her back for her friend to fasten it.

"That's Chanel! I've been going into Luscious for ages, and never found a bargain like that!" She zipped the dress up.

"Yeah, but it is faulty. There's a bone missing from the bodice."

"Let me see?"

She turned around again.

"Where?"

Hannah felt the fabric underneath her breasts. "Here, the left side is missing."

"Well, you can't tell. It looks stunning, Hannah. Honestly. And if your hunky CEO doesn't fall at your feet, then he most certainly is gay."

Hannah smiled. She did feel special. In fact, the dress gave her more confidence, somehow.

"Right, get it off. I'll drop it into Chang's on my way home from work in the morning. I can smell the perfume from here. Then, I'll pick it up on Wednesday afternoon, or Thursday, ready for your big date on Friday. How's that sound?"

"Would you? That'll be a huge help. Thanks, Diane."

"My pleasure. What are friends for?"

Wednesday, at lunchtime, Hannah headed down to the gym, and there, sure enough, was her bag and gym gear.

She shook her head, and headed into a cubicle to change.

As she pulled on the underwear, she paused. The panties hadn't been new—she'd had them for ages, yet they seemed much whiter than she remembered. The bra, too. She figured it must be something to do with the false lighting in the basement.

Steve Miller made a note in the day log for Don Henry, before leaving for the day on Thursday. He only caught up with the night staff in person once a month, but he felt this problem needed to be addressed sooner.

He'd noticed from the swipe card entries Don had been spending up to five hours a night in the security hub.

This was the most secure of all areas, due to AdCor's different divisions. All telecommunication, intranet, and broadband were streamed through the devices inside. Asset Tracker, a computer program designed to monitor all activity, would flag certain items, and log them with the IT department. From there, they checked the content, and reported anything unusual.

Bistrack was also controlled from the hub—all video leads were streamed and saved using the web, which meant a person could access and view anywhere within the AdCor network of offices. This included web content and even mobile phone texts. The only areas not accessed were the toilets, Max Myers' living quarters, and the security hub itself. The team called it the 'Big Brother Room.'

Steve had been down to the hub, and couldn't see anything amiss. He actually suspected Don had been pushing the two leather desk chairs together and catching forty winks. He knew *all* night staff did this kind of thing on occasion, but the swipe logs showed, in the last three weeks, Don had accessed the room every shift.

Steve knew Don would be ropable to be confronted, but he needed answers.

Don slammed his fist down on the day log, and kicked the cupboard beneath it. *There have been some discrepancies with your security log,* Steve Miller's message said. *Please stay on late in the morning for a debrief.*

Don was furious the interfering little man thought he had the right to question his routine. He wrote below it in his usual scrawl, *Unfortunately, I can't stay late due to a previous appointment.* He smiled to himself. *That will teach the old bastard.*

He felt elated and superior he had got one over on his boss, and then, he trundled off to put on his uniform and start his rounds. But, he knew Steve's issues wouldn't go away. He'd have to face him, eventually.

Don took his uniform from the locker, and hooked the hanger over the door. Then, he reached inside and removed a blue Adidas bag from the back. He unzipped it and pulled out a handful of items. A pair of shorts and cropped T-shirt, bra and panties—which had a small tear in the waistband—Reebok trainers and socks.

Don picked up the panties and held them to his face. Hannah's perfumed scent still lingered on them, and his heart compressed.

Don finished his shift at 6am, and headed to his flat in a rough part of Longsight, about a ten-minute drive out of the city.

His front door was slotted between a haberdashery shop entrance and a pizza shop entrance. He angrily kicked a pile of discarded pizza boxes off his doorstep, and out towards the rubbish bin beside the road.

He opened the door and ran up the wooden stairs directly in front of him. The flat wasn't the flashiest, but it served him well. It comprised of one large, open-plan room, which doubled as his lounge, kitchen and bedroom, as well as a small bathroom across the landing.

It was still only 6.30am, and much too early to carry out his plans, so he heated a cup of warm milk, and lay on the bed for a while, hoping to get a bit of shuteye.

A couple of hours later, he showered, and changed into jeans and checked shirt. He shrugged into his jacket, then opened the wardrobe and pulled out a burgundy cardboard shopping bag. Printed across the bag, in fancy black lettering, was the word *Luscious*.

With a spring in his step and a whistle on his lips, he headed for the door to deliver his gift.

Fifteen minutes later, Don parked his red Ford Taurus across the street and peered at the building opposite. He was no stranger to the flat, having been there once before, but it paid to be cautious.

He pulled out his phone and dialled AdCor. "Could you put me through to the marketing department, please?" he said, in a Scottish accent.

After a brief pause, Keenan Barber, a young, up-and-coming salesperson, who considered himself a hotshot around the office, answered the phone.

In the same accent as before, Don asked for Hannah.

Her breathy voice made him think she was expecting somebody else, and that irritated him briefly. He hung up, satisfied the coast was clear.

With his toolbox and the bag, he headed for the entrance and took the stairs to the fourth floor.

At flat 4b, he removed his pick gun from the toolbox, and was inside within ten seconds. He quickly scanned the flat.

Lifting a coffee cup up from the sink, he pressed his mouth to the lipstick mark on the rim and savoured the greasy film, as he rubbed his lips together several times.

In the bedroom, he removed the dress from the wardrobe, lifted up the plastic cover, and slid the dress from the hanger. Then, he took the identical replacement dress from the *Luscious* bag. He removed all the tags before swapping the hangers, and replacing the plastic cover over the new dress.

Now, whenever Hannah wore the dress he'd bought for her, it would be something special between the two of them.

Removing all his clothes, he climbed into her bed. Her scent surrounded him. His senses hummed.

He hugged the pillow, and mumbled, "I love you, Hannah. I hope you enjoy my gift." Then, he closed his eyes and slept.

A couple of hours later, he jumped out of the bed, smoothing down the duvet, threw on his clothes, bagged the old dress, and left.

CHAPTER 8

After work, Diane helped Hannah get ready. Hannah had never been adventurous with makeup, but Diane wouldn't take a blind bit of notice, and made her sit quietly while she let loose with her pencils and brushes. Instead of tying her hair into a neat and tidy knot, Diane insisted she left it unbound, using mousse and spray to make her red curls appear fuller and much tamer than usual.

But, even Hannah had to admit, the end result looked amazing.

The dress fitted her even better than it had earlier in the week. She did a twirl for Diane to show her the completed outfit, which included a pair of strappy gold sandals. But, she stopped mid-twirl.

"What's wrong?" Diane said.

Running her hands over the dress, Hannah shook her head. "It's been fixed."

"I'm sorry?"

"The missing bone. It's been replaced."

Diane shrugged. "Mrs Chang must've done it. She didn't say anything when I picked it up, and I only paid for the cleaning."

"Maybe they made a mistake. I'll call in tomorrow and pay them what I owe."

Diane left for work, and Hannah was as ready as she could be. She felt nervous, but wasn't too worried.

When the intercom buzzed, she jumped out of her skin. Like a little girl, she ran to the phone.

"Hello?"

"Ms McLaughlin?" A deep male voice came through the earpiece.

"Yes."

"My name's Jackson. I'm your driver for the evening."

"I'll be right down."

Jackson, a middle-aged bald man, was as broad as he was long. He held the limo door open for her, and once she was in, got behind the wheel and drove towards the city.

"Here we are, miss," Jackson said, as he slowed down outside a French restaurant in the Central Business District of Manchester. Jackson pulled the limo into the nearest parking spot, then ran around to escort her from the car.

Hannah took Jackson's offered hand, and left the comfort of the leather seat.

"Don't you have a jacket, miss?" Jackson asked.

It was a mild night, but he must've mistaken her trembling for shivering. "I'll be fine once I'm inside. Thanks."

Jackson accompanied her into the restaurant, then ducked back out of the doors.

"I'm meeting Maxwell Myers," she said to the head waiter.

He showed her to an empty table set for two, and Hannah panicked. *Where was Max?* Surely he wouldn't leave her to entertain Danny Leno alone—he knew she was wary of him.

Another waiter arrived at the table with a bottle of red wine, and proceeded to fill two glasses.

Just then, Max appeared from an area near the bar.

"I'm so sorry, Hannah. I should learn to turn my phone off in the evenings. In fact, I'll do it right now." He took his phone from his pocket and pressed the power button. "There. Done." He sat opposite her.

Shocked the one other diner was actually Max, and not Danny, she struggled to find any words. She smiled, nervously.

"Danny has been held up," he continued. "He's going to try to make it for after dinner drinks, but in the meantime, we may as well enjoy our meal."

She gulped, finding it difficult to swallow her saliva, never mind eat dinner.

Max looked her up and down. "I must say, you're looking particularly lovely tonight."

"Thank you." She was thrilled he'd noticed the effort she'd made.

The waiter appeared with the menus.

Hannah looked at the fancy French names, and had no clue what to order.

"Are you okay? Do you need some help?"

Hannah nodded. "I'm sorry. I don't speak French."

"No problem. Not everybody does. They should put the translation underneath in English." He shook his head. "So, what do you like?"

"Most things, really."

"Then, can I recommend the onion soup for a starter?"

She nodded enthusiastically. She could do soup. "Sounds lovely." At least her voice sounded calm and in control.

"Do you like shellfish?" He looked at her over the top of the menu.

"Love it." She smiled.

"How about the butter-poached lobster for the main? It's very good."

"Then, how can I resist?"

By the time the food arrived, Hannah was feeling much more settled. Max's laid-back attitude and easy sense of humour had her laughing.

"Oh, wow!" she said, as they put the rustic clay pot in front of her. The cheesy onion contents smelled divine. She cleaned her bowl, mopping up every last drop with the crusty bread roll.

After the equally delicious main course, Hannah was pleased when the waiter appeared beside Max with a message saying Danny Leno couldn't make it after all.

"Oh, what a shame," she said.

"I know you don't mean that. You're dancing an Irish jig on the inside, aren't you?"

"How do you know I can dance an Irish jig?"

He shrugged one shoulder, humour filling his dark brown eyes. "Oh, you know."

"No. I don't know."

He rolled his eyes. "Alright. So…I might have read your file."

"My file? My file wouldn't say whether I can dance, or not!" She laughed.

He rubbed his hands over his face and groaned. "Busted."

"So, how did you know?"

"I googled you. I watched several online videos from your school talent competition."

Hannah gave a little scream. "No way! Oh my God! No way."

He nodded, his sexy mouth twisted in mirth.

She buried her head in her hands. "I could just die right now."

"What? It was cute!"

"Cute!" She burst out laughing, shaking her head.

"Your hair was much wilder back then, though."

"No, not really. I've just learned to tame it with product."

"Does anybody else have red hair in your family?"

"Yes, my mother does. In fact, I'm very like her. If you look at old photographs, it's hard to tell us apart."

"So, were you born in Ireland?"

"No. My brother was, but my parents immigrated six years before I was born."

"Why England?"

"Daddy worked for an agricultural company specialising in heavy machinery back in Ireland, and, at the time, they were expanding throughout the UK. They offered Daddy the manager's position in a new branch. So, he, Mammy, and my brother, Shaun, who was eighteen-months-old at the time, left their beloved hometown for a new life, and settled just outside of Shropshire."

"Have they ever been back?"

"No."

"Not even for a visit?"

She sighed. "Nope. I don't know why, because I know they still get homesick."

"I couldn't move to a new country, could you?"

"No way. In fact, my brother and his wife have just gone back to Ireland with his work. My parents were distraught."

"Ireland isn't far though, in comparison. And with the ferry service, I bet you could get there faster than you could get to some parts of England—especially in rush-hour."

She laughed. "That's true, actually. I think what upset them the most is the thought they're in another country. But, Shaun was living in London before that, and they only saw him once or twice a year."

"Are your parents still working?"

"No. Well, yes—they work for themselves. They live just outside a little market town called Bishop's Castle. Daddy has his own workshop on the property, and he restores old plant machinery that he sells at auction. They also have a few animals, and grow their own vegetables and stuff. Mammy makes jam and chutney, and she travels around the local farmers' markets on the weekends."

"Sounds idyllic. Why on Earth would you want to leave?"

"Oh, you know. I love it there, but nothing happens from one month to the next."

"Yes. I do know, actually. I was born and bred in Sussex, but when I was thirteen, we moved just outside of Newby Bridge, a little place on the southern tip of Lake Windermere."

"Oh, nice. I've always wanted to visit the Lake District."

"Have you never been?"

She shook her head.

"You'd love it. We had a holiday home in Bowness-on-Windermere when I was a kid. Back then, my parents owned *The West Sussex Express*. When they sold it, they supposedly bought the lake house with the intention of retiring. A likely story. In fact, they were busier *after* they moved than they were before. Anyhow, they bought out HGT, the company that owned AdCor previously."

"Are they still alive?" she asked.

"Sadly, no. My dad got sick on a trip overseas. Ate something he shouldn't, and the proud old bugger didn't tell anybody how bad he felt. He died in an Indian hospital a week later. I was eighteen."

"That's awful. I'm so sorry, Max."

He nodded, his eyes glistening. "Then, my mum just gave up work from that moment on. Thankfully, they had enough reliable staff to make sure the company ticked along. But, the pressure was on me to step up almost right away."

"And your mother?"

"She died less than twelve months later. She had no desire to live without Dad."

"That's so sad. To love somebody so much you'd die of a broken heart." She felt tears pricking at her own eyes and had to pull herself together. She found it so easy to forget he was her boss.

It was raining when they left the restaurant. Thankfully, Jackson had moved the limo, and parked it directly outside the door.

Max said his goodbyes, and watched as she got inside, before he turned, and headed in the opposite direction.

She'd presumed he'd share the car with her—he *had* been drinking, after all. And, although they'd had an amazing evening, there wasn't any mention of doing it again. She suddenly felt deflated.

The wet street shone from the light of the street lamps as she reminisced about the night. Max had been great. He was a terrific listener and so funny. She smiled broadly just thinking about him. She knew she was falling for him. She also knew she was being incredibly foolish.

The limo stopped, and she was jolted back to reality as Jackson opened her door.

"Can I show you inside, miss?"

"There's no need. Thanks for everything, Jackson." She covered her head with her handbag and ran towards the stairs.

It was midnight and she felt alive. She was finally living the dream she'd had as far back as she could remember—to swap the laid-back lifestyle for the city, fall in love with a prince, and live happily ever after. Oh, well. Maybe her dream was right out of a fairy story, but tonight, the reality had been close enough.

CHAPTER 9

Steve Miller had been furious with the message left in the daybook, but he was adamant he would bring Don to task tonight. He planned to time it just right.

After his shift finished, Steve met up with an old friend in the city to kill a few hours. They ate dinner in Chinatown, and he got a cab back to AdCor at around 10pm. The beers he'd drunk over dinner fired him up even more, and he was more than ready to take Don down a peg or two.

Ken Barber, the youngest member of the team, was on the front desk. He jumped up, clearly shocked to see his boss at that time of night.

"Hey, mate. How are you doing?" Steve liked Ken. He was hard-working and pleasant to be around.

"I'm good, yeah." Ken gulped, clearly unsure of what to say.

Steve nodded. "Good to hear, mate. Hey, you haven't seen me, okay?"

"Of course, sir."

He knew he could trust Ken. He just hoped he'd left it late enough to catch Don at whatever it was he'd been up to. He approached the security hub, swiped his card and let himself in.

Don didn't hear him enter. He was too engrossed with the video links playing on six of the screens. Don paused one of the videos, rewound it, and played it back as the girl, who Steve now recognised as Hannah McLaughlin, undressed and stepped into a bathtub. Another screen showed the girl's emails.

"What the …"

Without warning, Don jumped to his feet. With lightning ferocity, he smashed Steve around the side of the head with his steel torch.

A thick spray of Steve's blood covered the fuse cabinet, before he slumped to the ground with a deathly moan.

Don sat back in the leather chair. He hadn't felt so pumped since he was first under fire in Afghanistan. Springing to his feet again, he jumped on the spot, letting out a guttural roar.

"Help me, please."

Steve's whispered voice jolted Don back to reality and the gravity of what he'd done. He ran to the storeroom across the hall and grabbed some hand towels, placing them around Steve's head to mop up the blood.

After lifting Steve into the chair, Don paused the cameras and looped them. Being a surveillance expert, he figured he'd rather not have a recording of the next bit, just in case something prevented him getting back to erase the evidence.

He wheeled Steve in the chair towards the lift, thankful the older man had decided to pay him a visit so late—any earlier and the place would have been like Piccadilly Station.

Semi-conscious, Steve kept groaning and pleading with him.

"You couldn't keep your big fucking nose out, could you? Oh, no. Always wanting to be one step ahead," Don muttered, his face in a continuous sneer. He slammed the heel of his hand on the lift button.

The doors opened with a *ping*.

Don struggled to get the stupid chair inside as one of the wheels caught in the gap. With another roar, he launched the chair over the threshold, slamming Steve into the wall opposite. Using Steve's security pass, he selected the eleventh floor.

When the doors opened, he pushed Steve and the chair out. Using Steve's pass again, he entered a sequence of numbers to send the lift to the top floor in fault mode. Once the lift light had stopped, he forced the doors open using his keys. A rush of cold air came from the open shaft.

He removed the towels from Steve's head. "Don't look at me like that, you pathetic fucking pig. You brought all this on your-self. You hear me?"

Steve, barely conscious, didn't respond, which riled Don all the more. He kicked the ignorant bastard several times, before pushing the chair towards the shaft. Without hesitation, he tipped Steve face-first over the edge, hearing him land, moments later, with a sickening *splat*. Don smiled, closed the doors, and called the lift again.

"Going down," he said to himself, with a self-satisfied smile.

Don returned to the security hub, pushing the empty chair, and began cleaning the blood away. Afterwards, he recorded two hours of empty corridors, and ran it over the footage from before Steve's arrival. This would show him turn up, and head to the lifts, but not where he went from there. He registered an alarm call on the computer system, showing the lift doors on the eleventh floor seemed to be jammed in the open position, and sent a text alert to all departments. Then, he sent the lift to the sky deck and locked it off. He reset the computer log for his rounds, and did a key check. He copied the previous night's screen, changed the date, but left the time sequence alone, and then, pasted it over the current loop. That would provide his alibi.

Satisfied with everything, he ran his eyes around the room one final time. Everywhere appeared spotlessly clean. He turned to the monitors and said goodnight to Hannah with a kiss to the screen. Before leaving, he ran the scramble code which would hide all the links and live feeds he had running—no one would find them. The army had been good to him, and the technical stuff they had taught him whilst in khaki was coming in very useful.

CHAPTER 10

Hannah woke to the sun blazing through a chink in the curtains. She winced, groaning, and ducking her head back under the covers. It was far too early to wake up.

After an hour of tossing and turning she gave up, wrapped herself in her long, pale pink satin robe, and headed to the kitchen to make a pot of coffee. She carried her mug and this month's *Glam* magazine, and settled on the balcony.

The community she was now a part of was coming to life, and she enjoyed people-watching from her perch above the streets.

A short time later, she heard Simon's door open, and his head appeared above the partition moments after.

"Oh, hello." She smiled lazily.

"Hello, beautiful. You look a little worse for wear. I heard you stagger in past midnight."

"I hardly staggered in, cheeky. And it wasn't *after* midnight, as it happens."

"Well, it certainly wasn't before. You barely made it through the door, before your carriage turned back into a pumpkin." He laughed.

"You're a nutcase."

"I've been called much worse. Anyway, can I get you a hair of the dog?"

Hannah grinned. "I've only ever heard my dad say that. And no, thank you. I'll pass."

"Are you sure? I've been down to the Turkish deli on the high street and bought six bottles of my favourite Zinfandel rosé."

"Six bottles! Are you planning on getting trashed?"

"They're not all for tonight. They were on special. Plus, I got four family-sized bags of peanut M&Ms—sheer heaven."

Exasperated by his energy, Hannah rolled her eyes. "I thought you were working this weekend."

"No. I decided there was no need, and, to be quite frank, I've switched off. It must be because I'm leaving in a few weeks. Anyway, what are your plans for the day, because I was thinking about firing up the barbecue, and getting stuck into some chilled rosé? What do you say?"

Hannah considered his offer for a second. She knew Diane was working all weekend, so she would be putting herself at Simon's mercy. She nodded. "Yes, that would be very nice," she eventually said. "What would you like me to bring? Not M&Ms, I hope?"

"No." Simon laughed. "That's for dessert, silly."

Saturday morning meetings were a regular occurrence for Max. He didn't relish them, but as head of the Northwest Division, it meant sacrifices. As he waited for the others to arrive, his thoughts slipped back to Hannah, and the evening they'd shared.

If he was honest with himself, he was deeply attracted to the quirky young woman. He'd always avoided any personal relationships with employees, but plenty had tried to change his mind. Especially his last PA, Daniella Vespucci. She had come highly recommended by the CEO of HGT Euro, based in Paris. She was apparently homesick, and longed to return to her family in Manchester. However, it wasn't long before Max found out the true reason. Daniella had been sleeping with her boss for over two years, but when his wife began to ask questions, he needed to get rid of her, and fast.

Daniella became a handful very quickly. She was too touchy feely for Max's liking, and made no bones about letting him know she had her sights set firmly in his direction. Then, one day, after a couple of months, she appeared in his office, wearing nothing but a G-string and suspender belt. He found her splayed wantonly on top of his desk.

After that, he decided she had to go, but the problem he had was how to do it legally, without breaching company rules and regulations. He needn't have worried. Soon after, he discovered she'd been seeing one of his project managers, John Farley, and had fallen pregnant—clearly her ploy to snare herself a husband from the start. When John confided in Max, he told him he should to do the right thing by her. Daniella and John were married in Scotland within weeks, and Max arranged a promotion for him to the Glasgow office.

That was the reason he avoided employees like the plague, but something felt different with Hannah, although he couldn't pinpoint why.

He glanced at his watch, and wondered what was keeping the others.

Moments later, Angela arrived looking deathly pale. "Max, we appear to have a problem."

The vibration of his mobile phone on the bedside table woke Don from a deep, satisfying sleep. He glanced at the bright red numbers of his alarm clock—9.23am. He reached for his phone.

"Hello."

"Is that you, Don?" Angela Beanie's no-nonsense clipped tones assaulted his ear.

"Yes, I was sleeping. What do you want?"

"I apologise for that, however, we have an urgent issue. Mr Myers has asked if you would come back to work, ASAP?"

Don rubbed at his face with his free hand and groaned. "Can't Miller deal with it?"

"Impossible, I'm afraid," Angela said, her voice giving nothing away. "Will you come?"

"I suppose I have no choice. I'll be there as soon as I can."

Within the hour, Don noticed two fire crews, police, and paramedics down the service lane to the side of the building, as he pulled into the car park. He rushed through the back entrance into the main reception. Everything seemed calm. If not for the two suited men Myers and Angela stood talking to, nothing was amiss.

Myers spotted Don, and acknowledged him with a nod of his head before excusing himself from the group.

"Don. Thanks for coming in." He shook Don's hand warmly and slapped his shoulder.

"No problem, sir. I saw the emergency services outside. What's happened?"

"Did you happen to see Steve Miller last night?"

"No. Was I supposed to? He doesn't usually stay behind after his shift."

Max shook his head. "Well, it seems he decided to come back last night to do a safety audit of the night shift."

"Are you sure? That doesn't sound like something Steve would do."

"That's what I thought, but he was definitely here. Although it isn't clear what for, or why he didn't log his movements."

"Am I missing something, sir? What exactly is the problem?"

Max pinched the top of his nose between his eyes, and sighed. "Follow me," he said. "We'll walk and talk."

Don fell into step beside the younger man.

"It appears, after you left this morning, we received a call from Mrs Miller concerned about her husband. She informed Angela he'd told her there was an issue he needed to attend to here last night. When he wasn't home by this morning, she began to worry."

"I'm sure she did. Maybe he went out on the town instead, and crashed on somebody's sofa."

"That was the opinion of Angela, at the time, although she didn't say as much to Mrs Miller."

Don nodded. "So, what changed her mind?"

"At 8.15am, an engineer arrived to say we had a fault showing on number three lift. They found it to be jammed at the sky deck floor. During an inspection of the bottom counterweight and safety systems, they spotted what looked like a body."

Don gasped. "A body?"

Max nodded. "The fire department and the police were called. But, it's quite clear from the photograph the police provided it's Steven Miller."

Don gasped and spun away, feigning total shock. He dramatically leaned against the closest wall, struggling to catch his breath. He made a show of trying to pull himself together, then turned back to his boss. "I'm sorry, sir. Do we know how it happened?"

"At the moment, they believe he fell from the eleventh floor. The memory card showed at 10.48pm, the doors on eleven had jammed open. They reset fifteen minutes later, at which point the lift went to the safety position on the sky deck."

"It doesn't make sense. Why would he...?"

Max sighed deeply, shaking his head. "The video evidence only shows Steven walking towards the lift. He appeared happy enough, and more importantly, he was alone."

"I can't believe it. He was such a careful guy. How can something like this happen? Why didn't he tell anyone he was coming?"

"I don't know," Max said. "He obviously had his reasons for

returning. We'll know more when we hear from the coroner with the autopsy report. However, the police think he may have received a text alert regarding a fault with lift three. His phone was smashed and will take time to check, but we're thinking he lost his balance and fell."

Don closed his eyes and scratched his forehead. "Poor Steve. This is such a shock."

"I know. But, until I sort this mess out, can I ask you to take over as Head of Security?"

"No problem, Mr Myers. I already do a lot of Steve's work, anyway. I won't let you down."

"That's great. Thanks. I'm relieved I can rely on you. Now, go and get some sleep, and we'll talk tomorrow."

"Yes, sir."

"Oh, by the way, Don. Maybe we should try to refer to him as Mr Miller, not Steve. It will show more respect, at this time."

Don turned and watched his boss walk away towards the lift. His eyes could have burned holes the size of cannon shells in Max's back.

"Who the fuck do you think you're speaking to?" he muttered, once there was enough distance between them. "Fucking mouthy bastard."

Hannah threw on her denim shorts and a pink T-shirt. There wasn't a cloud in the sky. A perfect day for a barbecue. She slipped on her sandals and headed out to the deli.

She loved the deli atmosphere. It was cosmopolitan and different to the market atmosphere back home. The owner, Ahmet, and his wife, Elgin, were Turkish. He was a huge, noisy man, who was always cheerful, almost too cheerful, and she was quite the opposite. Their entire family worked in the deli, and they all seemed to love it.

Ahmet remembered her from her last visit, and welcomed her inside. "How are you settling in, 'anna'?"

"Very well. Thanks for asking."

"Georgie," he called to a young man, who was, without doubt, one of his sons.

When the younger man turned, Ahmet put his arm around his shoulder, and guided him towards Hannah. "This is 'anna', the young lady I was telling you about."

Georgie flushed deep red, clearly uncomfortable with this obvious attempt at matchmaking.

Hannah raised her eyebrows at Georgie and smiled. The meaning wasn't lost on him, and he laughed, and ducked out of his father's embrace.

After stocking up on a few items, she spotted some delicious-looking tomato and pesto sausages, and bought some for the barbecue.

Before heading home, she called into Chang's, the dry cleaner. An Asian man behind the counter greeted her as she entered.

"Hello," she said. "My friend dropped my dress in to be cleaned on Wednesday morning …"

The man turned to the rack of garments. "Name?"

"Oh, no. I'm sorry. She actually picked it up again that same day."

He frowned. "Something wrong?"

"No. The opposite, actually. It had been repaired. A bone had been added to the corset. I wanted to thank you, and pay for your wife's time."

"And you didn't ask us to repair it?"

Hannah shook her head.

"Then, she wouldn't have repaired it. We can't just take it upon ourselves to repair anything."

Hannah was speechless. She stood staring at the man, completely confused. "Are you sure?" she eventually said. "Can you check with her? It was a black, fitted dress. I'm not angry. In fact, I'm thrilled."

The man opened the door behind him, and called something she couldn't decipher. Within moments, a small woman appeared —a worried expression on her face.

The man spoke in their own language, and the woman shook her head, her forehead furrowed deeply.

"Like I said, miss. It wasn't altered here."

"Okay. Sorry to bother you."

Completely confused, she left the shop, and headed for home. *Was she going crazy?* First the locker and the underwear, and now the dress.

She headed home, and, once inside, she ran herself a bath.

Lying in the fragrant bubbles, she smiled when she suddenly heard Simon, in his shower, singing in a deep baritone voice. *You're the one that I want.* She sniggered, imagining him doing the motions as well.

After a few more cringeworthy moments, she turned up her music, and sank deeper into the water.

Just before seven, Hannah opened her wardrobe, looking for something to wear. She came across the black dress, and pulled it out to re-examine it. Maybe she'd been mistaken, after all.

She sat on the bed, manipulating the fabric between her fingers, but the dress was perfect—nothing missing at all. Totally freaked out, she tried to think of a logical explanation, but there wasn't one. She hadn't been the only one to notice the bone was missing. The two women in the boutique had seen it, too.

CHAPTER 11

Max usually went home to the lakes on Saturdays, which was approximately a 90 minutes' drive away, but not today. Absolutely exhausted, he let himself into the self-contained flat adjoining his office on the top floor of the AdCor building. After showering, he fell into bed.

He was pleased the day was over. He'd never had a death at the office before, and Steve's death wasn't anything like a straightforward heart attack. Instead, it had been a particularly gruesome discovery. Not something he'd forget in a hurry.

"Are you ready? Are you still coming?" Simon called from his balcony.

She opened her door and winced, as a cloud of smoke wafted into her face coming from the direction of the barbecue. "Smells delicious," she croaked sarcastically.

"I'm just burning off the surface—it's been left out here all winter. Don't worry, I haven't started cooking yet."

"Pleased to hear it. I'm coming now."

"The front door's open. Just come on in," he said.

He handed her a glass of rosé, as she stepped onto the balcony, trying to dodge another plume of smoke.

"Look at you, all dressed up," he said, eyeing her up and down. "I should have said dress casual."

She glanced down at her favourite sunflower top and cut-off black trousers. "I am casual."

"If you call that casual, you must look stunning when you make an effort."

She felt her cheeks redden. "You're so sweet, thank you."

"How's the wine?"

She sipped at her glass, and blinked several times at the sharp taste.

"You hate it? I can get you something else."

She shook her head and laughed. "No. I don't hate it. I've just brushed my teeth, that's all."

She handed him the bag from the deli. "I bought some sausages when I went out."

"Are they the tomato and pesto ones?"

"They are. Have you had them before?"

He took a sip of his wine and chuckled. "I practically live on them when I'm home."

"Is this the usual way to entertain back home in Seattle?"

"Yeah, if the weather forecast is good, most people light the barbecue."

"Are you looking forward to seeing your family again?"

He nodded, suddenly serious. "My nan has been ill. Mom kept it from me, but now I'm going home, she thought she should prepare me."

Hannah reached out, touching his arm. "I'm sorry. That's tough."

"Anyway, less of this depressing talk. We're meant to be having fun." He lifted the lid of the barbecue, then went inside, returning moments later with a platter of meat.

"You've got enough there to feed the whole building."

"Slight exaggeration, but yes, I may have overdone it."

Hannah took a closer inspection. Lamb chops, fillet steak, chicken breast, *and* sausages. She groaned.

"Don't worry. You don't need to eat it all in one go—we can just graze over the evening. Are you warm enough?"

"I'm toasty. Thanks."

Simon loaded the grill with the meat, and brought a large bowl of salad out from the kitchen. "More wine?" He paused, with the bottle over her glass.

She nodded, noticing her glass was almost empty. "See, I told you I liked it."

They sat at the table and waited for the food to cook.

"I love sitting out here. I usually plant myself down early afternoon, and people-watch until the neighbourhood settles for the night."

"Don't you go out with your friends on your days off work?" she asked.

"To be honest, I've not met many people around here. My work life is hectic, and I stay in hotels with a lot of the labourers wherever the job is. By the time I get home, I'm glad of my own company." He got to his feet to check the grill.

With his back turned to her, Hannah looked him up and down. He was incredibly attractive—more so than Max, if she was honest. The way his jeans hung off his hips and moulded his legs would send most women into a frenzy. The plain white T-shirt he was wearing looked anything but plain, as it clung to his broad, athletic frame. The fact he was sensitive and funny was a bonus, not to mention he seemed to find her attractive, too.

Max, although gorgeous, wasn't interested in her, not sexually anyway. But, this red-blooded male in front of her, was.

"So, tell me. How's it going at work?" he asked, breaking her daydream.

"I'm loving it. Everybody is so friendly." A sudden vision of

Angela snapping at her and marching from her office flashed through her mind.

Simon squinted. "What was that all about?"

"What?"

"You winced."

"Oh, it's just my boss. She jumped down my throat earlier in the week."

"What for?"

"That's just the thing, I have no idea. She said something about my timekeeping, but I wasn't even late—well, not much, a minute, if that!"

"That's odd. Had you done something to upset her?" He handed her a plate and topped up her wine once again.

"I hadn't seen her in days. Unless, it was because I complained to security... But, no, it couldn't have been. I didn't do that until later."

Simon piled all the meat onto a fresh platter, then placed it on the table beside the bowl of salad. He sat down again. "Why did you complain to security?"

"Oh, my gym bag had gone missing from the lockers." She stabbed a sausage, and transferred it to her plate, cutting off a piece of chicken. "This looks divine."

"Why would anybody have an issue with you reporting a missing bag?"

"Because it hadn't actually gone missing. It seems I'd put it in the wrong locker."

He shrugged, and shoved a piece of steak in his mouth, chewing several times before continuing, "Easy done."

Hannah nodded and looked back at her plate.

"You don't think so?"

"Sorry?"

"I said, 'easy done,' and your eyes said different."

"Smart arse."

"Am I wrong, though?"

"No, you're not wrong. But, it sounds crazy."

"What does?"

"I don't believe I would've put the bag in the wrong locker. I'm a bit OCD about that kind of thing. My locker is the third from the left, third from the bottom, and third from the top."

"Was anything missing?"

She shook her head, and placed her knife and fork down. "This is where it gets crazy. I'm sure the stuff inside had been exchanged for similar, but much newer, items."

"Yes, you're right. It does sound crazy." He sniggered, wiping his mouth on a napkin.

"I did warn you. But, that's not all!"

"Go on."

"I bought a dress in the sale, knowing it had a fault in it. Anyway, Diane dropped it in at Chang's for me, and when I got it back, someone had repaired it."

"That's easy. Mrs Chang must've fixed it."

"Exactly what I thought, but I called in earlier to thank them, and they didn't have a clue what I was talking about." She took another mouthful of sausage.

"So, you suspect somebody is fixing and replacing your belongings?"

Hannah covered her mouth with a piece of kitchen roll while she finished her food. "I told you it sounded nuts. I've also had a feeling someone's been in my flat. But, that could be my wild imagination playing tricks on me."

"So, nothing is moved, or missing?"

"Nope. It's just a feeling. A certain smell when I arrive home. But, to be honest, I'm still getting used to the flat. It could just be the natural smell."

"What's it like?"

She shrugged. "Can't explain it. It's not horrible—just different."

"Do you want my advice?"

She nodded. "Of course."

"It's your first time living alone. When a flat has been left alone all day, it smells funky, until you fill it with your living smells—cooking, cleaning, and what have you."

"I suppose."

"At home, I bet your mum would have a meal waiting for you, and all the laundry done—am I right?"

She nodded, grinning. "Yes, you're right."

"I bet you never came home to nothing, and if you did, it would have seemed strange—right again?"

She shrugged. "Right again."

Once they'd finished eating, Hannah helped with the dishes, and headed back to the balcony.

"Here, I've got a blanket. It's getting quite chilly now," Simon said.

They turned the chairs towards the street, and sat side-by-side, sharing the blanket. They stayed that way, putting the world to rights, watching the sun go down.

Simon walked Hannah to her door, after polishing off three bottles of wine between them. She hadn't felt tipsy until she got to her feet and the room went a bit squiffy.

Just like last time, he bent in for a kiss. But, unlike last time, she welcomed it, pulling him towards her.

So what if he wasn't Max. He was more suited to her than Max would ever be. She was attracted to him, and he made her laugh. But, above all—they were two consenting adults.

She turned to open the door, but they barely made it through, before he pounced on her again.

"Do you have condoms?" she whispered.

He nodded, his eyes drinking her in. He pulled her towards him again and spun her against the wall. He gripped her hands in his above her head, so she couldn't move. She found it strangely erotic.

Tearing himself away, he panted, "I need to run next door before I lose all control. Be right back."

She took several deep breaths and headed to the bedroom.

When he returned, she locked her arms around his neck, as they collapsed onto the bed. She pulled his T-shirt off over his head, and launched it across the room, then buried her fingertips in his thick, chest hair.

Once again, he tore himself away to peel off his jeans and white cotton briefs. Then, tantalising her beyond belief, he slowly removed her clothing.

When he eased himself down on top of her, crushing his chest against hers, she wrapped her legs around his hips, and pulled him to her tightly.

"What does this mean, lovely Hannah? You're driving me wild."

"Shhh, don't speak." She'd lost all sense of logic and reasoning. She needed him. Right now.

———

Her head felt as if it was about to explode when she awoke hours later. Needing to pee, she eased herself out of bed, not wanting to disturb Simon. She needn't have worried. He'd gone.

Padding to the bathroom, she barely opened her eyes and winced at the fiery urine. They'd used a condom, so she hoped the burning sensation was caused by overuse, and not the beginnings of cystitis.

She considered calling Simon, as she climbed back into bed, but it was too early. She'd leave it until the mist and thunder had cleared from her head.

CHAPTER 12

Don was snapping the wristband furiously. He'd witnessed every second of Hannah's assault from the security hub, this time without interruption. He thought he was going to blow his top. *How dare the fucking pervert lay one finger on his girl?* Snap-snap-snap.

But, he wasn't going to lose control like he had with Clair. He'd made a huge mistake there, and ended up losing everything. This time, he'd deal with things much more efficiently.

As soon as he finished his shift, he sped over to Simon's flat, and let himself in.

He crept through the flat, noticing the wine glasses, dishes, and leftover food. He stepped on top of a pile of old records fanned out across the carpet beside a new Bang & Olufsen turntable, and smiled as the discs cracked and snapped. He headed for the only bedroom.

On the monitors, he'd watched the bastard sneak from Hannah's bed, once he'd had his fill of her. Don found him lying spread-eagled and naked on top of his own bed.

A packet of condoms lay open on the bedside table, and several small square packages had spilled out. Don imagined the man rushing to grab some in his haste to molest poor Hannah. With an almighty rage, he lifted the torch high above his head, and swung down, hitting Simon hard across the throat.

Simon shot up, both hands gripping the front of his neck. He couldn't breathe. Choking and rasping sounds came from him as he flailed about in the darkness, clearly trying to figure out what the hell had just happened to him.

After a minute or two, the choking gave way to a wet, gargle-like sound.

Don stepped forward and stood in a shaft of light made from a chink in the curtain. "You raping bastard! You fucking dead raping bastard!"

Although in a bad way, Simon must have sensed he was in mortal danger, and tried to flip himself off the other side of the bed. But, he was too far gone, and fell to the carpet on the other side of the room.

Don strode over to him. "She's mine, and you hurt her. For that, I'll take your life."

Holding the torch in both hands, Don crashed it down onto the young man's skull, letting out a guttural roar.

Don paced the room, until his heartbeat returned to a normal rhythm. Then, he pulled the curtain closed properly, before switching on the overhead light.

He was surprised there wasn't much blood—nothing on the bed, and only a pool spreading on the carpet underneath Simon's head. But, the stain wouldn't be noticeable from the doorway.

He ran to the kitchen for a plastic bag, then found some tape in a drawer. Returning to the bedroom, he taped Simon's mouth shut, then placed the bag onto his bloody head. Satisfied there was no exposed blood, Don dragged the naked man through to the kitchen.

In his toolbox, he'd brought everything he needed.

He checked for a pulse. It was weak, but the bastard was still very much alive, which was what he'd been hoping.

Don waited until Simon began to stir, before he carried out the next step of his plan.

He removed the bag, no longer concerned about the mess on the vinyl floor covering—he'd mop it up later. With a length of electrical cord, he strapped Simon's hands and feet together, and wrapped the cord around his neck. Then, dragging him into the small utility room to the rear of the kitchen, Don opened the chest freezer. He removed several lumps of meat, making sure there was enough room.

When Don grabbed the cord, it tightened around Simon's throat. Then, he lifted the semi-conscious man, and dropped him inside the freezer.

Simon's petrified eyes suddenly opened. He tried to cry out, but the tape prevented him making much sound, except for several high-pitched squeals. He began to struggle like a maniac. Each movement caused the cord to tighten further.

Don laughed. "Got yourself into a bit of a pickle, haven't you, boy? Squealing like a piggy, and trussed up like a turkey. The freezer's the only place for you."

Tears ran from the man's eyes, and a steady stream of piss flowed from his flaccid penis.

"Ooh, look! You're leaking from your turkey twizzler. You'll regret doing that, when you stick yourself to the sausages."

After more frantic wriggling, Simon's face turned scarlet, and his eyes bulged.

"Don't worry. I'll be kind, and close the lid to make it faster— I'm not a total fruit loop, you know." With that, he slammed the lid down.

Using his drill and pop rivets, he fitted a clasp and padlock to the lid, then went about tidying the flat.

———————————

A loud bang and muffled scream startled Hannah awake again.

She held her breath and listened but everything was silent. *It must have been a dream.* She groaned and pulled the duvet over her head once more. She couldn't face the world yet.

An hour or so later, she dragged herself out of bed, vowing to steer clear of the wine for a while. She hoped Simon was alright. He was coming over all heavy last night, and at one point, she suspected he was about to declare his undying love for her. She liked him a lot, but they were still missing that vital spark she felt when she was around Max. She thought she could settle last night, but now, she didn't want to just settle, not without finding out if there could be a future for her and Max.

Lying on the sofa with a thin blanket, she reached for her phone and sighed. She needed to get this over with.

A ringing sound led Don to the bedroom, and he found Simon's phone underneath the pillow on the bed. The display said, *Hottie next door.*

His finger hovered over the end button, but then he stopped, and instead, answered the call.

Her breathy tones filled his ear. "Hi, Simon. How's the head?"

Don silently held the phone close.

"Simon?"

After a few more seconds, she hung up.

Don relaxed and began breathing again. Then, he was startled by a different melodic tone. A text.

Hottie next door- *Hope you're feeling ok. My head feels like a brass band has taken up residence—never again, lol.*

. . .

He considered replying, but another message came through before he'd made up his mind.

Hottie next door- *I hope you're not upset with me. I like you, but last night was a mistake. I'd prefer to go back to being friends. Can we start again?*

Delighted she'd rebuffed the sleazy predator, Don punched the air with glee, before replying.

Yes, I agree. Huge mistake. I've received some bad news, and had to go away for a while. Speak soon.

Hottie next door- *Oh no! Is it your nan? Are you heading back to the States already?*

Yes, and yes. I'm waiting for a standby flight. I'll be in touch.

Hottie next door- *Is there anything you need me to do?*

If I send you my work number, can I get you to call them tomorrow, and explain?

Hottie next door- *Of course I will. Hugs. Safe flight.*

. . .

Without knowing, Hannah had given him the perfect explanation. Now, there was no reason he couldn't use the flat, so long as he kept the noise down. He couldn't get closer to her if he tried. It would suit his purposes perfectly.

He stripped the bed, and cleaned up the dishes and food from the night before. Then, he put all Simon's clothes in two large rubbish bags, intending to put them in the clothes bins for the homeless outside his local Asda.

Once everywhere was tidy, he walked toward the double-skinned brick, dividing wall between the flats. Knowing Hannah was on the other side made him warm inside. He reached into his jacket pocket and pulled out Hannah's white panties. Then he stripped off all his clothes, and lay on the carpet facing the cold brick, placing the sweet, musky-smelling panties to his face.

Her scent relaxed him, and he sighed, closing his eyes, happy in the knowledge he'd managed to protect her from the scumbag in the freezer. *She's mine. Forever.* He drifted off, dreaming of a time when they would be together as a couple, a contented smile on his face.

Don woke with a start an hour or so later. Getting ready to leave, he dressed, and returned Hannah's panties to his jacket pocket. The keys to the flat were on the hallstand.

The tricky bit would be to get past Hannah's front window without being seen.

As an afterthought, he checked on Simon. He unlocked the padlock and lifted the lid. Don belted out a laugh, as he took in the scene before him.

Simon's cheeks were red raw, and a fine layer of frost coated his entire body. A stream of snot had frozen, and hung from one nostril. Don thought he was already dead at first, until he noticed

Simon's eyelid had frozen open, stuck to the side of the freezer, and his eyeball was rolling around aimlessly.

Don figured he must be blind already, as the eye didn't seem to focus on anything at all.

"Wow! You know what, you sick fuck? The *super freeze* function really works! But, don't worry, you'll be out in time for Christmas."

Don's laughter and the slamming of the lid would be the last things Simon would hear, as he succumbed to the freezing cold darkness awaiting him.

Hannah didn't surface again until early afternoon. With a raging thirst, she stomped to the kitchen for a drink. After knocking back two full glasses of iced water, she scanned the contents of the fridge. She needed to eat something, but nothing appealed to her in the slightest. She returned to the sofa, and closed her eyes once again.

CHAPTER 13

On Monday morning, Hannah found Devlin, the marketing manager, perched on the edge of her desk. He had several members of staff around him, who all seemed to be listening intently.

Devlin hopped to his feet when he noticed her. "Okay, then, back to the grind." He clapped his hands, and the crowd dispersed.

"What's happened?" she asked, placing her bag down on the desk.

"Oh, didn't you hear?" Devlin's eyebrows arched upwards. "They found Steven Miller dead at the bottom of the lift shaft."

Hannah gasped. "Oh my God! That's terrible!" She immediately thought of Max. No wonder he hadn't been in touch with her all weekend. He must be devastated.

"How did it happen?" she asked.

Devlin shrugged. "He fell, as far as I know. There was a fault with the lift, and he must've tried to fix it, or something. Poor bastard. Imagine falling all that way! My stomach does a flip when I'm going down *inside* the lift."

"Oh, don't." Hannah shoved his arm. "It makes me feel ill just thinking about it."

Angela Beanie arrived to take the Monday morning meeting, and Hannah's heart sank further. *Where the hell was Max?*

Angela asked to speak to Hannah after the meeting. She was as tight-lipped and curt as she'd been the previous week.

Hannah longed to ask if she'd done something to upset her, but she didn't feel she knew her well enough to be so informal.

After pouring them both a coffee, Angela indicated they sit beside each other on the sofa. "So, how's it going?"

Hannah nodded. "Great. I'm loving my job."

"I hear Danny Leno asked for you to be on his campaign?"

"Yes. That's right. We were supposed to meet on Friday, but he was held up."

"So I hear." She smiled, her eyes expressionless. "Can I be frank with you, Hannah?"

"Of course, you can." Hannah's stomach dropped.

"Being the new girl here, you should be wary of making enemies."

"Enemies? I don't understand."

"I don't know how it works at the *Daily Post*, but there is a kind of hierarchy here. Some of your colleagues have worked hard to get to their positions, and you come along with one notable deal under your belt, and you're getting preferential treatment. People are talking—calling it favouritism."

Hannah was flabbergasted. She shook her head, trying to dissect Angela's words and the underlying meaning. "I'm sorry. I didn't realise I was being treated any differently. As far as I knew, Danny Leno asked for me personally. That's hardly *my* fault."

Angela curled her lip scornfully and her nostrils flared. "Do you really think Danny Leno would have asked for you, just like that? After one meeting, you'd had him eating out of your hand? Pull the other one."

"I don't follow you. If not him, then who asked for me?"

"Oh, Hannah, Hannah. You *are* naïve. Didn't you even suspect when Mr Leno didn't show? It's the oldest trick in the book."

"What is? You don't mean … Max?"

"Of course, I mean Max. But, don't flatter yourself. He does the same with every pretty new employee."

Hannah could feel her cheeks burn up as tears pricked her eyes.

The older woman reached out and patted Hannah's knee. "I'm sorry to upset you, dear. But, I couldn't stand by, and let him make a fool of you. Most of the women know the score; they're worldly-wise, but you're so innocent and trusting."

Hannah wiped the tears from her face. "I feel so stupid."

"Don't beat yourself up about it, kid. It happens to the best of us, at one time or another."

After a hectic weekend, Max took off to the lake house for some much needed sleep. He thought about calling Hannah, but figured it wouldn't look good calling her at work, so decided to wait until later.

Their evening kept playing over in his mind. He was pleased Danny hadn't made it, in the end. He almost called her from the taxi on Friday night on his way back to his apartment at AdCor, but, feeling like a love-struck teenager, he ended the call. However, he now wished he had called. Once he'd found out about Steven, he hadn't had five minutes to himself. He was worried Hannah would think he didn't care, considering he'd left it so long.

The drive to the lake house always chilled him out. He put the roof down on his silver Mercedes Cabriolet, and the stresses of the business and chaos of the city fell away the closer he got to his destination. The last twenty minutes of the journey had stunning water views, and that was when he completely switched off from work.

His parents had purchased the property years ago with the

intention of retiring, but although they soon returned to the grind, and had the flat added onto to the main office, they still kept the lake house to escape to whenever they could.

He turned off the road into the driveway, drove past the little cottage where Charmaine and Lenny, his housekeeper and caretaker, lived. The large stone house peeked through the trees. He hit the garage door opener, and drove straight in to the four-car garage.

He grabbed his bag, and ran up the interior stairs to the living area on the first floor. Charmaine always made sure the fridge and larder were well stocked in anticipation of his return. After devouring a cheese sandwich, he went out onto the veranda, and climbed into his hammock.

Mid-afternoon, Max woke with a start. Although pleased he'd caught up on some much-needed rest, he hadn't meant to sleep quite so long. He had a lot of work he should be getting on with.

He found several emails from Angela when he turned on his laptop, but one in particular surprised him. She told him Hannah had pulled her to one side that morning, and asked to be taken off the Leno campaign.

Why would she do that? They'd had a great time on Friday, even though Leno hadn't showed, and she hadn't seemed at all bothered. Today was only Monday, so it wasn't as if anything could have happened over the weekend. He was more determined than ever to call her at home later.

Don returned to Simon's flat straight from work on Monday morning. He lugged up a holdall filled with his personal items, and after making the bed, crashed for a few hours.

He was vaguely aware of Hannah taking a shower next door, just after 8am, and he smiled contentedly, and snuggled further into the duvet.

Around lunchtime, he woke, showered, and made himself two slices of toast, courtesy of the contents of the fridge. Then, he set about hacking into Simon's laptop.

It didn't take long. Don was a seasoned IT expert. Once in, finding all the man's stored passwords was a breeze. He read several emails to get the gist of what was happening in the man's life, preferring to face potential problems head-on, rather than have them knock at the door.

Firstly, he emailed Simon's mother. From what he could gather, Simon was intending to return to the USA soon, and warning bells would sound if he just didn't show up. So, using the same wording from the previous emails, he told her he'd been offered a job too good to turn down, and he would be in touch as soon as he could.

The next email he sent was to Simon's boss, reiterating what Hannah had no doubt told them, if she'd kept to her word.

Once all the loose ends were tied up, he set about logging in to the security cameras he'd set up next door. It was strange to be able to see Hannah's home from every angle, and know he was so close.

On his days off, he would be able to sleep less than three feet away from her—watch her every movement, and record each snuffle and snore. The mere thought of it caused his entire body to tingle.

CHAPTER 14

Hannah made it through the rest of the day on autopilot. Every time she allowed her thoughts to replay Angela's brutal words, she flushed deeply.

Feeling like a fool, she could hardly wait to get home and spill the whole story to Diane. She'd been working all weekend, so Hannah hadn't told her about her fling with Simon yet.

Angela sent a message after lunch, informing her she'd officially removed Hannah from the Leno campaign. As she read it, tears pricked her eyes, and she ran to the bathroom hoping nobody had noticed the cry-baby new girl.

After crying all her makeup off, she felt wretched for the rest of the day. Diane gasped when she answered Hannah's knock later on.

"What's wrong, sweetie? Come in. Come in." Diane rushed her through to the kitchen, and sat opposite her at the small bistro table. She listened while Hannah poured her heart out, gasping and sighing at all the right moments. But, she was clearly shocked to hear about Simon's moonlight flit.

"I know! I tried to call a couple of times, then I sent a text. I thought he was ignoring me, because I'd been a little standoffish once the passion had died down, but he messaged me back eventually, and said he was already at the airport."

"Poor Simon. I knew his grandmother was sick, but I didn't think she was *that* sick." Diane got to her feet and filled the coffee pot.

"Same. He'd only told me about her the night before, and I knew they were close. He must've been devastated to get the dreaded call."

"I'll email him tomorrow. He should be home by now," Diane said.

"Oh, good. Can you tell him I said hi? I don't have his email address."

"Of course I will, and I'll forward you his address. What are you going to do about your boss?"

Hannah shrugged. "Not a lot I can do. He's made a fool of me, that's for certain."

"Thank goodness this Angela chick had the decency to be honest with you."

"I know you're right, but I actually think she got a kick out of it."

Diane shook her head. "What kind of person could get a kick out of something like that?"

"I don't know, but I'd put money on her being one of them."

"She might be wrong. I mean, look at you—you're a stunner. I reckon he'll be falling over himself to get back in your good books."

"I doubt it. But, I must admit, I'd love you to be right," Hannah said sadly.

"Trust your auntie Diane. You'll be on like Donkey Kong by the weekend."

Hannah laughed. "We'll see."

After coffee, Hannah left Diane to get ready for work, and headed to her own flat.

As soon as she stepped in the door, the strange smell hit her again. She shuddered, and reminded herself of what Simon had said—the flat just needed her input in order for it to feel loved, and smell like home.

She couldn't face cooking, so she ordered a pizza, and took a shower while she waited for it to be delivered.

As she turned the water jets off, the phone began to ring. She grabbed a towel, and quickly rubbed her hair before wrapping it around her body. The ringing had stopped by the time she reached it. She checked the caller display, and her stomach dropped. It was Max.

Backing away from the phone, as though it was some sort of incendiary device, she leapt out of her skin as the doorbell sounded. *What the hell was wrong with her? Why did the womanising prick make her feel like this?*

She answered the door still wrapped in the towel, dripping water everywhere. Not that the pizza delivery guy minded—his eyes almost boggled out of their sockets.

After finishing his paperwork, Max headed to the cottage to catch up with Charmaine and Lenny. Lenny was actually an old friend of his from school, who had found himself in a pickle after losing his job at the local sports centre. The timing couldn't have been better, as it coincided with Max needing to replace Katherine and Colin, the elderly couple who'd been in the position since his parents ran the place.

For Lenny, it was as though he'd died and gone to heaven. To be paid to stay home and potter around the place, giving them bags of time off, was a dream come true.

But, Max didn't mind. He knew the place was much too hard for him to deal with himself, and he wasn't able to make it home every weekend. He needed people he could trust and rely on to keep the place up to scratch in his absence.

Lenny was sitting on the tiny veranda of the cottage, as he walked around to the front. "There you are, buddy. I heard your garage door open earlier, and came to check it was you—it's unlike you to be here during the week. Is everything alright?"

"Oh, sorry. I meant to warn you I was coming. I had a full-on weekend. One of my security officers had an accident. He fell down the lift shaft."

"Shit! How the hell did that happen?"

"It's a total mystery. The police believe he was trying to find the fault, and lost his balance."

Lenny squinted his eyes. "You don't think so?"

Max shrugged. "Seems crazy he would do that. He'd worked for me for years, and was Head of Security, so not a stupid, young thing."

"Do you think somebody pushed him?"

Max shook his head rapidly. "No. Nothing like that. The security footage shows him approach the lift shaft alone."

"So, what are you thinking?"

Max laughed. "You know me so well, Len. Steve was a hardworking, older man, nearing retirement. I know he struggled with the more physical side of the job, so he'd have to hang up his uniform for good soon enough."

"So, you think he did it on purpose?"

Max nodded. "I haven't said anything. It would kill his family, if that were the case. Better everybody thinks it was an accident."

"Will he get a pay-out?"

Max nodded. "A hefty one. As Head of Security, an insurance policy was part of his package."

"So, if he was going to do it at all, it makes sense for it to be at work?"

"Exactly."

"Fancy a beer?" Lenny got to his feet, as Charmaine appeared in the doorway, two bottles of Mexican beer in her hands.

"Beat you to it." She laughed.

They settled around the wooden outdoor furniture, and chatted about the house and local gossip. Max left after an hour or so and strolled back to his place.

At six-thirty, he called Hannah's phone, but it went unanswered.

Hannah was wrapped in her robe, curled up on the sofa in front of the TV. She'd eaten half of the pizza by the time the phone rang again.

She debated whether or not to answer it, but she'd never been any good at letting a call go unanswered. "Hello?" she said, after the fifth ring. Her stomach was in knots.

"Hannah? It's Max Myers."

"Hi, Max." Her voice sounded childlike to her ears.

"I'm sorry I haven't been in touch since Friday evening, but I'm sure you've heard about Steven Miller."

"Yes, I did. Shocking news."

"I intended to call you tonight, anyway. I've escaped for a few days to the lake house, but I'll be back on Thursday for Steven's funeral."

"Okay," she said, wishing he'd get to the point.

"But, I've received an email from Angela Beanie. She said you'd requested to be taken off the Leno campaign."

"Yes. That's correct."

"May I ask you why?"

"It's just not for me. I've only been working here two minutes. I don't want the rest of the team to think I'm getting preferential treatment."

There was a silent pause on the other end of the phone. "But, you're not. Danny Leno requested you," he eventually said.

"Still, it's not very fair on the others."

"Was it because he didn't show on Friday? I thought we had a good time."

"It's nothing to do with that. And, yes, I enjoyed myself. But, you're my boss, and I'm your employee. I don't want to blur the lines."

"Can we meet on Thursday? After work."

"I'd rather not. I don't want people talking."

"Screw everybody else. I like you, Hannah. I thought you liked me?"

"Yeah, well, I refuse to be just another conquest. If you insist on a meeting, I'd prefer it to be in the office within work hours."

"Another conquest? I don't make a habit of feeling like this! In fact, this is the first time."

"I'm sorry, but I need to go. I'll see you on Thursday at some point, Mr Myers." With that, she hung up.

Tears flowed down her face, but she was proud of herself. She wouldn't be treated like just another star-struck employee. No way.

No longer hungry, she slid the pizza box onto the coffee table.

CHAPTER 15

On Thursday morning, Max left the lake house bright and early hoping to miss the rush-hour traffic. The weatherman on the local radio station seemed far too cheerful, informing the morning listeners the weather would turn cloudy, and there was a seventy-five percent chance of rain.

But, Max was a hundred percent sure it would. In fact, it had already begun spitting, and the sky had turned dark and moody-grey, exactly what they didn't need, considering they had Steve's funeral scheduled for 2.30pm.

He knew there was no shelter outside the crematorium. Not only would it be solemn, but it would also be windy and wet.

He scrolled through his contacts using the steering wheel buttons, and called Angela's number.

"Hello?"

"Hi, Angela. It's only me. Sorry to call you so early, but I've just heard the weather forecast for today. I think we'd better arrange a large gazebo for the funeral. Can you organise that for me, please?"

"All in hand, Max. I spoke with the funeral home last week, and asked them to check weather predictions on the day. I told them if the chance of rain was forty-five percent or above, they should arrange a gazebo to be erected out the front for a dry entrance from the car park."

"That's excellent, Angela. I should have guessed you'd be one step ahead of the game. I'd like to say how pleased I am with your overall efforts, and I'll arrange for us to have a chat as soon as things settle down. Is that okay?"

"Thanks, Max. But, I'm only doing what you pay me to do."

"You're always helping me reward loyalty and hard work. You're not exempt from that, you know."

"Thanks. I appreciate it, Max."

"Oh, and I received your email about Hannah McLaughlin. What exactly did she say to you?"

"Not a lot, really. Just that she wanted to be taken off the campaign."

"Can you do a bit of digging for me? I have a feeling she's being bullied. She was raring to go on Friday."

Angela didn't say anything.

"Are you there, Angela?"

"Yes, I'm still here. I have a feeling she may be getting a bit of stick for her relationship with you."

"What relationship? We had a business dinner—nothing more. Find out who's causing trouble, and have them waiting for me in my office when I get there."

"That might be a little tricky. You see, she won't say who it is. But, leave it with me. I'll see what I can find out." She ended the call.

A short while later, Max pulled the car up to the barriers of the underground car park at AdCor, although he couldn't remember driving the last few miles since leaving the motorway.

He took the lift to the top floor. He preferred the flat adjoining his office to the lake house in a lot of ways. It was nothing special, just a converted office space, with a practical double bed along the far wall, a two-seater sofa placed to take in

100 | NETTA NEWBOUND

the outstanding city views, as well as the flat screen TV, and a compact bathroom.

He sighed, as he noticed Angela had dug his funeral suit out of the fitted wardrobe. The plastic covering with ticket attached showed she'd had it cleaned for him, too. He hadn't thought about that.

He showered, and changed into casual clothes, planning to put on his suit a little later.

Sitting at his desk, he switched on his laptop to check his emails. One had come in from Don Henry, explaining he and two guards would attend the funeral, and any others who wished to pay their respects would attend the wake at the family home after 5pm. Don also said he and the other two would cover the night shift tonight. Max didn't need to reply.

He swivelled in his seat to face the window, just as a flash of lightning lit up the dreary sky. A boom of thunder followed immediately after. Max shook his head, as the heavens opened.

Hannah was surprised to find Angela sitting at her desk when she arrived that morning.

"Ah, Hannah, there you are. Can we have a little chat?" Angela said.

Hannah glanced around the busy office and nodded. Then, she followed the other woman out to the communal area.

"Max called me this morning," Angela said. "He's angry, and is demanding to know who's been talking to you."

"Don't worry. I won't say a word."

"See to it that you don't. I only told you in the first place, because I didn't want him making a fool of you. Needless to say, my job would be on the line, if he knew it was me."

"I said I won't say anything, and I meant it."

Angela's face was set in a stern expression. She turned to leave, without another word.

Hannah headed back to her desk. As she was returning from lunch later on, she spotted Max. He and several members of staff were gathering in the foyer, ready to go to Steven Miller's funeral. She couldn't help notice how handsome he looked in his charcoal grey tailored suit, crisp white shirt, and black and grey paisley tie. But, he didn't notice her.

She was more than a little annoyed he hadn't sought her out that morning, especially after the phone call on Monday night.

As they followed the funeral procession, Max couldn't stop thinking about Hannah. He decided to ignore her wishes, and turn up at her flat later, bearing gifts. He was looking forward to seeing her in her own environment. Away from prying eyes, he was certain she'd be more at ease, rather than calling her to his office during business hours.

They parked outside the crematorium, and Max patted Angela on the shoulder, nodding at the pouring rain. "Thank goodness for your forward planning."

They ducked from the car and gathered underneath the large white gazebo. Moments later, Steve's casket was carried inside from the hearse, and placed at the front of the chapel by six burly men.

Max, Angela, and the security staff filled the back row of the tiny room. Max admired how the whole scene was tastefully done. After liaising with Steve's wife, Angela had arranged the flowers, chairs, and music. All costs were being charged to the company.

The service was emotional, but pleasant, as funerals go. After the formalities, Max got in line to pay his respects to Steve's wife and close family. Then, he stopped directly in front of a framed picture nestled amongst the flowers. Steven was in his police uniform, and, although it was years ago, he'd hardly changed. His chiselled good looks had stayed with him through to his sixties. The easy smile and twinkly eyes had been captured perfectly, and Max felt choked up. He would miss Steve very much.

Stepping aside to allow the line of mourners to take turns, he glanced at Don, who was hugging Mrs Miller. He couldn't hear what was being said, but he could tell Steve's widow wasn't comfortable with him. Max knew how she felt. Although he couldn't put his finger on it, Don made him feel the same. He wasn't a patch on his predecessor.

As Don moved to the flower table, Max decided he'd find another Head of Security. Don was fine as assistant head, but he lacked the people skills to fulfil the role to its full potential.

Don, who had his back to him, was now looking at Steven's photo. Max could see the other man's reflection in a huge mirrored plaque on the wall. He was smiling. Well, not really smiling, more of a self-satisfied smirk. Suddenly, Don caught sight of Max in the mirror, and his expression changed dramatically, this time to a menacing, piercing glare.

Startled as someone grasped his arm, Max spun around, tearing his eyes away from the other man. Mrs Miller looked up at him.

"Oh, I'm sorry. I didn't see you there," he said.

"Mr Myers, I meant to thank you for all your support. We will be forever grateful."

"No thanks needed," he said, glancing back to where Don had been. There was no sign of him. "Steven will be sadly missed, and not only as a valued employee. I classed him as a good friend."

"And he you, Mr Myers."

Max scanned the rest of the room over his companion's head, but couldn't see any sign of Don. He had a bad feeling about this. "It has been a privilege and an honour to be able to assist today. If either you, or the family, need anything, you call me. Oh, and please, call me Max."

"It's comforting to know that. Thank you, Max. And I insist you call me Nora."

He patted her arm. "I will, Nora."

"Are you coming back to the house for a bite to eat?"

"I intend to, although I can't stay long, I'm afraid," he said.

"I understand."

As she walked away, Max once again searched for Don. He had a prickly feeling at the base of his neck. Things were definitely not as they seemed. He'd always had a sixth sense, mainly in business, but occasionally with people. It had saved him many times from making poor business decisions, and helped him succeed, once he had learnt to trust his inner voice. This was one of those occasions. He would need to do some digging next week into the background of his temporary security head.

CHAPTER 16

The office was very quiet for a change, not the usual buzz. Hannah presumed everybody had gone to the funeral. Either that, or they were skiving off while the management were away. But, even those people who *were* there seemed subdued. She knew Steve Miller was popular around the office, but she hadn't known him very well. He'd solved the mystery of her missing gym clothes, and then politely contacted her again, asking if she was settling in okay, but she got the feeling he was a genuine guy.

Unable to concentrate, she headed to the day room, and poured herself a cup of stewed coffee.

She was still feeling the effects of the night she'd spent with Simon. It had been ten months since she'd had a boyfriend, and she hadn't been willing to take it any further, even then. *What the hell was wrong with her?*

And the man she wanted was totally out of bounds, yet she couldn't shake the feelings she had for him. Stupidly, if she didn't know better, she'd say she was falling hard.

She had got Simon's email address off Diane, but although she sent him quite a wordy apology, he hadn't replied. She'd also noticed his car was still parked in the usual spot. But, then, it would be, wouldn't it? If she was heading overseas indefinitely, the last thing she'd do was leave the car at the airport. It would cost an arm and a leg.

Don Henry left the funeral, after proving he was far superior to the lot of them. He'd played his part with Miller's old bitch of a wife, consoling her, and taking great satisfaction in the fact she would never know he'd murdered her husband.

His only concern now was Maxwell-fucking-Myers. Don had seen the way he'd been looking at him, and would have no choice but to sort the bastard out, if anything came of it.

After arriving back at the flat, he checked Simon's phone and laptop for any correspondence. There were several text messages from Diane, and someone called JD asking for Simon to confirm he was okay, and two emails, one from Simon's mother, giving him a telling off only mothers know how to do. The second email was from Hannah, who waffled on and on about how much she wanted to remain friends—blah, blah, blah. *Didn't the stupid girl realise the favour he'd done for her?*

He replied to them all, sticking to the original story. To Hannah, he apologised for taking advantage of her, knowing there would be no chance of a future together.

He glanced at his watch at 4.30pm. Although pushing his luck, he needed to let himself into Hannah's flat briefly to alter the position of one of the bedroom cameras.

He had no need to break in. He'd fixed the locks by removing the small brass pins from inside the barrel, and now any similar key would open the door. He walked directly into Hannah's flat and through to the bedroom. He pulled her bed out from the wall. On the far side of the bed, he removed the side table, and placed it and miscellaneous other items on the floor. Then, he reached up to the corner of the room, and altered the position of the camera in a disused motion detector. Racing against the clock, he hurriedly pushed the furniture back.

As he pulled the door closed behind him, a woman suddenly appeared from next door.

"Hello. You gave me a start," she said. "Can I help you?" She glanced from him to Hannah's front door.

"No, I'm fine, thanks. If you're looking for Hannah, she's not home from work yet," he said, his mind reeling.

She nodded. "I heard the front door opening, and thought she must have got home early. I'm Diane. I live next door. You must be Max. Hannah's told me all about you." She looked him up and down taking in his smart black suit.

Don smiled, and shook her hand. *What the fuck did she mean? Why would she think he was Max?* "Pleased to meet you, Diane. I must rush."

"Me too. I'm off to work. I'll walk down with you."

Thankfully, Don had his keys in his pocket. He'd intended leaving anyway, before Hannah returned home, so he smiled, and fell into step beside the short, dumpy doctor. "Do you work at the infirmary?" he asked, as they jogged down the stairs.

"For my sins. And I'm lucky enough to score the night shift, too. Now, let me tell you, night shift in ER isn't for the faint of heart." She smiled.

"I can imagine."

They stepped out onto the street, and Don motioned he was heading in the opposite direction. "Nice to meet you, Diane."

"Yes. You, too. We'll have to catch up properly sometime."

"You can count on it," he said, as he watched her walk towards the train station.

Hannah arrived home just after six. When her knock on Diane's door went unanswered, she let herself into her own flat. She dropped her bag, kicked off her shoes, and began running a bath. She felt totally done in and highly emotional. She'd hung around at the office for an extra half hour, hoping Max would find the time to seek her out. But, Diane was so wrong—he couldn't care less about her.

After soaking in vanilla-scented bubbles for half an hour, she was ready to fall into bed. She ate several rye crackers topped with canned tuna, washed down with a cup of milky tea.

As she slid between the sheets, she heard a vague tapping sound.

What the hell was that?

She held her breath, waiting for the sound again. Sure enough, a few seconds later, she heard it again.

Getting out of bed, she crept to the window, and peeked around the edge of the curtains. Her heart missed a beat when she saw a man dressed in jeans and denim jacket. She immediately knew who it was. She'd recognise that delicious posterior anywhere.

Max turned and smiled that heart-stopping smile of his, and lifting his arms, indicated he had two full shopping bags.

"What the...?" Shaking her head, she dropped the curtain.

She switched on the overhead light and baulked at her reflection in the mirror. She didn't have a scrap of makeup on, and her nipples stuck out like fingertips through the fine fabric of her nightie. She pinched her cheeks, and licked her lips, as she shrugged into her robe.

Max was leaning against the doorjamb, as she opened it. He smiled and raised his eyebrows, as though trying to establish if he was going to be welcome, or not.

"What are you doing here, Max? I was in bed."

"Really? Are you sick?"

"No. Why?"

"Because it's not even seven-thirty."

"I've had a busy day, if you must know."

"Are you going to ask me in? These bags are pretty heavy."

She gave an exaggerated sigh and stepped backwards, allowing him to enter. "What have you got in the bags?"

"Dinner. I'm going to cook for you."

"I've already eaten," she said.

He screwed his lips to one side. "Ah, yes. I didn't actually think this through, did I?"

A reluctant smile tweaked at the corners of her mouth. "Not really. What did you bring?" she asked, as she led him through to the kitchen.

He placed the bags on the benchtop. "I was going to make chicken in a white wine sauce, dauphinoise potatoes, and broccoli."

"Sounds delicious. If only you'd let me know earlier."

"I wasn't sure if you'd answer my call, after the telling off you gave me the other night."

"So, you thought you'd just turn up, and hope for the best?"

"Pretty much—yeah."

She rolled her eyes. "Do you want a cup of tea or coffee?"

"I have a lovely Australian Shiraz in here somewhere." He rummaged in the bags and lifted out a bottle of wine. "Fancy a glass?"

Hannah searched the cupboard for a couple of decent glasses, but she only had mismatched ones. "I don't own many glasses, and the ones I do have are meant for white wine, sorry."

He shrugged. "Doesn't matter. A glass is a glass."

She handed him a corkscrew. "So, are you going to tell me why you're here?"

"Because I've not been able to get you out of my mind since last Friday." He pulled the cork out, and held the bottle towards her.

She leaned her glass towards him. "So much so, you waited almost a whole week to see me again."

"Hardly fair. I did have the death of a friend to contend with on Saturday morning. I was working with the police most of the weekend, only going home for some rest on Monday. I called you that very evening."

Hannah shrugged.

"I'm still a little confused by what you said, by the way," he said.

"I don't see why." She sipped her wine, and walked through to the lounge.

He followed.

Once they were seated at either end of the beige velour sofa, she placed her glass on the coffee table. "You're my boss, Max. We're from opposite ends of the spectrum. This will never work. Plus, like I already said on the phone, I don't want to be just another conquest." She couldn't believe she was talking to her boss like that, but he was in her house, outside of office hours. That made them equal in her eyes.

"Now *that's* the part I don't get." He shuffled to the edge of the seat. "I've never dated anyone from the office. Not once. So, who's been saying differently?"

Hannah picked up her glass again and stared into it, not wanting to drop Angela in the crap.

"And so what if I'm your boss? It doesn't mean we can't enjoy each other's company. I haven't asked you for anything else. Have I?"

"No. Not yet. But, I was told you make a habit of schmoozing all your young, pretty employees."

"That's bullshit, Hannah. Tell me who's been lying to you."

"I'm not going to break their confidence."

He got to his feet and walked from the room.

Hannah's stomach fell. *Was he leaving?* When he returned with the wine bottle, she wanted to cry. She realised, at that moment, she wouldn't have allowed him to leave. She didn't know why, but she believed him. *And so what if he'd had affairs with lots of different women?* She was hardly whiter than white herself.

He filled her glass again, and returned to his seat. His stomach growled. "Sorry." He smiled.

"You're starving. Shall I make you some..." She racked her brain, trying to remember what she actually had in the fridge. "...toast?"

"Toast would be lovely. Thanks."

"Hardly lovely. Just haven't had a chance to go to the shop."

They both headed back to the kitchen.

"What shall I do with this lot?" He patted the bags.

"Take it home, I suppose."

"There's no point. I don't have a cooker in the flat, and I'm not dragging it all the way to the lake house."

She put two slices of bread in the toaster.

"I could always come back tomorrow and cook for you, if you like? Just to cook for you. No strings."

"What if I want strings? What if I want ropes and chains, and strings?" She looked at him hopefully.

His beautiful eyes twinkled. "Let's see if you still feel the same after you've tasted my cooking, shall we? And then we'll renegotiate from there. Deal?"

"Deal." She giggled.

CHAPTER 17

"What the fuck?" Don screamed at the monitor. "Why is this happening to me?" He tore at his hair, and bit down hard on his lip as he paced the compact security hub. *Well, he wouldn't have her. No fucking way was he going to let Maxwell-fucking-Myers have her.* Snap-snap-snap.

He kicked the swivel chair, then picked it up and slammed it back down to the floor. Bits of black plastic and chrome flew in every direction.

Standing in the corner, his forehead placed against the cool wall, he forced himself to breathe slowly, calming himself down. Snap-snap-snap.

Then, he set about clearing away his mess.

After doing his rounds, he checked on Ken and Aaron, the two youngest, and most gullible, members of staff, before exiting via the service doors.

It was 1.47am at Cheadle Royal Infirmary. The emergency department was always busy, but thankfully, Diane enjoyed her work.

The world of emergency medicine was her calling, and she thrived on the chaos and the individuality of every person, every case, and every scenario.

Paramedics had brought in a 21-year-old black male a couple of hours before. He'd been shot twice with a small calibre pistol, once in the neck and once in the shoulder. He didn't look like the normal type of thug they usually admitted.

Because the police didn't know him, the young man's family hadn't been informed. The officer in charge was trying to piece together what had happened to lead him to this potentially fatal attack, but none of the supposed witnesses had admitted to seeing anything.

He'd had an emergency tracheotomy performed at the side of the road to help him to breathe, which had stabilised him for the trip to the hospital.

Once there, Diane established both of the bullets had exit wounds, and had managed to miss any major arteries, but the lad was in a bad way. Any muscle or nerve damage would be dealt with if he actually survived, which, in her professional opinion, seemed unlikely. The next few hours would be critical. She cleaned and dressed the wounds, and arranged for six units of blood, before placing him on life support.

Although the patient needed to be admitted to ICU, because of overcrowding, they had no choice but to administer critical care in the stabilisation room, a room off the ED, while they waited for a bed. Diane had found she needed to use the room more and more in the past few months. It was quiet and peaceful in there. Apart from the sound of the life support systems, you could not hear any chaotic activity out in ED, and it was technically a place for cases with little or no chance of recovery.

Unofficially, patients would be placed in the room, and monitored for around two hours. In most cases, the patients would pass away within that period. One in twenty-five would stabilise, and be taken to intensive care. The savings in man-hours, medicines, and care were huge, justifying to the financial team the use of the room. It was a costing issue pure and simple.

Don stood in the shadows waiting for his opportunity to deal with his loose end. He watched as Diane finished with a patient, and turned towards the Stabilisation Unit to check on the young gunshot victim she seemed concerned about.

He was ready.

Inside the room, the combination of low lighting and the life support system created an eerie glow. She walked toward her patient, checking the monitor, and examining his pupils using her penlight. Hearing the door open, she turned.

"You're not allowed in here, sir. Please wait outside, and I'll be with you shortly."

He continued towards her.

"Sir?" Then, she seemed to notice his uniform. "Oh, sorry, I didn't realise. Can I help you?"

As he approached, he watched the smile drop from her face, as she suddenly recognised him.

"What are you doing here? You don't work for security."

"You're right. I don't!" he said.

Suddenly, with the stealth and speed of a trained killer, he produced a hunting knife in his blue, latex-gloved hand. Before she could react, he stepped forward, and thrust the knife deep into her chest, twisting it slightly to the right—pointing across to her left shoulder, and he hugged her closely with his other arm. He knew this would pierce her heart, causing it to bleed out into the lungs and chest cavity. One thrust, an almost instantaneous death, leaving very little blood outside the body. Clean, very clean. This happened to be his favourite, close combat kill position.

He held her, until the life drained from her eyes. "You

should've kept your nose out, shouldn't you? You stupid, stupid woman."

He allowed her lifeless body to slump over the bed, and placed the handle of the knife into the boy's right hand. Using his elbow, he crushed the tracheotomy tube cutting off his air. The boy began to shake around in a small pool of Diane's blood. He made a gurgling sound. Thirty seconds later, the flatline confirmed he was dead.

Don exited into the busy ED, leaving via the medic's access. He discarded the gloves in the yellow biohazard bin.

Everything was almost back on track, excluding Max. Pleased with himself, he zipped up his jacket, and walked into the night, heading back to work.

Hannah went to bed with a huge grin on her face, and it remained in place for the whole of the following day.

She avoided Angela, fearing the woman would see right through her. She didn't know if Max was telling the truth, but she wanted to give him the benefit of the doubt. However, she knew how awkward it would make things with Angela, who was her direct boss. And, if Max was being honest with her, she didn't know why Angela would have lied to her in the first place.

When she got home from work, she knocked on Diane's door, but she wasn't home, again. She was itching to tell her friend her news.

She rushed into her flat to get ready for Max. He intended to do the cooking, so she guessed he'd arrive quite soon.

Max arrived at Hannah's door just after 6pm. He'd brought flowers, and was casually dressed in jeans, trainers, and his favourite pale blue Ben Sherman oxford shirt. He had a thin cotton jacket over his arm.

He couldn't remember feeling this jumpy since his first date back in college. Back then, it was the first time he'd really felt something for a girl, and he'd arranged to meet her outside the movies.

"Grow a pair, Maxie-boy," he grumbled to himself, then he took a deep breath, and rang the doorbell.

Moments later, Hannah flung the door open, and her face lit up when she saw him.

Her welcome helped settle his raging heartbeat.

Insisting she leave him to it, he set about his business in the kitchen, while Hannah put her feet up, reading her book in the lounge.

Hannah sipped on a glass of wine, while she listened to Max banging and chopping. He popped in every so often to top up her glass, but wouldn't allow her into the kitchen. She could certainly get used to being treated like this.

Startled by the doorbell, she bumped into Max in the hall.

"Are you expecting anybody?" he asked.

"No. Unless it's my neighbour. She usually calls in for a drink, but I thought she'd left for work already," she said, as she walked to the door.

The sight of two uniformed cops caused her to gasp.

"Good evening, ma'am. Are you the registered occupant of this flat?" one of the officers said.

"I am, yes."

"I wonder if we could step inside for a second. We need to ask you a few questions."

Feeling suddenly guilty, the way she always did around the authorities, she backed up allowing them to enter. She glanced towards Max, who was standing in the kitchen doorway, and his forehead crinkled as he saw who was behind her.

Max wiped his hands on a towel, and stepped towards her. "Is everything alright?"

"Sorry to disturb your evening, sir. We just need to ask you and your wife a couple of questions, and we'll be out of your hair," said the older, grey-haired officer.

"Max isn't my husband. He's just... he's just a friend," she stammered.

She ushered them into the lounge.

The younger cop pulled out a pad and pen, then glanced at his colleague.

"Firstly, do you mind confirming your name for me, please?" the older officer said.

"Of course. Hannah McLaughlin."

"How long have you lived here, Ms McLaughlin?"

"Not long, three or four weeks. Why?"

"How well do you know your neighbour, Diane Nagel?"

Hannah's mouth dried up. "Well, I guess. She's a good friend. Why?"

The officer ignored her question. "When did you last see her?"

"Erm... Tuesday or Wednesday. We often have a coffee together when I finish work, and before she leaves for hers, but I haven't seen her for a couple of days. Is she alright?"

The officers glanced at each other. "I'm sorry, miss, but I have bad news."

Hannah gulped, and Max reached for her hand. "Go on," she said.

"I'm sorry to have to tell you, but Ms Nagel was killed at the hospital last night."

CHAPTER 18

Hannah felt as though she was in a bubble. She could see the officer's mouth moving, and warbled sounds infiltrated her mind, but she couldn't hear a word. Diane, her lovely, funny, and only friend, was dead.

Forcing herself to breathe, she shook her head. "How? Who killed her?"

"It's still under investigation, but it appears a young man, who'd been admitted with gunshot wounds, must've had a knife on his person. We're not certain until we get the SOCO report, but he apparently stabbed your friend, before dying of his own injuries."

She shook her head. "It doesn't sound right." A sob escaped her, and she turned towards Max.

He wrapped his arms around her tightly. "It's okay, Hannah, let it all out."

When she regained a little composure, she wiped her eyes, and turned back to the officers. "I'm sorry, but I don't understand. How could somebody so sick find the strength to kill Diane?"

"As I said, it's still under investigation."

"So, why are you here?"

"Routine. We need to look into all aspects of a murder victim's life to see if there are any discrepancies. One thing I've discovered since being a police officer is that criminals will go to extraordinary lengths to cover up a crime."

"So you think it may not have been this guy after all?" Max said.

"That's up to the homicide team to establish. We're just interviewing anybody who knew the victim to try to build a picture of her life. Did she have any enemies you knew of? Any boyfriends, including exes?"

"No. She told me she hadn't had a boyfriend in months, and even then, it wasn't anything serious. She was too focussed on her job. Plus, doing permanent nights messed up her chances of meeting people."

"How did she seem the last time you saw her?"

"Normal. She was happy." She buried her head in her hands. "It just doesn't make sense," she sobbed.

Max rubbed her shoulder, and she gave him a grateful smile.

The younger officer cleared his throat. "Do you have a key to her flat, by any chance?"

Shaking her head, she wiped her eyes on the sleeve of her T-shirt. "No, sorry, I don't. I think Simon might have one, because she said something one day, but he's in the States."

"Simon?"

"At 4c. We were all friends."

The older officer placed a card on the coffee table. "Well, that'll be all for now, Ms McLaughlin. If you think of anything else, you can reach me on this number. Oh, and you may hear some movement next door over the next couple of days, when we gain access. Hopefully, you won't be disturbed too much."

Hannah nodded.

Max saw the officers out, and returned to her side. "Are you alright?"

She slowly shook her head. "I can't believe it. Who would want to hurt Diane? She was the kindest, most caring person I've ever met."

"I don't know." He put his arm around her, and pulled her head to his chest.

Although her tears had dried, she felt an overwhelming sense of doom, as though in the middle of a nightmare. The type that if she tried to run away, she'd find she was running on the spot.

In less than a week, she'd lost her two amazing neighbours.

"The food!" she said, lifting her head.

"Are you hungry?"

She shook her head. "No. Not anymore. But, you've gone to a lot of trouble."

"It's not important. We can heat it up later, if you get hungry."

"Thanks, Max. I'm so grateful you were here tonight. I couldn't imagine being on my own right now."

"I'm going nowhere. Not until you want me to."

"You know, just a couple of weeks ago, I was telling Mammy I couldn't have been luckier with my neighbours. And now, they're both gone."

"Both of them?"

"Yes. Simon got a call from his family in Seattle, telling him his grandma was very sick. He had to up and leave immediately. And now, I don't have any friends." The tears finally spilled from her eyes.

"Hey, silly. You have me."

"You know what I mean. You don't count."

He huffed, blinking several times. "Charming."

She smiled sadly. "I can't stay here. I'm going to have to find a new flat."

"What? Tonight?"

"Of course not tonight. But, I won't feel right being here alone anymore."

"Go and pack a bag, while I clean up the kitchen." He drew her upright.

"I don't get you."

"We can spend the night at my apartment, and then, after my meeting in the morning, we'll go to the lake house for the weekend."

"But—"

He put a finger on her lips. "As friends, remember? Now, go on. Bag."

She went into her room, and found her weekend suitcase in the bottom of her wardrobe. Feeling fragile and highly emotional, she grabbed a few outfits, her nightie, underwear, and toiletry bag. But, her perfume was missing off the bedside table. "That's odd," she murmured.

Then, she saw it, peeking out from underneath the bed. As she dropped to her knees, she noticed the bed *and* the bedside cabinet had been moved—the indentations in the carpet pile were off by a couple of inches. She got a prickly feeling at the nape of her neck.

Somebody had been in her bedroom.

As he completed his rounds, Don was floored to see Hannah on the monitor, arriving with Maxwell Myers at the car park level. The rage within him was almost too much to control when he saw his boss take an overnight bag from the back of the car. Snap-snap-snap.

"You okay, Don?" Ken said.

"What?" He spun on the spot, totally forgetting he wasn't alone.

"You've turned a strange colour. Are you feeling okay?"

"I'm fine!" Don stomped away.

He watched as the lift light went all the way to the top, before calling it himself, and travelling up behind them.

The corridors were empty, and the lighting muted, which was normal for that time of night. He crept to Max's office door and listened. Nothing. There was no entrance to the apartment from the main corridor, so he opened the office door and silently walked to the internal door.

In a fury, he listened to the hushed whispers. Under no illusions what they were getting up to inside. This was the only room that he couldn't see into. He felt as though he'd been violated, mugged of his possessions, and there was absolutely nothing he could do about it.

Hannah loved the night-time city views from Max's compact apartment. She wasn't too thrilled to see one double bed, however.

He saw her reaction to this, and assured her he would sleep on the chair in his office.

He'd brought the wine and two plates of food from Hannah's flat, and set about warming them in the microwave. He poured the wine, and sat beside her on the two-seater.

She wiped her eyes from a fresh bout of tears, before taking the glass from him. "Thanks, Max. I do appreciate this, you know?"

"I know."

"And I'm sorry our first proper date was ruined. I'll make it up to you, I promise."

"Nonsense. It's hardly your fault."

"I know. But, I'd like to."

He nodded. "We've got plenty of time for that. And, besides, our first date isn't over yet. We have the whole weekend away to make nice memories."

A few minutes later, he checked on the food, bringing two delicious-smelling plates over to her.

"This is the life." He clinked his glass on hers, before digging into his dinner.

Hannah still had no appetite, and only managed a couple of mouthfuls. She apologised, and helped him do the dishes afterwards, before settling down again on the sofa.

Over the next few hours, she broke down a number of times, but Max held her tight, allowing her to grieve. She told him about Diane, and the few memories she had of her lovely friend.

When she had nothing left to say, he told her about his childhood and the death of his parents, and about his best friend, Lenny, and Charmaine, Lenny's wife, who worked at the lake house.

They spent the evening talking and holding each other. When he eventually kissed her, she felt like everything had fallen into place. She just wished she could share her happiness with Diane.

Although she hadn't known her friend long, she could honestly say Diane had been the best friend she'd had since leaving school. She knew Diane would be overjoyed for her, but it felt a little wrong to be feeling this way, while her friend lay on a slab.

As dawn approached, they drank coffee, and watched the morning sun radiate the buildings opposite with its tangerine fingers, as if prodding everything to life.

"We need to get some sleep, otherwise I'll be falling asleep in my meeting."

"Who's your meeting with?" she asked.

"Just the weekly video conference with all the other branches."

"Will Angela be there?"

He gave her a sidelong glance. "Yeah. Why do you ask?"

"Oh, just wondered. You won't say anything about... about us?" she asked shyly.

"Of course I won't. It's nobody else's business."

"Good."

She didn't know why, but the first person who came to mind, when she realised somebody had been in her house, was Angela. She knew how stupid it sounded, but she couldn't shake the thought at all. Angela was the only person who knew her address. She'd also had access to her gym bag.

Max pulled her to her feet. "Come on. You get into bed. I'll come back for you after my meeting. Then, we can get on the road."

"You're not going to your meeting now, are you?"

He glanced at his watch. "No. I have a couple of hours yet, but I'll try not to disturb you."

"Do you want to get in bed, too? It seems silly you sleeping curled on the chair. You'll crick your neck."

"If you're sure?"

"Positive."

They fell asleep in each other's arms, still fully dressed.

When Hannah woke a few hours later, she was alone.

She used the bathroom, grabbed a change of clothes and her toiletry bag, and hopped in the shower.

Max was sitting on the bed again when she returned.

"Oh, hello. I didn't hear you come in," she said.

"I expected you to still be snoring. You were dead to the world when I left this morning."

His words made her think of Diane, and her breath hitched as she turned away.

"I'm sorry. Bad turn of phrase. Forgive me."

She smiled sadly. "I still can't believe it. I'll have to contact Simon and let him know—he'll be devastated."

"Use my laptop while I have a shower, if you like. Then, we can get going."

"I will do. Thanks."

He went into his office, and returned with his laptop. "*Captain Max* is the password. That's a capital *C* and a capital *M* —one word."

"Really?" She sniggered.

"Yeah. What's wrong with that?"

She straightened her face, and shook her head. "Absolutely nothing."

"Good." He opened the wardrobe door, and selected a pale blue checked shirt and jeans.

"So, are you?"

"Am I what?" He turned, as he reached the bathroom door.

"A captain?"

"That's for me to know, and you to find out."

She barked out a laugh. "Do you know how childish you sound?"

He poked his tongue at her, entered the bathroom, and closed the door.

CHAPTER 19

Don couldn't sleep. He'd returned to Simon's flat once his shift had finished, and played back the previous evening's footage. The brief thrill of hearing what the police had to say about Diane's death was ruined by the way Maxwell-fucking-Myers continually pawed at Hannah, as though she was his possession.

Snap-snap-snap.

Awash with rage, he paced up and down the flat in the dark. He'd seen and heard everything between Hannah and Myers. Although they weren't physical, as such, their exchanges seemed even more intimate than sex.

Snap-snap-snap.

He was relieved they were no longer next door, because the way he felt, he knew he would've been tempted to rush in there, and carve that bastard into a thousand tiny pieces right in front of her eyes.

Snap-snap-snap. Snap-snap-snap.

Needing to vent the volcano of rage within him, he grabbed the claw hammer from the windowsill, knocking over the box of half-eaten pizza he'd brought with him, and ran to the freezer.

He unlocked the padlock, and lifted the lid.

His rage let loose, pounding the hammer into the frozen mass which was once Simon Fowler's head. It wasn't surprising it had no effect—he was frozen as solid as a woolly mammoth found in Siberia.

After a while, Don stopped mid-swing, totally exhausted. Simon's skull, above the eye sockets, had collapsed. Don stared at it for several seconds, then calmly dropped the lid, and fastened the padlock.

He placed the hammer on the hallstand, with several clumps of bloody matter attached to it. He needed to lie down, before he fell down. He'd always thrived on very little sleep, but found he was struggling lately.

He climbed on the bed, and collapsed on the pillow.

The offices were mostly deserted as, arm in arm, they took the lift down to the parking floor. Max was loading the bags into the boot, when Angela suddenly appeared. If looks could kill... Hannah wanted to stop, drop, and roll under the car, but it was too late. By the expression on her face, Angela knew exactly what was going on.

She approached them, her eyes scanning the bags.

"Hi, Angela. I thought you'd left already," Max said.

The bitch made a show of ogling Hannah, before she turned back to her boss. "Just leaving. I had a few things to catch up on."

"Oh, I'm just giving Hannah a ride home."

Hannah smiled at her.

"Home? I see." She lifted her chin in acknowledgement, and narrowed her eyes, as she stared at Hannah's face.

Hannah couldn't wait to get away from there. She nodded at Angela, and jumped in the passenger seat.

Max and Angela exchanged a few more words, then Max slid

into the driver's seat, started the car and drove towards the bollards.

They burst out laughing, as they drove onto the street.

"Did you see her face?" Hannah asked.

"She wasn't impressed, that's for certain."

"She hates me."

Max glanced at her. "Nonsense. Why would she hate you?"

"Oh, ignore me. I'm excited to see your home. Maybe next weekend, I could take you to see mine?"

Max shuddered, and shook his head comically. "I don't know about that."

"Why not?"

"Well, my family home only has me in it. Your family home has your mum and dad. I can imagine what they'll say when they hear their only daughter is having a fling with her boss."

"Is that what we're having?"

He glanced at her again. "See? I'm not good at this kind of thing. Why do I feel I'm in the doghouse?"

"You're not in the doghouse. Not yet." She grinned, and glanced at her phone, before returning it to her pocket.

"Expecting something?"

"I didn't email Simon in the end. I don't know how often he checks his inbox, so I texted him instead."

"And he hasn't responded?"

"Nope." She shook her head.

"What's the time difference?"

"I never thought about that."

"From memory, I think Washington is around 8 hours behind us. Or is it ahead?"

She laughed. "That's a big help." She looked at her watch. "So, according to you, it could either be 3am in Seattle, or 7pm."

Max chuckled. "Exactly."

Hannah watched out of the window, as all signs of the city fell away.

"You hungry?" Max asked, after they'd been driving almost an hour.

"Starving."

"Why didn't you say? I forget people usually eat in the morning. I don't bother until lunch."

"I'm fine. I think it's because I didn't eat much last night, you know, with…"

"Of course. I know a great gastropub in Carnforth."

"Sounds great. I've heard of Carnforth, but I don't know why," she said.

"Carnforth is a lovely little village. It's famous for the railway station—it was used as the set for the old black and white movie *A Brief Encounter*."

"Was it? I've actually seen that, I think. Did the housewife have an affair?"

He nodded. "That's the one. We can have a look inside, if you like? In fact, we could eat there. Apparently, there's a tearoom which was built to replicate the original set."

Hannah raised her eyebrows. "Really? I'd love to."

Max took the next exit off the motorway, and less than five minutes later, pulled into the car park of the Carnforth Station and Heritage Centre.

The wide-fronted, pretty stone building comprised of the station entrance, with a rug shop on one end, and a pub called The Snug on the other.

Hannah smiled, and took Max's offered hand, as they headed to the main door.

After taking their time browsing around, and photographing the quaint, old-fashioned railway station, a member of staff offered to take a photo of both of them underneath the replica clock made famous by the movie.

Max stood behind her, and wrapped his arms around her, pulling her in close. Hannah's stomach flipped at the realisation this was their first photo together. The first of many, she hoped.

After taking several more photos of The Refreshment Room, they both ordered roast ham, egg and chips, as well as a pot of tea to share.

"Hey, look at this," Max said, pointing to the price list. "They have pre-decimal prices here—a full English breakfast would have cost just five-bob."

"Five *what*?"

"Five bob. That was probably around five pence."

She laughed. "You wouldn't get a mouthful of beans for five pence nowadays."

When the food came, she ate with gusto, almost finishing before him. She would have, if she could, found room for the last four fries. She sat back, feeling stuffed.

"Better?" he asked.

"Much better, thanks. I really enjoyed that."

"I could tell. And you have a blob of mayo on your…" He pointed to the side of his mouth.

She grabbed her napkin and swiped at her mouth.

He chuckled.

"What? Were you joking?"

He nodded. "You should've seen your face."

"Idiot." She grinned, and threw the napkin at him.

He caught it, screwed it up, and placed it on his plate. "Shall we get going? We still have the best part of an hour's drive."

As they approached the car, Max gasped.

Hannah spun around to see what was wrong, and followed his gaze to his car.

A deep scratch ran along the entire passenger side of the Mercedes.

Being his night off, Don had planned for his first evening to be lying beside his darling Hannah, albeit on opposite sides of the adjoining wall. But, now, that bastard Max had whisked her away for the weekend.

When he woke up, he showered and dressed. He knew Max's house was beside Lake Windermere, but he was unsure where. That wouldn't stop him.

Just five minutes on the laptop proved fruitful, and he jotted down the address, grabbed his bag, and headed to the front door. A heavy knock made him freeze mid-step.

Hardly breathing, he stood dead still, praying whoever it was hadn't seen his silhouette through the textured glass.

More rapping followed. "Open up! Police!"

What the fuck? Shit! Don reached for the hammer, which still had clumps of, now defrosted, brain matter on it. He peered through the spy hole, and he could see a cop in uniform. *Just one? This wasn't a raid.*

He slowly opened the door. "Yes, officer? Can I help you?" He still held the hammer in his hand, just behind the door.

"I apologise for disturbing you, sir. Are you the occupant of the flat?" Don had to think fast—he would kill this fucker if need be, but wasn't sure what the cop wanted yet.

"No, it's my friend's place. I'm looking after it for him while he's in the States."

"What's your name, sir?"

"Ken. Ken Barber. Why?"

The officer jotted it down. "And what's your friend's name?"

"Simon Fowler. Can I ask why all the questions?"

"All in good time, Mr Barber. When did your friend leave for America?"

"Last week."

"And have you been staying here ever since?"

Don shook his head. "No. This is the first time I've called by."

"I see. We needed to ask your friend a few questions regarding one of the neighbours. Do you know Diane Nagel, from 4a?"

Don shook his head, trying to show zero emotion. "No. I can't say I do."

The officer handed Don his card. "Could you ask your friend to email me?"

"I will, but can I tell him what it's about?"

"A woman was murdered."

"The neighbour? The one you were asking about? Did it happen here?"

"Yes, it was the neighbour. But, it didn't happen in her flat. If you could pass on my details, I'd appreciate it."

"No problem, officer."

"Have a nice day, sir." He tipped his hat, and turned away.

Don stayed where he was, peering from a crack in the door, the hammer just out of sight, yet at the ready. He could hear the cop talking to somebody else.

"No answer at 4b, John. We'll have to come back later."

Stepping from the door alcove, Don peered around the corner, and watched as two officers headed for the staircase.

He was shaken up. He'd thought killing her at the hospital would keep the investigation away from the flats. Patient kills doctor—end of story. But, he would have to watch his step now. There was a sighting of him, at the flat, even though he had given them his drippy colleague's details.

Looking out to the street, he watched the two cops leave the building, and drive off. He grabbed his bag, dropped the hammer back on the hall table, and left for the Lake District.

CHAPTER 20

Clearly distraught, Max looked around the car park. "The bastards."

"Who did it?" Hannah also looked around, wondering who he could be talking about.

He shrugged. "Did you notice the scratch when you got in the car earlier?"

"To be honest, I was so distracted by Angela, I just jumped in. And it was quite dark, so I probably wouldn't have noticed it anyway."

He shook his head, and unlocked the car. As he opened the door for her, he said, "Never mind. It's just a car—the insurance will cover it." But, she could tell by the way his jaw clenched he was pissed off.

They drove a little way in silence, each occupied with their own thoughts. When they turned off the motorway, the scenery changed, and so did Max's mood.

Hannah couldn't wait to see the lake. She'd always loved the water. She dreamed of raising a family beside a beach or lake, throwing sticks into the water for the dog to fetch, and jumping over waves with the toddlers. She didn't tell Max about it, though;

she wouldn't see him for dust if she started talking about babies and settling down at this stage of their relationship—they'd barely got past first base.

"The scenery is stunning around here," she said.

"Yeah. I love it. I always feel the stress melt away when I get to this spot."

"This is the furthest north I've been. How sad is that?" she said.

"You must have been further in other directions, though?"

She shrugged. "I've been on holiday to Malaga with a friend of mine, so that's the furthest I've travelled. But, within the country, we used to holiday as a family in Great Yarmouth or Aberystwyth. I love the coast, but we only got to see it for a week or two every year. Dad likes what he likes, and never really diverts from that, so we went east or west, and never north or south."

"You don't know what you've been missing. I'm looking forward to showing you the sights."

"I can't wait."

"Not far now." He smiled.

Although she was excited to see his home, it was the thought of spending the entire weekend with Max she was looking forward to the most.

Suddenly, the deep cobalt blue of the lake came into view, and her breath hitched.

"It never fails to take my breath away," Max said.

When he finally turned into a driveway, she gasped at the cutest little stone cottage she'd ever seen. But, he didn't stop at the cottage. He drove past, and through the trees to a stunning, multi-level home.

He pressed a button on the sun visor, and the garage door began to open. Moments later, he drove into a garage so large it could have fit the quaint cottage in the centre of it, with room to spare.

"Wow!" was all she could manage.

When they got out, Max re-examined the paintwork of the

car. He shook his head in disgust. "I'll never understand the mentality of some people."

Startled by a sound behind them, they turned as a man appeared around the corner on a ride-on mower.

"Ah, here's Lenny, the friend I told you about." Max waved.

Lenny killed the engine and jumped off the mower. "Hey, buddy. I wasn't sure if we'd see you this weekend, with you only going back a couple of days ago." He glanced at Hannah. "Hi."

"This is Hannah. Hannah meet Lenny, my oldest friend."

"He means, we've known each other a long time, not that I'm ancient." Lenny laughed, his hazel eyes twinkling.

Hannah giggled, as she took his outstretched hand. "I did wonder."

"Hey. Cheeky!" Lenny nodded at her, looking at Max, as if to say, *'You've got a live wire here.'*

"What are your plans for the weekend, Len?" Max asked.

"Oh, you know—the usual. Why do you ask?"

"I thought I might introduce Hannah to Trixie. Let her check out the competition."

Hannah's stomach dropped. *What the hell?*

"Wouldn't miss it for the world. I'll tell Charmaine. She'll organise some food."

"Great. Not too early—say around nine."

"Lookin' forward to it. Lovely to meet you, Hannah." He gave a salute, and ducked under the closing garage door.

"Seems nice," Hannah said.

"He's great. His wife, too. You'll get on well with Charmaine." He pulled the two cases from the boot, and headed to the extra wide internal staircase.

She followed him. "So, come on. Put me out of my misery. Who's Trixie?"

Although he had his back to her, she could tell by the way his ears moved that he was smiling. "You'll have to wait. It's a surprise. You're not jealous, are you?"

He stopped on the landing, pointing with one of the cases. "This is the bedroom floor. My bedroom's on the left. I'll put your things into the room across the hall. Is that okay?"

"Sure." She followed him into the bedroom, and gasped again. Oak trim framed each lemon and white wallpapered wall, and matched the doors and bay window. Another door led to a compact bathroom and walk-in-wardrobe "Oh my gosh! It's so lush." She sat on the edge of the bed, stroking the fine white fabric "What's the thread count on these sheets?"

"Is that a real question?"

She laughed. "Forget it. Come on. I can't wait to see the rest of the place. How many bedrooms are there?"

"Four." He left her bag on the window seat, and headed across the hall to drop his own case off.

His room was even more exquisite. Hannah was astounded. The duck egg blue and gold wallpaper matched the plush bedspread. Brushed gold-coloured accessories were dotted around the room. French doors led to a beautiful wooden deck, with stunning water views. The bathroom off that room held a double-sized, corner Jacuzzi bath, a freestanding shower unit, bidet, sink, and toilet. A fifty-inch TV was fitted into the wall opposite the tub.

"Oh, Max. This is beautiful."

"Wasted on me, though. I considered selling it a while ago, but I love it, and I feel my parents all around me when I'm here."

"Oh, no! Then, you can't sell it."

He smiled sadly, and tucked a tendril of her hair behind her ear.

Hannah gasped. The way he gazed into her eyes made her suddenly self-conscious.

Taking her hand, he escorted her up the second wide, beige-carpeted staircase to the upper level.

The open-plan living space was divided into three areas—a state of the art kitchen filled the entire front wall, with an island-breakfast bar separating it from the rest of the room. The lounge and dining room occupied the extended rear of the building, and overlooked the stunning back garden and incredible water views. The semi-circular deck resembled something you'd find in a home and garden magazine—in fact, the whole house did. The end of the garden dropped away quite steeply on one side, and a walkway led to a private jetty jutting out into the water.

A small stone building was located to the side of the jetty.

Hannah turned to find Max sitting on the sofa, with a grin pasted on his face. She laughed. "Sorry. But, this house is extraordinary. I expected a little quaint cabin, not this." She held her hands out, and twirled on the spot.

He patted the cushion beside him. "Never apologise. I could watch you all day."

She smiled shyly, and sat beside him.

He took her into his arms, and kissed her deeply. "I've been dying to do that all day," he said.

"Me too," she said, feeling lightheaded.

Afterwards, he took her for a stroll around the garden, telling her tales of his childhood.

He showed her the massive tree he used to climb, from which he would dive into the water.

"But, it's so far from the water. It's a wonder you didn't have a nasty accident."

"You don't see danger as a kid. But, I was heartbroken when my mum hired a contractor to chop my favourite branch off."

"Good on her. I don't think I could cope with any child of mine doing something like that." They stopped at the jetty, gazing out to the water.

"You can't wrap them up too tight, or they'll never learn," he said.

She shrugged. "I'd take away the hazard, like your mum did."

"Meany. Boys are built different to girls. They need all that physical, blood-pumping stuff. It doesn't mean they'll have a fatal accident if you let them climb a tree. You just need to teach them how to climb the tree safely."

"I can't believe we're having our first disagreement, and it's about how to raise children." She laughed.

"Some things need to be established early. For instance, I would have to insist our son, when he turns six, would be sent to boarding school." He raised his eyebrows, as though challenging her.

"Six! Oh my gosh! No son of mine would be sent anywhere. I'm sorry, but no. I've decided not to have your baby."

He grabbed her hand, and moved in closer, lifting her chin with his other hand. "Are you certain about that? Maybe there's something I could do to persuade you."

Her pulse quickened, as she gazed into his eyes. "Hmm, maybe. Depends on what you have in mind."

His gentle kiss gained momentum, and literally took her breath away. He wrapped his arm around her waist, pulling her up, and closer to him.

Hannah moaned against his warm and sweet-tasting lips—completely smitten.

His hands moved up to clasp her face, his tongue swirling around hers, exploring her mouth.

An irritating buzzing sound distracted Hannah. She pulled away as a small motorboat passed—the two male occupants gawking at Hannah and Max.

Blushing, she moved away from him.

"Come here, woman," he growled.

She squealed, and ran off towards the house, Max close on her heels.

CHAPTER 21

The place seemed deserted when Don approached the lake house. The small cottage was visible from the road, and nothing like he'd imagined the great Maxwell-fucking-Myers would own. It was too plain and not at all flashy.

He returned to his car, and drove off in search of something to eat and a drink. He'd come back after dark.

Hours later, Max woke and smiled, as he gazed at Hannah's sleeping face.

Making love to her had confirmed what he already knew—they were perfect for each other. She was everything he'd dreamed of.

Although reluctant to leave her side, he needed to use the bathroom, so he slid his arm out from underneath her head, and plumped the pillow so as not to disturb her.

Moments later, he donned his robe, tying the belt loosely around his waist, and headed off towards the kitchen—he was once again ravenous. Charmaine always kept the fridge well stocked.

He padded on bare feet up the stairs, and set about preparing a feast for them both.

Surprised by the dimming light, he glanced across the lake at the setting sun. They must have slept for hours, which wasn't surprising since they'd hardly slept the night before.

Max arranged a platter of olives, sun-dried tomatoes, a selection of different cheeses and crackers.

He was startled when two hands snaked around his hips, as he was uncorking a bottle of red wine.

"Oh, hello, you." He kissed the tip of Hannah's nose. "I was about to come and wake you."

"I panicked. I didn't know where I was for a second." She was wearing his shirt and nothing else, and he felt the familiar stirrings again.

"You know, there's nothing sexier than a woman in a man's shirt." He put the bottle down and reached for her, cupping her bare buttocks in his hands, and grinding against her stomach.

"Tempting as that suggestion is..." she said, pressing back against him, "...I'm starving, and might just pass out, if you don't feed me soon." She twirled away from him, and he smacked her bottom playfully.

Don returned to the lake house, and parked along the road. Walking back towards the property, he ducked through the bushes where he had a perfect view into the lounge.

The light from the television lit the room enough for him to make out two people lying on the sofa. Picking up a rock, he launched it through the window, and stepped deeper into the bushes.

Max and Hannah were snuggled together on the flokati rug, when a drumming sound, he recognised as somebody running up the external steps, startled them.

He grabbed a blanket from the sofa, and threw it over Hannah's nakedness.

"What is it?" she said.

Just then, Lenny hammered on the French door.

Max jumped to his feet and pulled his robe closed, tightening the belt. He opened the door. "Shit, Len. What's up?"

"Some bastard just threw a rock through the cottage window." Lenny panted.

"You're joking. Hang on, let me get dressed and I'll meet you out the front."

He locked the door, as Lenny charged off. "Wait here," he said to Hannah, and ran down the stairs to the bedroom.

Lenny was agitated when Max met him a few minutes later out on the driveway.

"So, tell me again. What happened?"

"We were watching TV, and a fucking big rock came through the window."

They set off in the direction of the cottage.

"Were either of you hurt?" Max asked.

"No. But, several of the small panes and the frames are shattered. The glass covered the coffee table and lounge chair. Luckily, neither of us were sitting on it."

They rounded the front of the cottage, and Max could see what he meant. A huge hole around five inches in diameter was in the middle of the wooden, six-panel window frame, and several of the cross members were obliterated, too.

"Jeez, man, someone meant business here tonight. Have you any idea who it could have been?"

Lenny shook his head. "It's totally random."

Charmaine came to the front door, clearly shaken. "Did you see anybody?"

"No. Go on in, babe. We'll get it boarded up." Lenny kissed his wife, and ushered her back inside. "Close the curtains," he called after her.

Max strode out to the road, and glanced up and down. Several cars were parked along on either side, but nothing struck him as odd or different to normal.

Lenny appeared through the bushes. "They were probably hiding in here. Nobody would see them, and yet, they could get a perfect view into the cottage."

Max followed him back through the bushes. "Well, whoever it was, will be long gone now."

"Seems pretty creepy, if I'm honest. We never close the curtains, and anyone could be gawking at us. But, why throw a rock?"

"Probably kids. Don't worry about it. Have we got anything we can use to board it up with until morning?"

Lenny nodded. "Yeah, I'll get it sorted now. I've a few boards in the boat shed. I planned to get Trixie out tonight, anyway."

"Are you sure you don't need a hand?"

"Na. I'm fine. You get back to your guest. She seems nice, by the way."

Max grinned. "She is nice. I have a good feeling about her, Len."

***

Just as Don thought, he'd got the wrong address. Maxwell-fuck-ing-Myers appeared on the road.

When he'd gone back in, Don approached the property again. He watched the other guy knocking the loose glass out of the frames from the inside. Once again, there was no sign of Max or Hannah.

After a short while, the guy left the cottage, and walked to the rear of the property. Don, still in the safety of the bushes, followed him towards the lake.

Just then, he saw the other, flashier house. He hadn't considered there could be two houses at the one address.

He stayed in the bushes, watching the other man inside a shed down beside the water. He heard a motor fire up. It was a boat shed.

He smiled. At least now he wouldn't have to sleep in the car.

Observing from a distance, in case Myers returned, he soon realised the man was just another employee. Myers would be up in the huge house, with *his* girl.

Snap-snap-snap.

Once he was sure Myers was well and truly gone, he moved towards the boat shed. It looked as though the man was preparing the boat for a trip, arranging fishing rods, opening the blinds, and cleaning down all the surfaces.

Maxwell-fucking-Myers was taking Hannah for a romantic day out on the lake.

A while later, the man passed close by Don, lugging a huge board—clearly to fix the window with.

Don skulked back to his car.

CHAPTER 22

Hannah had worked herself into a frenzy—convinced she was the target of someone's wrath. In fact, she was certain Angela was the culprit, though she knew how crazy it sounded.

"Did you see anyone?" she asked, when Max returned a short time later.

"Not a soul. They were long gone. Probably just kids." He sat beside her on the rug. "Hey, what's wrong?" He lifted her chin to look into her face.

"You'll think I'm stupid."

"I won't. Tell me. What is it?"

She exhaled noisily, and moved back a little, turning to face him. "Since I moved here, and started my new job, I've had a feeling someone's been stalking me—entering my flat, when I'm not home."

"Really?" His forehead creased.

She nodded. "But, that's not all. My sports bag went missing from the gym locker. Steve Miller found it for me—it had been put away in the wrong locker. There was nothing missing, but I knew the contents had been tampered with."

"In what way?"

"That's where it gets creepy. My underwear had been replaced with newer, very similar stuff, but it wasn't *my* stuff."

"That *is* creepy. Are you sure?"

"Not at first, I thought I was being paranoid. But, then, I kept feeling someone had been in my flat—especially my bedroom. Then, do you remember the black dress I wore to the restaurant that night?"

"Yeah."

"Well…" she shook her head. "I can't believe I'm telling you this, but I'd bought it in a sale the week before. It should've been hundreds of pounds, but it had a wire missing from under the boob area."

"Oh, I didn't notice."

"That's because the dress had been replaced, too. I didn't realise myself, at first, but suddenly there was no fault."

"That would mean someone's paid hundreds of pounds to replace your dress, without you even knowing about it. I mean—who would do that?"

"I dunno."

"So, what else? Because I can tell by your face there's more."

"The other night—after we found out about Diane—I went to pack a bag, and couldn't find my perfume. Then, I found it under the bed. Plus—the bed had been moved. The indents in the carpet were off by an inch or two."

"So, that's all of it? We've been together ever since, so there can't be more. Or can there?"

She nodded again. "Your car, and now the window. What if it's all connected?"

"No." He shook his head. "I agree the other stuff you told me sounds odd, and yes, I'd be concerned about it. But, nobody knows about us, or about this place."

"Somebody does."

"Who?"

"Angela."

Max laughed. "And what? You think Angela scratched my car, and broke the window? Or all of it? You think she's been in your flat and swapped your clothing?"

"I knew you'd think I've lost my marbles. But, it all makes sense."

"What does? What am I missing?" he asked.

"She's in love with you."

Clearly confused, Max scratched his head. "You think Angela did this to you, because she's in love with me?"

She nodded. "I'm certain of it."

"I'm sorry, Hannah. But, this doesn't make sense to me. Angela is just my PA. There's never been anything inappropriate between us. She's hardworking and loyal. Not only that, even I didn't think you and I had any future, until a couple of nights ago."

"I know all that. And, honestly, I feel terrible saying this to you. But, that day, when we first met, there was clearly some chemistry between us."

"Yes, but…"

"Then, the day we bumped into each other in the canteen, she was waiting for me at my desk, and tore a strip off me for being late. But, I wasn't late. I was bang on time."

"Really?"

She sighed, and tried to smile. "And there's more. Angela warned me off you—even told me to pull out of the Leno campaign."

"*Angela* told you I'd been sleeping my way through all the employees?"

Hannah nodded again. "Sorry, Max. That's why I couldn't tell you. She's my boss, when all's said and done."

"Not for much longer, she's not."

Hannah gasped. "What will you do? We have no proof."

Max rubbed his unshaven chin. "We need to play it safe, try to catch her out."

She nodded, suddenly dreading Monday morning.

"And don't worry. We'll work it out together." He hugged her tight. "I hate seeing you so upset—first Diane, and now, this."

Relieved he actually believed her, she gently stroked his face with her hand. "Thank you, Max. It means a lot."

They made love again, but this time, without the lustful urgency of earlier. They spent hours exploring each other's body, and afterwards, lay sweaty and spent in each other's arms.

Much later, Hannah extricated herself from her human restraint, and padded to the balcony, wrapped in the blanket. She sat on a recliner, and dozed to the sound of the lapping water.

"Oh, there you are," Max said from the doorway.

She held her hand out towards him. When he took it, she dragged him closer, moving to allow him to sit. She climbed onto his knee, and wrapped them both in the blanket. "Oh, Max. It's so beautiful here."

"I'm glad you like it. When my parents bought the property, there was just the fishing lodge, which is now Lenny's cottage. It was a lot rougher in those days, but my dad could see the potential. His dream was to build this stunning lake house, and for them to retire here."

"That's so sweet."

"Dad drew up the plans. He and Mum were at odds over the design, but he stuck to his guns."

"Oh, no! Did she like it, once it was built?"

"Begrudgingly, yes. She didn't want to, and he practically had to force her through the front door. But, after wandering around the bedrooms stony-faced, she looked at me and Dad, and beamed."

"Thank goodness for that!" Hannah laughed.

"They were always like that with each other. Such different opinions, but they were closer than any couple I've ever met. That's why I've waited so long to bring anyone home. I needed to feel the kind of connection they had."

"You've never brought a girlfriend home before?"

He shook his head. "I've had several dates. Lots of friends have tried to set me up, but it's never felt right—until now." He glanced at her, his forehead furrowed.

"Oh, Max. That's the sweetest thing anybody's ever said to me. And just so you're in no doubt—I feel exactly the same."

They watched the sunrise while in each other's arms. Moody shades of mauve and indigo were broken by a spectacular show of pinks and yellows mirroring back on itself across the still water.

"It's beautiful," Hannah whispered.

"Just like you." He kissed her deeply. "Come on, I'll make you some breakfast." He guided her to her feet, and followed her inside.

Don slept fitfully on one of the boat bunks. As the sun rose, he grabbed his things together, and headed for the door of the boathouse.

When he rounded the corner, he stopped, and jumped back for cover. Hannah and Maxwell-fucking-Myers were lying together on an outdoor chair, chewing the faces off one another.

Snap-snap-snap.

His fury was getting harder and harder to control. Suddenly, the band snapped, and fell to the ground.

CHAPTER 23

Even though she'd spent part of the evening in Max's bed, Hannah didn't feel confident enough to shower in his bathroom. Besides, her bag was still in the spare room. So, leaving him making breakfast, she headed downstairs to freshen up.

Thinking about heading home tonight reminded her of the problem they had with Angela. She didn't regret telling Max everything, but it didn't stop her worrying about how he intended to deal with it.

The thought of being targeted by a crazed stalker freaked her out a little. Although, if Angela was capable of being violent, surely she'd have shown that side of herself by now.

After showering, she dressed in shorts and a strappy blue top, and then headed back up to the kitchen. "Mmmm, something smells delicious."

"Just in time. Go sit yourself down. I've laid the table out on the balcony."

She did as he asked, and he followed her out with two plates filled with strips of crispy bacon, poached eggs, and grilled tomatoes. On the table, there was crusty bread, freshly squeezed orange juice, and a pot of coffee.

"Gee, you've been busy. And I thought you didn't eat break-fast?" she said.,

"I'm willing to make an exception for you. Plus, we worked up quite an appetite last night, didn't we?" He bent to kiss her, before taking his seat.

Her phone rang from her handbag beside the sofa. She gasped, and glanced at him. "It might be Simon."

"Go get it."

She ran inside and fumbled in her bag. "Hello," she said, without looking at the screen.

"Good morning, sweetheart."

"Oh, hi, Mammy." She winced, as she glanced out at Max and shrugged.

He winked.

"Just checking in with you. Kimmy Jackson from across the road is doing the stall for me today, and Daddy's taking me for a drive and a bite of lunch."

"Oh, that's nice."

"Are you not home? I tried the landline first."

"Er, no. I'm staying with a friend."

"Really? Why?"

"We came to the Lake District for the weekend. I must go, Mammy. We're just about to eat breakfast. Can I call you from home tonight?"

"Of course you can. Have a lovely day, sweetheart." Hannah switched off the phone, and returned to the table.

"Sorry about that, Max. It's just I still haven't heard from Simon." She sat back opposite him, and tucked in to her food.

"Try to call him."

"In the States? It'll cost a fortune."

"Use my phone. It's fine."

She shook her head, and placed her hand over her mouth while she chewed her food. "No. It's okay. I'll email him later."

"I don't mind, honestly. Plus, it's a company phone, so you may as well use it."

"Okay. I'll check out the time difference, and call him later."

"Are you looking forward to today?" he asked.

She shrugged. "I think I've worked it out. Is Trixie a dog?"

"Nope!"

"A horse?" She grinned. "Are we going horse riding?"

His eyes twinkled. "Nope!" He glanced at his watch. "I'd better get ready. Keep guessing. I'll be back shortly."

She growled in mock rage, and he laughed, as he ran down the stairs.

Half an hour later, he led her down to the garden. Holding her hands, he made her walk backwards towards the lake.

Giggling hysterically, she almost toppled over a couple of times.

Max nodded to someone out of her vision, and moments later, an engine started up.

Hannah began to turn.

"Tut, tut, tut. No peeking."

"Oh, come on." She pulled her hands from his, and spun around.

Lenny waved at her from the top deck of a stunning wooden boat. *Trixie-Belle* was emblazoned down the side.

Hannah was speechless.

"So? What do you think?"

She shook her head and smiled. "I'd worked out it was going to be a boat when you headed for the lake, but wow!"

"She's a launch. A beauty, isn't she?"

"She's that, alright." She gazed over the graceful lines of the launch. It was a mixture of natural and white-painted wood. The top deck was exposed, apart from a canvas roof, with two seats facing the dashboard and steering wheel. Two doors opened to several steps dropping into the bottom deck.

"Fancy a tour, madam?" Max smirked, holding his hand out.

"Don't mind if I do." She took his hand, and, after a couple of wobbly moments, stepped onto the back deck of the boat.

Down the steps, two single beds sat either side of a table. A small cooker and benchtop on the right faced a wall of built-in units. A triangular double bed was in the very front. Highly varnished wood was fitted throughout.

"Do you sleep on here?"

Max nodded. "I have done, but don't see the point, to be honest. If we go out for a fish, it's easier to come home to bed. Anyway, come on, I want you to meet Charmaine."

As they climbed the steps, she noticed a short, stocky woman, with shoulder-length, dark, wavy hair, dressed in bright pink shorts and a tight white T-shirt.

Hannah hit it off with the other woman almost immediately, but a melancholy mood came over her. Charmaine reminded her of Diane, from her build, to her easy smile, and sense of humour.

"Right, are we all set?" Max said.

Everyone nodded.

He bent, and opened a cupboard underneath the dash, taking out a hat. He placed it on his head, showing Hannah. Cap'n Max was embroidered across the front.

Hannah smiled. "Of course. I forgot all about that."

"Move over, sailor," he said to Lenny, who scooted out of the captain's chair.

Max looked at home behind the wheel, and Hannah had lustful thoughts while watching him expertly manoeuvre the boat away from the jetty, and out to the centre of the lake.

She sat beside Charmaine, on the bench running around the edge of the deck, while the men showed off. The motor was so loud, it prevented them from talking, and each time one of them tried, they ended up laughing.

After zooming around the outside of the lake, the boat eventually stopped. The men raced around, dropping anchor, and organising the fishing rods.

"Do you fish, Hannah?" Charmaine asked.

"I have, years ago. But, I've got a phobia about touching raw fish." She shuddered. "It's so wet and slimy."

Charmaine barked out a laugh.

"Now she tells me." Max shook his head.

"To be fair, I would have told you, had I known we were spending the day *fishing.*"

"Ah, there is that." They all laughed.

"Anyway, I don't mind watching you, and I've got my book on my phone, if I get bored."

A couple of hours later, Max had caught two large brown trout, and Charmaine and Lenny one each. They packed the rods away.

"I made us a picnic lunch, in the hope we'd have some fresh fish to go with it," Charmaine said. "You do *eat* fish, don't you?"

Hannah nodded. "I love it, once it's cooked. Just can't help you gut and fillet it, sorry."

Charmaine placed a hand on Hannah's arm. "That's the men's job. We're just responsible for cooking and eating it."

"I'm fine with that, then." Hannah laughed.

CHAPTER 24

Before picking the lock, Don tried the door, and, surprisingly, it opened.

The cocky bastard doesn't even lock his house up when he heads out for the day.

He knew there was nobody home—he'd watched them all sail away, as though they hadn't a care in the world.

The stupid house was upside down, as far as he was concerned. The bedrooms were downstairs, and the living rooms up. As he scanned the bedrooms, he noticed the messed up master bedroom with discarded clothing, Hannah's and Max-fucking-Myer's himself, strewn all over the carpet.

He reached for his wristband, and, remembering it wasn't there, an instant rage suddenly surfaced. Yanking his penknife from his jeans pocket, he roared, pouncing onto the bed on all fours, and began to slash at the mattress and pillows. The blue and gold bedspread was soon torn to ribbons, with feathers and mattress stuffing spilled onto the carpet.

Exhausted, he got to his feet, and took a few steps back to inspect his handiwork. He hadn't intended doing that, but he felt quite proud of himself, even though they'd now know somebody had been in the house.

Before he left the room, he picked up a pair of red lace panties, and shoved them into his pocket, rubbing his semi-hard cock through the fabric.

Upstairs, he picked up a piece of well-done bacon off the grill pan, and wrapped it in a slice of buttered bread from a plate under some cling film.

Then, he opened the fridge, and took several swigs from the carton of milk.

Afterwards, he busied himself by installing two tiny surveillance cameras—one in the lounge and one in Max's bedroom. He'd hated not knowing what was happening with Hannah the past couple of days. And he wished he'd installed a camera in Max's apartment, when he'd had the chance.

Don was beginning to think he'd made a huge mistake with Hannah. If he'd taken her out of the picture in the first place, that would have been it. But, now, because of her, he'd killed two people already, and goodness knew how many would end up dead, before he claimed her for himself.

Clair Dietrich had been lucky, all those years ago. He'd been inexperienced and sloppy. After picking her up from a nightclub, he had driven her to the flat he had rented in one of four high-rise buildings. He'd made sure the flat was soundproofed prior to taking her there, but, stupidly, he hadn't blanked out one of the higher windows. He hadn't thought it would be an issue, since she had been tied to a small aluminium deck chair.

He'd undressed her, of course. Not for any sexual satisfaction, but her clothes just made it more difficult to care for her, and it wasn't as though it was cold in there—the heating had been cranked up 24/7. He'd cut a hole in the fabric of the chair to catch her waste in a steel bucket placed underneath. He washed her twice a day, even spending hours brushing her hair until it gleamed. But, after a couple of weeks, just as Clair had begun to settle down and trust the relationship between them, she was spotted by a contractor working on the roof opposite, who called the police.

The first Don knew about it was when his flat was raided by a squad of armed officers, and of course, what they found looked bad, but they never actually asked Clair if she'd been abused. They just looked at the situation, and drew their own conclusion.

At his court-martial a few months later, it was deemed because the victim – *the victim!* – hadn't been sexually assaulted and only mildly physically abused, Don would be medically discharged with PTSD, and not dishonourably discharged and imprisoned, which would put the British army in the spotlight once again, which they really didn't need.

Shaking his head at all his memories, he methodically began trawling through the drawers and cabinets, trying to dig some dirt on his squeaky clean boss, but he found nothing.

Satisfied he'd done everything he needed to do, Don slinked back to his car via the bushes, and headed back to Manchester.

After a slap-up lunch of grilled trout, potato salad, and coleslaw, Hannah took herself off to the top deck to take in the sun's rays.

She attempted to read her book, but her eyes were heavy, and she kept reading the same line over and over. She gave in and dozed for a while.

Soft butterfly kisses along her neck woke her a short time later. She opened her lazy eyes, and smiled at Max. "Hello, you. You stink of fish."

"You say the nicest things." He laughed.

She snorted and wrapped her arms around his neck, kissing him deeply.

"It's beautiful out here, isn't it?" he asked.

"Perfect. I don't want today to end."

"There'll be plenty of other days."

"I know," she said sadly.

"What's wrong? Are you worrying about Angela?"

She nodded. "A little. Aren't you?"

"No. She's brought it on herself. Even if she's not responsible for the scratch on the car and the cottage window, she's guilty of warning you off me, and that, in itself, is unacceptable." He traced his fingers in circles on her exposed stomach.

"I guess. I wish it was all over, that's all. I hate trouble and bad feelings."

"Don't worry. I'll make sure she doesn't upset you ever again."

She smiled, but the feeling of dread wouldn't leave her.

"So, what do you think of *Trixie?*"

"She's beautiful, although I'm totally shocked at the style of boat. I expected you to have a flash, fibreglass speedboat, not this classy old lady."

"She came with the house. In fact, Dad and I found her rotting in the boat house."

"Did you? So, who restored her?"

"We did. Well, of course it was Dad more than me, but I helped, where I could."

"And the name?"

He shrugged. "It was already named *Trixie-Belle*, and Mum thought it was tacky. She asked Dad to rename her, but when he looked into it he found that, according to legend, it's bad luck to change the name of a boat."

"Really?"

"Apparently, there's a way to do it safely, but the truth is, Dad didn't want to. He told Mum it would be a lot safer to start calling *her* Trixie, than to change the name of the boat."

Hannah chuckled. "And what did she say?"

"She dared him to try it, and never mentioned it again."

"Sounds as though your dad knew exactly how to get his own way."

"He taught me everything he knew." Max wiggled his eyebrows comically.

CHAPTER 25

"Ready to head back, Max?" Lenny called from the back of the boat.

Startled, Hannah woke, gazing up at the bluest sky she'd ever seen, and remembered where she was.

Max lifted himself onto one elbow, rubbing the sleep from his eyes. "Yeah. Be right with you."

"Aw, do we have to?" Hannah whined, pouting like a spoiled child.

"I'm afraid so, sausage. But, we can come back next week." He got to his feet, and stretched.

"Sausage?" She goggled at him.

"Yes. My little sausage." He grinned.

"I don't know if I like that!" She grimaced.

"You'll get used to it." The cheeky twinkle had returned to his gorgeous brown eyes.

"Will I now? So, you haven't gone off me, then?" She lifted into a sitting position, crossing her legs in front of her.

He bit his lip and narrowed his eyes, as though thinking about the question.

She slapped at his foot. "Hey!"

"Joke. Of course I haven't gone off you. But, still early days, I guess."

Hannah squealed, and swatted at his retreating back. She followed him, and, once again, sat with Charmaine, while the men did their thing.

Fifteen minutes later, they pulled up to the jetty at the bottom of the exquisite garden.

Lenny helped the ladies disembark, and then he and Max continued to close down the boat.

"Max, I'll go on ahead and pack my bag," Hannah called.

"Okay. The door's open."

"So, did you enjoy today?" Charmaine asked, as they walked up towards the house.

"I did. Thanks. But, you should've let me help prepare lunch."

"Don't be silly, it was only a few salads. And besides, it's my job."

"I'm sure it's above and beyond your job description. Working weekends and entertaining your boss's girlfriend."

"Well, of course *that* part wasn't work. There are perks to any position." She giggled. "But, Max is rarely here, and when he is, he's no trouble. I often feel guilty for accepting my pay, when I feel as though I haven't done anything to earn it."

"From what he's told me, you earn every penny."

They reached the front of the house, and Hannah paused. "Well, it was lovely meeting you, Charmaine. I hope we can do it again."

They hugged, before heading in different directions.

Don arrived back at Simon's flat, before Hannah and Maxwell-fucking-Myers had returned from their boat trip.

He cooked some eggs and made a pot of strong coffee. Then, he sat back waiting for the show.

First off, he heard the slam of the front door, followed by somebody running up the stairs. He couldn't tell who.

Hannah began singing to herself, and Don realised she was alone.

After a few minutes, she appeared in the doorway of the master bedroom. She stood still for a moment, before darting around the room, collecting her clothing from the carpet. Then, she picked up a piece of white fluff, a puzzled expression on her face.

Just then, another sound from outside the room was followed by a male voice calling out to her.

"I'm in here," she said flatly.

Hannah turned to greet Max as he entered the room. She held her lime-coloured blouse in one hand and the white fluff in the other.

"What the hell?" Max said, looking from her, to the bed, to the mass of stuffing all over the floor.

Don belched out a laugh, and slapped his thigh. The attack on the bed hadn't been intentional, but it couldn't have played out better.

The person who'd slashed at the bed must have been in a total frenzy, considering the damage they'd done. Hannah watched, shocked, as Max pulled the loose coverings off the mattress and examined the deep slashes in the surface of it.

Max spun to face her. "Have you been upstairs yet?"

She shook her head, and steadied herself against the doorframe.

"Wait here."

Never one for doing as she was told, she followed close behind him. She almost jumped out of her skin when he reappeared at the top of the stairs.

"Shit, Hannah! You made me jump."

"Have they done anything up here?"

"Not that I can tell. But, I'm calling the police. I've had as much as I'm going to take now."

"Do you think it could've been Angela again?"

"What do you mean *again*? We don't even know for sure if it's her at all, but I'm not messing about anymore. We can leave it to the police."

Surprised by his attitude, she backed up to the sofa, and sat down heavily, curling her legs underneath her. She felt sick. She'd been certain somebody was messing with her mind, but now, she'd dragged Max into it.

"I'm sorry for snapping, Hannah." He crouched in front of her and held her hand.

"That's okay." She nodded.

"We'll get to the bottom of this, I assure you."

He pulled his phone from his pocket, and walked towards the breakfast bar. She listened as he gave his details and a brief explanation of the crime to the police, then he hung up.

"They might not be here for a few hours," he said, sitting next to her.

She quickly looked at her watch—4.34pm.

"Don't worry, sausage. We don't need to go back to the city tonight, unless you want to, that is?"

"What about work?"

He shrugged. "Are you forgetting it's my company?"

"No, but…"

"Don't worry about your job. I want to keep you away, until the police look into everything. We don't know how unstable this person is." He gently encircled her shoulders with his arm. "Oh, my God! You're shaking."

Once she'd calmed down, they went to let Lenny and Charmaine know what had happened.

They walked around the back of the cottage to a small stone patio where Max tapped on the window.

Charmaine was in the kitchen, peeling potatoes. She threw the peeler onto the bench, and called Lenny before unlocking the door and inviting them inside.

Lenny ran down the stairs, tucking his T-shirt into the waist of his jeans. "Hey, mate. Take a seat." He gestured to the sofa.

Hannah noticed the boarded-up window, as she sat beside Max on the sofa. She winced inwardly at the damage—several of the panel frames were completely smashed.

"We've had an intruder," Max said. "They've slashed my bed and all my bedding."

Charmaine gasped.

"Who'd do that?" Lenny said, shaking his head. "How did they get in?"

"I didn't lock up. But, to be honest, I never do, until I'm leaving for the city. I've never needed to before."

"Yeah, we're the same. You don't usually see anybody at this end of the lake."

"That's two acts of vandalism in twenty-four hours," Charmaine said. "You need to call the police."

"I have. They won't be here for a while. But, we'll stay here tonight anyway."

"Do you want to stay for dinner? I have plenty," Charmaine asked, raising her eyebrows.

Max glanced at Hannah.

She shook her head. "Not for me, thanks. I feel quite sick, to be honest. It was such a shock."

Charmaine crossed the room to crouch beside Hannah. "Lenny, make some hot sweet tea, will you? She looks deathly pale."

Max reached for Hannah's hand. "She thinks she knows who's responsible, and that they've been stalking her for weeks."

"Who?" Charmaine asked, wide-eyed.

"Angela. My PA and head of Human Resources," he said.

Charmaine screwed her face up. "Really? Why?"

Max glanced at Hannah. "You tell her."

"Because she fancies him." Hannah nodded at Max. "She's already warned me off him once. Plus, she was the only person who knew we were together, and she has access to Max's private details, so could easily find this address."

Charmaine exhaled noisily and returned to her seat. "Crazy bitch!"

"Who's a crazy bitch?" Lenny said, appearing with a heavily laden tray.

Charmaine explained to her husband what they'd been talking about.

"Jeez, man. What will you do about it?" Lenny asked Max.

"To be fair, Angela might not be responsible. It's one thing warning Hannah off me, but it's quite another to break into her flat and my house, and purposefully destroy our belongings."

"So, someone's been in your flat, too?" Charmaine asked Hannah.

Hannah nodded. "I've no real evidence, but some of my belongings have been tampered with—even replaced, which I know sounds crazy."

"The police will need to look into it," Max said. "In the meantime, we'll stay here for a day, or two. I can work from here, no problem." He glanced at Hannah for confirmation. "Is that alright?"

"Of course. I'm just relieved you believe me."

"What's not to believe? I've seen it with my own eyes." Max indicated to the damaged window.

"You think the same person is responsible for the window as well?" Lenny asked.

"I do, yeah. Who else would bother traipsing all this way around the lake, just to lob a rock through the window?" Max said.

"Make sure you lock up tonight," Lenny said, pouring the tea.

Max took a cup from his friend. "The same goes for you. Be extra vigilant. We don't know how far this person is willing to go."

CHAPTER 26

Don was wild with himself. His actions had caused Maxwell-fuckin-Myers to insist Hannah stay away for longer. However, he had discovered something remarkable—they thought Angela Beanie was responsible for everything, which made him howl with laughter.

He'd never liked Angela. And he could tell the feeling was mutual, so he decided to play a little game with the lot of them.

The police still hadn't arrived at the lake house when he had to leave for work, but he would be able to log into the surveillance cams from the security hub.

After taking over from the day staff, he spent an hour getting set up for the evening. Once Ken was occupied, Don left him to it, and headed straight for the security hub, where he temporarily looped the cameras to the staff lockers.

Then he removed Hannah's bag from his locker, and shoved it into the back of Angela Beanie's, along with the original black dress. He just wished he'd brought a souvenir from the lake house to stitch her up completely.

Back in the security hub, he logged into the lake house cameras, and sat in wait for the police.

"Can I make you a sandwich?" Max said, as they returned to the house. "Are you hungry?"

"Maybe later. I don't think I could stomach anything right now."

He rubbed her shoulder, as they snuggled on the sofa staring out at the glassy lake and scenic mountains in the distance.

"I wish the police would hurry up. It's making me feel jittery waiting for them," she said.

"They'll be coming from Penrith, probably. And don't forget it's Sunday—we'll be lucky if we see them before morning."

"Really? What if it was an emergency?"

"Then, they'd send out an emergency vehicle. But, I told them it wasn't. The intruder had already left."

She rummaged in her handbag for her phone. No calls or messages. She sighed, and threw it back into the bag.

"Do you want to call your mum? You said you would this evening."

She nodded. "I will, later. And I'll try Simon, too, if that's alright? Not that he can do much from Seattle, although he might want to send flowers."

"We could arrange flowers from you both, if you like. Then, at least he won't feel bad if he misses the funeral," Max said.

"That's a good idea. Thanks, Max. My mind isn't functioning properly at the moment."

He hugged her to him, and she sighed. For all that was wrong around them right now, being with him felt so right.

The police arrived just before 9pm.

Hannah had been dozing in Max's arms on the sofa, and she woke with a start when they heard loud rapping at the front door.

"It's okay, sausage. It's just the police," he said, heading for the stairs.

She heard the police radios, as the officers trudged up the stairs, and she folded the throw and sat upright.

A portly uniformed officer, who appeared close to retirement age, entered first. He was puffing and panting, as though he was about to keel over. A younger, attractive, blonde female officer came up behind him.

Hannah greeted them both with a handshake, and they introduced themselves. She didn't take in their names.

"Can I get you a drink?" Hannah asked, as they sat side-by-side on the sofa she'd just vacated.

"A cold drink would be appreciated," the man said, wiping his forehead with a handkerchief.

Hannah glanced at the other officer, who nodded in agreement.

From the kitchen, she listened as Max explained the two incidents.

Hannah returned with a jug of orange juice and two glasses. After pouring the juice out, she knelt on the carpet beside Max, who was sitting on the only other chair.

"And do you have any idea who might hold a grudge against you, sir?" the male officer said.

Max shuffled in his seat, and placed a hand on Hannah's shoulder. "Well, there's more, actually. But, I didn't know about it until yesterday."

The officer lifted his head, suddenly interested. "Go on."

"Well, Hannah works for me in Manchester. She moved from Shropshire a few weeks ago, and since then, she's experienced a few unexplained occurrences."

The officer looked at Hannah and nodded. "Can you tell us about these occurrences, miss?"

Hannah cleared her throat. "They started out as just a feeling someone had been in my flat. Nothing I could pinpoint, but there was a strange smell, especially in my bedroom."

"Go on."

"Then, my gym bag went missing from my locker at work, and, when I got it back, it appeared to have been tampered with. Everything was there, but different—as though several of the items had been replaced by similar but newer stuff."

The female officer's eyebrows furrowed, as she continued to jot in her pad.

"Strange," her colleague said. "Anything else?"

"Yes. The same thing happened with a new and very expensive dress I bought in a sale. I got it for a fraction of the original cost, as one of the bones was missing from the bodice. But, a couple of weeks later, when I wore it for the first time, I noticed the bone wasn't missing. It seemed like a totally different dress."

The officers glanced at each other, as if to say, *'Is this chick for real?'*

"I'm aware of how crazy it sounds, believe me. That's why I haven't reported it before now."

"It is strange, but carry on," he said.

"On Friday, I noticed someone had definitely been in my flat. The bed had been moved several inches. The indents in the carpet were a dead giveaway. It's a heavy antique bed, and won't move easily, so it had been moved on purpose. But, I'd just discovered my neighbour had been murdered at work, and so, I didn't really pay it much attention at the time. Max had told me to pack a bag, and we would come here for the weekend."

"Yes," Max said. "I took her back to my apartment in the city for the night, and the next morning, we left to come here. The only person who knew we were together was my PA, Angela Beanie. She saw us in the car park before we left. Then, I discovered a deep scratch along the passenger side of my new car. After we found the scratch, Hannah told me about Angela warning her off me a few days prior."

"So, you think this Ms Beanie is responsible for today's damage?" The female officer spoke for the first time.

"I'm not certain. I would've said I trusted her with my life until yesterday. But, the fact is, she told lies about me, and cautioned Hannah to stay away. This is totally out of character for the woman I *thought* I knew, so, until I'm convinced otherwise, I have to believe she's possibly behind all the other things, too."

"I see." The officer scratched his head. "Do you have Ms Beanie's address, by any chance?"

"No. But, I'll give you my Head of Security's details at AdCor, and he will assist you with everything you need."

CHAPTER 27

Don listened to the police interview. He suddenly had a new respect for his boss, when he heard Max tell the cop to contact *him*, his Head of Security!

Within moments of the police leaving, his phone rang—it was Max.

He puffed out his chest, and smiled before answering. "Don Henry."

"Don, it's Max Myers."

Don first heard Max's voice in his ear, and then the delay from the speakers. He winced, and quickly ducked out of the room. "Hey, Mr Myers. What can I do for you?"

"I've given a police officer your details. He will be asking you for some personal information on Angela Beanie. Please give him everything he needs."

"Will do, sir."

"Oh, and this is a little bit delicate, so I'd appreciate you keeping it to yourself, but if Ms Beanie comes into work in the morning, could you put her in the board room, and ask her to wait for Eric Gallagher, the company solicitor?"

"Of course. Can I ask why, sir?"

"I don't really want to go into it at this stage, until I'm certain, but I'll need you to assist Eric, if that's alright. I know this will mean you staying behind for a few hours, but as you're the senior member of the security team, I'd rather leave it with you."

"Not a problem, sir. Consider it done."

"Excellent. And one other thing. I'll be working from home for a day or two. Could you call me once Ms Beanie has been escorted off the premises?"

"No problem. You enjoy the rest of your evening, sir."

His night shift flew by, and Don was on cloud nine. It was only marred slightly when he watched Max carry Hannah from the lounge. And although he couldn't see them in the spare bedroom, he heard them loud and clear. He reached for the new band on his wrist. Snap-snap-snap.

Angela Beanie's priggish face was a picture the next morning. He met her as she breezed in from the car park, and she barely spared him a glance when he cleared his throat. "Good morning, Ms Beanie."

"What? Oh, good morning, Donald. Has Mr Myers arrived yet?"

"Not yet. In fact, it's my understanding he won't be in for a few days."

She went to press the lift call button, but he placed his hand in the way.

"What the...?"

"I'm sorry, but I need you to accompany me to the boardroom. It's important." Eric Gallagher had called to say he was on his way in, but was running a little late.

"Can't this wait, Donald? I'm going to be extra busy today, especially now you tell me Mr Myers won't be showing his face."

"This is at Mr Myers' instruction I'm afraid, ma'am."

She did a double-take at him, as though he'd just spat in her face.

It was all Don could do to maintain a professional demeanour, and keep his face from cracking into a broad, beaming grin.

"What is this about?" she snapped.

"I have no idea, I'm sorry. But, Mr Myers assures me we'll find out soon. However, it's imperative we go to the boardroom and await further instruction." He loved the way the words rolled off his tongue, and the underlying sinister message behind the seemingly innocuous request.

They travelled to the boardroom in silence. Angela Beanie gave several curt nods to a few of the staff they passed.

She slammed her briefcase and keys down on the large oval table, and yanked her chair out with a pissed-off sigh.

"Can I get you a coffee?" he asked.

"No. Thanks. Can we just get this over with?"

"I honestly don't know what *this* is. We have to wait a little while. I'm sorry." Don had to pluck at his wristband several times to stop him grinning from ear-to-ear. He knew he was getting far too much pleasure out of watching her squirm.

It was a further twenty minutes before Eric arrived, and by then, you could cut the atmosphere with a pair of chopsticks.

"Finally!" Angela said, as the middle-aged man breezed in.

Eric's mop of brown hair appeared windswept, causing Don's lip to curl in contempt. Men should behave like men, in his opinion. He had zero tolerance for namby-pamby shit, like designer clothing and hair stylists for men—that stuff should be left to the weaker sex.

"Will you hurry up, and tell me what this is all about," Angela snapped.

Eric seemed to be stretching the whole 'getting prepared' performance out, just a tad.

"All in good time, Ms Beanie." He clicked open the clasp of his briefcase, and took out a burgundy diary.

Angela's face had turned scarlet. Tight-lipped, she huffed air from her nose.

"So..." Eric hitched his chair forward, and placed his diary on the table. "It has come to my attention Mr Myers has been the victim of several acts of criminal damage."

Angela gasped. "Is he alright?"

"As I said, he's been the victim of criminal damage."

She shook her head irritably. "And what's that supposed to mean?"

"Somebody has deliberately damaged his property over the weekend, and it appears to be personal."

"Oh my God. So, what does he need us to do?"

Eric sighed. "Actually, Angela, he doesn't want *you* to do anything. He's standing you down, with full pay, pending a full investigation."

"What do you mean?" She jerked to her feet, sending her chair flying backwards. "Does he think *I* have something to do with it?"

Eric said nothing. He didn't need to—his face said it all.

"Why? Why the hell would he think that? It's ludicrous."

"He wants me to let you know the police have been notified, and will be contacting you this morning sometime. Now, if you don't mind, Don will help you collect your belongings, and escort you from the premises."

"Eric, you've known me for years. I could no more go against Max than you could—surely you know that."

"It's not up to me, I'm afraid. Apparently, he has reason to believe it could be you, and, as his solicitor, it doesn't matter what *I* think."

"Then, the least you can do is tell me what I'm supposed to have done."

Eric ran his fingers through his girly hair, and reached for his diary again. "There are several things. He discovered a deep scratch on his new car."

Angela snorted. "Sorry, go on."

"A rock was thrown through the window of a cottage on his property at the lake, and yesterday, somebody entered his house, and tore up his mattress."

"This doesn't make sense. Why would he think it was me?"

"Apparently, you warned his girlfriend to stay away from him last week."

"His girlfriend! If you mean that little trollop he's been drooling over—he's only known her five minutes."

"Her name is Miss McLaughlin. Did you warn her off him?"

She nodded. "Yeah, but…" She closed her eyes, and rubbed her temples. "I may have tried to put her off him. It's not professional. But, how did he come to accuse me of the other stuff from that?"

"Listen, Angela. I shouldn't be telling you any of this, but somebody has been stalking Miss McLaughlin, entering her house, stealing her belongings, etcetera."

"Well, it's not me. What's been stolen?"

He glanced at his diary. "A dress and a gym bag."

"Hang on, the gym bag was found. She'd put it in the wrong locker."

"Yes. But, the things had been replaced for new."

Angela looked around at Don for the first time. "Are you listening to this?"

Don nodded.

"They're accusing me of stealing her clothing—what the fuck would I do with them—they'd bury me. Hannah's hardly a lightweight; she's twice my size."

Suddenly annoyed, Don stepped forward. "Can we get a move on? I'm supposed to be home in bed by now."

Angela's mouth dropped open.

"Of course." Eric got to his feet, and began placing his things back in the briefcase. "Needless to say, don't try to contact Max. He'll be in touch, once the police have done their thing, and if *you* know you're innocent, then you've got nothing to worry about, have you?"

Don walked Angela to her office, where she collected several items off her desk. The receptionist on the top floor tried to get her attention over some crisis or other, but Angela just held her hand up, silencing the woman mid-sentence.

Bitch, Don thought.

On the way down to the car park level, Angela swung by her locker. The expression on her face was priceless when she spotted the gym bag, and she slowly pulled it out, glancing from the bag to Don, her mouth agape.

"Well, what do we have here then?" he said, shaking his head. He took the bag from her, and opened it up.

"I—I don't know where it came from. I've never seen it before." Her face had turned a sickly shade of grey. "You do believe me, don't you, Don?"

He shrugged one shoulder. "It doesn't matter what I think, Ms Beanie. I'll hand this in to the police when they arrive later."

"This is a set-up. Someone is trying to lose me my job. Surely you can see that."

Several people passing by stopped to have a nosey.

"Calm down, Ms Beanie. You're causing a stir," Don said.

"I don't fucking care!" She was shouting now. "Let them see what the management is doing to me."

He took the bag in one hand and gripped her by her upper arm, forcibly escorting her to her car. She was clearly unhappy, but knew it was pointless fighting against him—he was far bigger than her. The powerful feeling this evoked in him gave him the stirrings of an erection.

After taking her security passes from her, he watched Angela drive from the car park. Then, he turned to the crowd of spectators, which had seemed to appear from nowhere. "Carry on, there's nothing more to see here."

He secured Hannah's gym bag in the security hub, and dialled his boss's number.

"Oh, Don. Thank God. How did it go?"

"She denied everything, of course, Mr Myers. But, when I accompanied her to her locker, she tried to say the gym bag she found in there was nothing to do with her."

"Gym bag? What's in it?"

"Several items of workout gear, some underwear and a black dress."

Max gasped. "So, it *was* her. I honestly thought we were barking up the wrong tree, but Hannah was right."

"It appears that way, sir."

"Have the police been in touch yet?"

"No. But, I've left an envelope for them with Carlos. It has all Ms Beanie's contact details, as well as mine. And I've told them I'll be back here no later than six this evening."

"Great, thanks buddy. I owe you one. What did you do with Hannah's bag?"

"It's in the security hub. Ken and Big Brian are the only ones with a security pass, so if the police want it before I return later, they'll need to get hold of one of them. Unless you want me to put it into your office?"

"No. That should be fine. You get off, Don. You must be shattered."

CHAPTER 28

Max ended the call, and then turned to face Hannah who was kneeling on the sofa, her hands clamped to her mouth. "Don found your missing gym stuff and black dress in Angela's locker."

She shook her head, and stared at nothing in particular. Her mind was in chaos. Although she'd suspected Angela, she thought it would be a lot harder to prove it. "So, now what?" she eventually said.

He shrugged. "It's up to the police, I'd say. I'm in shock. I'd have trusted her with my life, you know?"

She held her hand out to him. "Oh, Max. You must be devastated."

He sat down beside her. "I know it sounds stupid, but I honestly thought we'd discover it wasn't her. I've always prided myself on being able to read people. I've worked closely with Angela for a few years now, and I didn't even suspect. Then, you come along, and have her worked out immediately."

"Only because of the warning. I thought she was really nice, up until then."

"The police haven't even been to interview her yet. I thought they'd be there first thing this morning."

She glanced at her watch. "It's only just gone nine. I'm sure they'll be there soon."

When Max went to tell Lenny and Charmaine of the developments, Hannah checked her phone. She still hadn't heard from Simon. She'd tried to call him the night before, but the phone was going straight to voicemail.

She didn't even know when the funeral was, if she *had* managed to get hold of him. She checked the internet for the hospital number and dialled.

After being put through to three different people, she established that Diane's funeral was to be held on Thursday, at 2pm – no flowers.

Don let himself into Hannah's flat, dropping his bag on the floor, and falling backwards onto the bed. He was exhausted. With everything he had going on, he hadn't managed more than four consecutive hours' sleep in weeks. It was catching up with him.

He altered the position of his erection through the fabric of his trousers. It had been throbbing continuously since manhandling Angela from the building, and he knew it wouldn't go away without assistance.

He wearily got to his feet, and stripped off his clothing. Gripping the base of his cock roughly, he found Hannah's skimpy red panties in his bag, and rubbed them across the glistening tip.

He groaned and climbed into the bed. He tried to envisage Hannah standing before him, stroking her milky white tits seductively. But, it was no use. Thoughts of another beautiful redhead came into his mind, as she always did as soon as he got aroused.

He suddenly slapped his penis hard, and groaned again, as he wrapped his hands tightly around himself.

When he closed his eyes, he was transported back almost forty years.

. . .

The woman cuddling him was naked, her full, pink-tipped breasts crushed against his nine-year-old chest.

She was warm, and smelled of sunshine and sandy beaches. He thought back to the night before, how his daddy had rubbed and sucked her until she cried out. Don had thought he was hurting her at first, until she started begging for more.

A strange rushing feeling began in his underpants, and he rocked his hips slowly.

His mother reached down, and slapped at him.

A sudden pain in his groin caused him to cry out in pain.

"Now, now, naughty boy. You know that's not allowed."

"I'm sorry, Mummy. I didn't mean to."

"Stand up and drop your trousers. Come on. Quick, quick."

He shook his head rapidly. "No, Mummy. I'm sorry. I promise it won't happen again."

"We'll see, shall we?" She gripped him roughly by the wrist, and pulled him to his feet. "Drop your trousers. Do it!"

Tears streamed down his face, as he fumbled with trembling fingers to open the button of his stripy grey slacks.

"Now, lift your shirt up." She taunted him.

"No, Mummy, please."

She nodded, indicating he should do as she said.

He lifted his shirt, leaving him feeling exposed and silly.

"Okay, what is it you like, little man?" She hoisted her heavy breasts, tweaking at the nipples slowly.

He tried not to look, but he felt his eyes drawn to them. They were beautiful, but they gave him the strangest feeling. He placed his hands in front of him, covering his boy bits.

"Lift your shirt up, Donald. I won't tell you again."

He did as he was told.

"Ah, seems you like my boobies. Am I right? Am I?" she said, rubbing her boobs—bouncing and wobbling them in front of him.

"Please, Mummy," he begged.

"Or is it this?" She lounged backwards on the chair, and opened her legs.

His heart was racing, and his breath was coming out in little bursts. His eyes glued to the curly red triangle of hair. Then, he felt a movement in his privates. He winced, and cried out, falling to his knees in shame.

"I told you you'd do it again. You can't be trusted can you, little man?"

Don opened his eyes, and dragged himself back into the present. His huge erection throbbed painfully. It was the same every time.

His parents had spent years training him not to get sexually excited. And because of that, he'd never had a sexual partner. Any time he had got close to a woman, with each erection came vivid memories of his mother's voluptuous curves, and the shame and humiliation of having his privates slapped and laughed at.

He tried to drag his thoughts back to Hannah in the bath, slowly soaping her lovely little breasts. He inhaled her scent from the bedclothes, as he rubbed her panties on the silky length of his cock.

As he closed his eyes, he was back there—in his childhood home in Hattersley, an overspill estate of Greater Manchester. He had now learned his parents were sex mad, but as a kid, it was normal for him to sit on the sofa watching TV, while they had fucked and sucked each other beside him.

He would mostly ignore them, but as he got older, it became harder and harder to tear his eyes from their glistening, naked flesh. His father's skin was dark, and his hair jet black. But, his mother was pale. Blue veins showed through her translucent white skin.

Don would pinch and push at himself—petrified of them seeing his engorged penis, but it was no use. That part of his body had a mind of its own. And when they had spotted it, his father would march him to his room, bend him over the end of the bed, and strap his behind with his leather belt until it was red-raw. This caused his erection to shrink.

One day, after being caught masturbating to a lingerie magazine, his mother had hit the roof. She locked him in his bedroom, while they waited for his father to come home from work. He was fifteen years old.

Don had been petrified, knowing what was to happen as soon as his father knew what he'd done. He'd pissed himself when he heard the car pull into the garage.

Within moments, his father burst through the door.

"I'm so sorry, Dad. I tried, I really did, but I just couldn't help it. It hurts."

His cries had been ignored. "Drop your trousers, boy. Hurry up. Do it."

Don knew not to argue with his father when his eyes bulged that way. He staggered to his feet, terrified his father would notice the wet patch on his black corduroy trousers. But, he was too far-gone to notice anything.

Don dropped his trousers and turned, bending over the end of the bed. He heard his father undo his belt, and slide it out of his belt loops. Don gripped the bed sheets, as he braced himself for the first whack.

But, what he got was totally unexpected.

His dad dug fingers into Don's buttocks and waist, and a white-hot, blinding pain followed.

Don screamed, but the sound wouldn't come out. He begged and called for his mother. But, as his father pumped away ferociously behind him, they slowly moved around the side of the bed. It was then he had got had a glimpse of his mother, smiling and rubbing at her privates in the doorway.

That was the last day he saw her. The last memory of his beautiful mother was her getting off on her only son being raped by his own father.

They left him curled in a ball on the carpet of his bedroom.

He waited until he heard them retire several hours later before getting to his feet, wincing in pain.

He'd known his parents weren't normal. They'd behaved the same way all his life, but that didn't stop him loving them. Yet, there was no coming back from something like that—rape.

Packing a few of his possessions, he let himself out the back door, never to return.

Don sat up on Hannah's bed, and wiped the mess from his stomach. Then, he snuggled down, and slept better than he had in weeks.

CHAPTER 29

While Max busied himself with work-related issues, Hannah called her mother. She didn't tell her about the trouble she'd had, feeding her a white lie instead.

"I've been putting in some extra hours at work, so I've got a couple of days in lieu. I'll be home for Wednesday."

"Oh, lovely. Whose house are you staying in?"

"Just a girl from work." She raised her eyebrows when Max glanced up at her, shaking his head. "Anyway, I'll tell you all about it next time. We're just heading off out. If you need me, call my mobile."

"Okay, sweetheart. Have a lovely time."

She hung up, and tried Simon's number again. Voicemail. She didn't know what else she could do. When he finally got his messages, at least he'd see how many times she'd tried.

"Knock, knock," Charmaine called from downstairs.

"Come on up," Max replied.

"Hi," she said, as she trudged upstairs. "I came to see if you want me to do some housework?"

"No need, Char." Max got up from his desk, and kissed the top of her head. "It's still pretty tidy."

"What about the bedroom? After the mess the intruder made?"

"Hannah cleaned that up this morning, while we were waiting for word from the office about Angela."

"Oh, how did that go?"

"I called over earlier to tell you, but you weren't home. Take a seat. I'll make a pot of coffee."

Charmaine sat on the sofa beside Hannah. Between them, they told her what Don had found in Angela's locker.

"So, that's it, then. She must be guilty of the rest, too. What did the police say?"

"Last we heard, they hadn't spoken to her yet. If they haven't called by this afternoon, I'll chase them up."

Max carried the pot and three mugs over to the coffee table.

"Do you need me to go for groceries? I only shopped for the weekend," Charmaine said.

Max shook his head, and gazed at Hannah. "I was going to suggest we go for a drive into Penrith."

"Yeah. Sounds good," Hannah agreed.

He turned back to Charmaine. "Thanks anyway. I'll need Lenny to get rid of the old mattress, though. We'll put it on his truck for the time being. I'll have a look for a new one when we're in town today."

"Yeah. Just let him know when you're ready, and he'll be right over."

A short time later, Charmaine left, and they busied themselves getting ready for their trip to Penrith.

Max's phone began ringing, as they pulled out of the garage. He hit a button on his steering wheel, and the call went through to the speakers.

"Maxwell Myers," he said.

"Hello, Mr Myers. It's Detective Aiden Johnstone from the Greater Manchester Police Department."

"Good afternoon, Detective."

"This is just a follow-up call, regarding the complaint you made yesterday evening."

"Yes."

"I've interviewed your employee, Ms Angela Beanie, and she is adamant she had nothing to do with your break-in, or any of the other incidents you mentioned. However, your Head of Security, a Mr..." He paused and they could hear paper shuffling. "...Henry said he was with Ms Beanie when she packed up her locker this morning, and a gym bag belonging to Ms McLaughlin was discovered."

"Yes. Don told me. What did Angela have to say about that?"

"She denied it, obviously. However, she has no alibi for any of the dates you gave."

"I'll bet she doesn't. So, what now?"

"We have a few more enquiries to make, and then, if nothing else comes to light, I guess we'll be charging her."

"Right. Well, thanks for letting me know. Will you keep me updated?"

"I will, sir. Enjoy the rest of your day."

Max exhaled noisily, and turned to face Hannah. "So, that's it, then. Just like that. Fuck only knows how I'm going to fill her position now."

"What happens in a case like this? Can you fire her, with immediate effect?"

"I would think so. I'll need to check with Eric." He indicated the phone. "Do you mind?"

"No. Go for it."

She listened as he called his solicitor, who said he'd draw up the termination notice right away. Then, he rang another number.

A woman answered, all breathy and sexy. "Hi, stranger."

Max glanced at Hannah and smiled, shaking his head at her raised eyebrows.

"Hi, Cheryl. I'm in a bit of a fix. I need to replace my PA, as soon as humanly possible."

"Really? What happened to the ice queen?"

"We've had a parting of the ways, I'm afraid. Do you have any decent candidates on your books?"

They heard her tapping on a keyboard. "Not many people of her calibre, to be honest, Max. She also headed the Human Resources team, didn't she?"

"She did. But, I'll employ someone else to do that, if need be."

"I'll pull some strings, and see if I can get an ad drawn up today. I'll have it on the website later on, if possible."

"Great. Thanks, Chez, and you may as well do me an ad for Head of Security when you get the chance. No hurry, though; the guys seem to be managing okay since Steve…well, you know."

"Yeah, I heard about that—poor guy. I've got Angela's job description in the archives, but I never had one for Steve's position. Can you send it through to me? I'll get it written up."

"Will do, love. Thanks for that." He hung up, and glanced at Hannah. "What?"

"You!" She made a stupid face. "Oooh, Cheryl, Chezzer, love," she squeaked.

"Idiot." He laughed.

"How far is the place we're heading?" she asked.

"Around forty-five minutes, but I want to stop at Tebay Services for lunch."

"Motorway services? Doesn't seem your type of thing."

"Wait till you see them—it's far superior to any others I've been to. They have *the* most amazing farm shop."

The drive north was pleasant, although all motorway, but she was enjoying the scenery, and being in his company.

"Check out this cluster of trees coming up on the right," he said.

Hannah stared at the trees, thinking what an odd place to plant a forest, but it wasn't until they were adjacent to it that she could see the shape. "It's a heart," she gasped.

Max nodded, his beautiful eyes sparkling.

"Who planted that?"

"I've heard several stories. One is that a farmer planted it to show how much he loved his wife, and another was it was planted in the memory of a man who was killed at war. I don't really know which, if either, is true. But, the one my mum told me is there were two neighbouring farming families, who had a long-standing feud. One family had a son and the other a daughter who inevitably fell in love, but, when the secret of the affair got out, the families banned them from seeing each other, and told them they were forbidden to marry. So, one night, the lovers met for one last time at the point where their farms joined, and, in each other's arms, they committed suicide. Both families were distraught at the tragedy they'd caused so they planted the wood in their memory."

"That's so sad. Why didn't they just run away?"

He shook his head. "I've no idea. It does seem a little tragic to me. They could have eloped to Gretna Green, which is only a little further north, and married, without their families' blessing."

"I'd hate to get married without my family's blessing though, wouldn't you?"

"Of course, but not so much I'd kill myself over it."

"Just different times, I guess," she said. "People would have been so ignorant of things—imagine living up here—isolated from everything, having no telephone, internet, or television. Snail mail would be the only form of communication. You'd have no choice but to believe anything your family told you—whether it was lies or not."

"Yeah, I suppose so. Shit, I don't know how people lived without all the modern conveniences we have today."

"I think it would have been so much nicer back then—to live off your own land, make your own clothes, and to go to church on a Sunday."

Max shuddered. "Sounds like hell to me. Now my parents are

gone, I'd have to live all alone on my land, with no family, and die a lonely old man."

"Don't you have any family at all?"

He shook his head. "None. Lenny and Charmaine are the closest thing to family I have."

"That's so sad."

Max pulled off the motorway, and Hannah could tell it was different to most motorway services. The buildings were constructed from traditional local stone. The place was buzzing with people, and it seemed it wasn't just passing tourists who stopped in there, but locals, too. In fact, it seemed to be a tourist destination in its own right.

"Told you." Max grinned.

"I love it. My mum would be in heaven here," she said, as they stepped through the door of the farm shop. All local produce and condiments filled the shelves. The butchery was also locally sourced, as were the fruit and vegetables. But, it was the cheese counter which had Hannah drooling. They bought a selection of cheese, as well as a few of the most amazing-looking pork pies Hannah had ever seen.

Then, with her stomach growling, they headed next door to the restaurant.

Hannah was blown away with the quality and range of food on offer. After much deliberation between two of her all-time favourites—macaroni cheese and steak in ale pie, with mashed potato and a selection of seasonal vegetables—she ordered the pie. Max chose Haggis, a Scottish dish made of offal, which didn't appeal to Hannah at all. Although, once it arrived, she thought it looked and smelled delicious.

Afterwards, feeling stuffed and ready for a sleep, they drove the final distance to Penrith in silence.

"There's a castle!" Hannah suddenly sat upright in her seat.

"Well, the ruins of one, yeah. Do you like castles?"

"I love them. We have Clun Castle near where I grew up in Shropshire, but that's much smaller than this."

"Next time you're here, I'll take you to Carlisle. The castle there's amazing, and it's close to the ruins of Hadrian's wall."

"Would you? I'd love that."

They parked the car outside a large furniture store, and strolled, hand-in-hand, through the store to the bed department, where they had a hilarious half hour testing out the different mattresses on display.

"I don't know about you, but I could go to sleep now," she said, as they lay on a plush, pillow-topped mattress.

"Seems this is the one, then." He called the salesperson over, and placed his order.

As they walked back to the car, Max glanced at his watch. "Okay, we could either head home the way we came, or we could have a quick look around Bowness, and travel home the back way?"

She grinned. "You know I'm going to say the back way. I want to see as much as I can while I'm here."

They headed back down the motorway, and took the exit for Bowness-on-Windermere.

"I thought your lake was Windermere?" she said.

"Yes, it is. But, I'm more Newby Bridge end. Bowness is the busiest area for tourists."

"How big is the lake?"

"A little over ten miles long."

"Wow. And how wide?"

"Obviously, that varies, but I don't think it's wider than a mile at the widest point."

"Less than moon river, then?"

"Sorry?"

Moon river – wider than a mile," she sang badly.

Max groaned, and she playfully punched his bicep.

Although she loved the higgledy-piggledy streets at Bowness,

Hannah found it much too commercialised, and felt a little claustrophobic when they strolled along the side of the lake, eating ice cream. She was relieved to get back to the car.

"How much further is your place?"

"Around five miles. Our house is about three miles this side of Newby Bridge."

He switched on the engine, and glanced at his watch.

"Are you okay?" she asked.

"I keep thinking about work. Angela's been a crucial part of the business since she came on-board a few years ago. She's slowly taken so much off my plate, I really don't know where I'm going to start."

"Do you want to head back to Manchester tonight? I could help, if you like—not that I know much about her position."

"Not today. We can leave first thing in the morning, and be back there in plenty of time."

CHAPTER 30

Don woke up, feeling cleansed and refreshed, a few hours later. He made the bed, and left Hannah's flat as he'd found it.

Safely next door, he showered, and threw a pile of laundry into the washing machine. Then, he settled down on the sofa, while he ate a pot noodle.

Afterwards he checked on the cam website, and discovered Hannah and the fuckwit had gone off for the day, which pissed him off—but not as much as usual.

Although he hated what his parents had done to him, he always felt better after releasing some of his pent-up emotions. The fact he could only ejaculate whilst thinking about them was diabolical, considering they were the ones who had punished him in the first place.

Thinking about his parents again caused his stomach muscles to clench. The love he felt for his mother was warped and confusing. He knew that. *What normal person lusted over the memory of his own mother? But, what normal parents treated a young boy the way they did?* They fucked him up good and proper.

After leaving, aged fifteen, he got himself a few odd jobs here and there, before eventually joining the army. On one of his trips home, he discovered his mother had died.

Even the way she'd died wasn't normal—she'd choked on a chicken bone in the middle of a party. If it wasn't so tragic, it would be funny. He hadn't seen her since leaving home, and although he sometimes yearned for one of her cuddles in the dead of night, he hadn't missed her—not really.

He made his father pay the price, though. Don followed him home from the pub one night, after he'd clearly consumed his weight in ale.

Don closed his eyes, as he recalled every minute detail.

The drunken old man came staggering down the back alley towards him. He was singing maudlin songs, and kicking a can along in front of him.

When he looked up, he saw Don standing before him, dressed in full uniform. His father saluted, and tipped his imaginary hat. The old bastard didn't even recognise his own son.

But, Don didn't budge. As his father got closer, he could see the older man's thought processes playing out across the lines of his face. Time hadn't been kind to the once-handsome man. His complexion had a yellowy tinge, and his eyes were dull, bloodshot, and lifeless.

He suddenly gasped as recognition dawned on him. "Donny? Is that you, my boy?" His father approached, slowly, clearly unsure at first.

Don stared ahead in silence—memories of their last time together played like a movie in his mind.

"It is! It's you! Say something to your old dad. I can't believe how you've grown." The old man reached his hand out towards him.

Don stepped back, as though the touch might sear his skin off.

"Donny? Don't be like that. I'm thrilled you're home." His face suddenly clouded. "Did you hear about your poor old mum?"

"Yes, I heard. And I laughed. In fact, I'd have paid good money to see her fight for one last dying breath."

"Donald! What's got into you? That's your dear, sweet mother you're

talking about." The old man shook his head and sneered, as he looked Don up and down. "The army's changed you. And not for the better, let me tell you."

"You think that, do you?" Don took several hurried steps forward, causing his father to lose balance. The stupid old bastard sprawled out on the cobbles, terrified.

Don felt empowered by the old man's fear. Gone was the no-nonsense hard man—the man who had got off on terrifying everybody in his path —the man who had brutally raped his own son when he was just fifteen. In his place, was a dithering wimp—a faded, empty replica.

He hadn't planned what he did next. Overcome with all kinds of emotion, he yanked his father to his feet, and threw him face first over the nearest rubbish bin.

Spurred on by his father's cries, he ripped the other man's pants down to his ankles, and, before he even realised what he was doing, he'd penetrated the disgusting old bastard. Don's normally flaccid cock had stood tall, flexing its muscles, and bucking for all it was worth.

Moments later, Don emptied himself all over the wasted, pathetic buttocks of his father, zipped up his fly, and walked away.

Before he turned the corner, he glanced back and smiled at the pitiful sight. His father, pants still around his ankles, was crawling on all fours up the alley, whimpering like an injured mutt, a pleasurable sight Don would take to his grave.

He was suddenly startled by somebody knocking on the door.

Crouching down, he scrambled to the bedroom, and peered through the window.

A short, bald man, wearing black jeans and a bright red T-shirt stretched over his fat gut, bounced on his heels, his arms crossed behind his back, as he waited for someone to answer the door.

After a minute or two, the man walked away.

Don couldn't see further than Hannah's front door from his position at the window. But, it appeared as though the man had gone. He didn't feel safe hanging about, though, not until he knew who the hell he was.

He threw on his uniform, which he usually left at work. But, because of all the hoo-ha that morning, he'd come home wearing it.

With a final peep through the window, he shuffled from the flat, pulling the door closed behind him.

Startled by the sound of voices, Don glanced up planning to turn on his heel, but it was too late. The man from earlier appeared at the nosy doctor's doorway.

"Simon?" he asked.

"Who are you?" Don squared his shoulders at the other man.

"I'm Edward, Diane's brother. We're clearing out Diane's flat. You heard what happened to her, haven't you?"

"Err, I did, yes. The police told me. Nasty business. I'm very sorry for your loss." Don continued towards the stairs.

"The celebration of her life is on Thursday at 2pm in the function rooms at the Bramhall Inn. I know she thought a lot of you. The family would love you to join us."

Don nodded. "I'll see what I can do." He shuffled past the other man. "I'm sorry, I have to dash, or I'll be late for work. Thanks for letting me know about the funeral."

"Erm—celebration of her life," the man corrected. "Dress in bright colours only."

"I will do. Thanks again."

Don couldn't get down the stairs and out of the building fast enough.

CHAPTER 31

On the way back to the lake house, Max called his solicitor again. Hannah liked him using the handsfree kit, so she could hear what was going on, without having to interrogate him.

"Eric, it's me again. I just want to check I'm within my rights to get Cheryl to start advertising Angela's position?"

"Hi, Max. Yes, go for it. I called the police station a while ago, and they told me they were in the process of charging her. So, it wouldn't take a rocket scientist to figure out she no longer has a job. I've got her termination of employment notice here. I'll put it in her mailbox on my way home later."

"So, they've charged her, then? I must say, I'm still in shock."

"To be honest with you, so am I. When you called me this morning, I was certain there had been some kind of mistake. Angela's always struck me as..." Eric paused and laughed. "...oh, it doesn't matter."

"Go on."

"Well, she's always reminded me of the frigid spinster type. She appeared to eat, sleep, and live for her job."

"Her dedication to her job's not in dispute, though. It's what she got up to in her spare time that's the issue."

"Yeah, I guess you're right. I'll let you know when I've dropped the letter off."

"Great. Thanks, Eric."

Max seemed deep in thought for a few minutes—driving as though on automatic pilot.

Hannah placed her hand on his leg, and he jumped, before smiling at her and stroking her hand. "You okay?" she asked.

He nodded. "I will be. I know it sounds silly, but I feel bereft. For years I've spoken to her every day—even on weekends. In a lot of ways, she took on the role of a parent. I truly thought she had my back."

"It doesn't sound silly at all. In fact, I think it's normal to feel devastated. She's betrayed your trust, after all."

Eric rang at around 7pm to tell Max he'd bumped into Angela when he'd stopped by to drop off the termination notice.

"She swears she's innocent, Max," Eric said. "And I couldn't help but feel sorry for her. She broke down sobbing when I gave her the notice."

"Sobbing? Angela?" Max scratched his head.

"I know, right? I didn't know where to put myself. She's not the easiest woman to console—it was like hugging a hunk of granite."

"But, she's been charged?"

"Yes."

"And she's accepted the termination notice?"

"Yes."

Max sighed. "Thanks, Eric."

They spent the rest of the evening with Lenny and Charmaine, drinking wine and eating the selection of cheese and mini pies they'd bought from the services, but Max wasn't very good company. He couldn't shake the heaviness he felt every time he thought about Angela. By ten o'clock, he was blatantly yawning, and their guests left not long after.

"Are you alright?" Hannah asked when he returned to the living room, after locking up after them.

"Just exhausted. I've hardly slept the past few nights, what with one thing or another."

Hannah raised one eyebrow. "Like that is it?"

A smile played at the corners of his mouth. He eased himself down on the sofa beside her. "You *have* been very demanding, but I wasn't meaning because of you."

"Demanding, eh? Well, we can always sleep in separate beds, if you can't take the pace." She tipped her head to the side, awaiting his reaction.

"You wouldn't be able to stand it. I'd wake in the middle of the night to the sound of your little feet skittering across the carpet towards me."

"I don't skitter! Cockroaches skitter."

"Okay. So, what *do* you do, if not skitter?"

"I slink—or maybe glide silently and demurely."

"I heard you running down the stairs this morning, and you sounded like a fairy elephant."

She playfully backhanded his chest. "Hey, you!"

He laughed, heartily. Then, he pulled her onto his knee, and kissed the tip of her cute nose. "Shall we go to bed? We'll have to be up early, if we intend to be in the office for eight-thirty."

The office was rife with hushed whispers and sidelong glances when she arrived the next morning. She'd made the best of what clothing she had with her. Max seemed stressed, and she didn't want to tell him she needed to head home to change first.

She hung her handbag on the back of her chair, and shrugged

out of the lightweight, black cotton jacket. "Hi, Dawn," she said to her colleague's back.

Dawn swivelled around, and raised her eyebrows in a knowing fashion. "Hello, stranger."

Hannah sensed a little frostiness from the usually friendly woman. "I'm sorry I didn't come in yesterday, but I did notify reception."

"No skin off my nose. And besides, rumour has it, you'll be taking over from Angela Beanie soon anyway."

"Is that what's being said?"

Dawn nodded, a sly smile playing around her wrinkled mouth.

"I don't know who told you that, but it's not true."

Another couple of women walked over, and stood behind Dawn.

One of them, Kate Darling, had her hands on her hips, and it was clear by the scowl on her face she had plenty to say. "Decided to grace us with your presence, I see."

Taken aback with the extent of their hostility, Hannah silently stared at each of the women's faces in turn.

"Too good to even talk to us, are you?" Kate curled her lip in obvious contempt.

Hannah's stomach dropped to the floor. "I—I don't know what you've heard, but it's all lies."

"Oh, so you're not screwing the boss?"

"I…" Hannah's mouth had dried up, and she had difficulty swallowing.

Kate and her friend, whose name had escaped Hannah, shook their heads and walked away.

Dawn gave a quick apologetic smile, before turning her back again.

Stunned, Hannah sat down heavily, tears pricking her eyes. She thought nobody but Angela and a couple of the security staff knew about her and Max. She hadn't expected to be confronted and treated like this by her workmates.

Her desk phone rang, and Hannah almost leapt from her seat. "Hello?"

"Hannah, it's me," Max said. "I need to warn you, the cat's out of the bag about us."

"No shit!"

"I take it from that response, you already know."

She bit her lip, trying to stop the tears spilling from her eyes.

"Hannah? Are you okay?"

It was no use. She hung up, and raced to the bathroom, passing Devlin on the way.

"Well, hello, sexy lady," the sleazy bastard said.

"Not now, Devlin."

Once inside, she ran into a stall, and locked the door. Above the sound of her sobs, she heard the flushing of a toilet in the adjacent stall. She wiped her eyes on a wad of tissue, and forced herself to calm down. The last thing she needed was even more attention for having a meltdown in the bathroom.

"Are you okay in there?"

Hannah recognised the melodic rhythm of the voice as Geeta, a gentle Indian woman, who also worked in her office. Hannah opened the door, and smiled apologetically.

"Hannah. What is it, my dear?" She held her arms out, and Hannah felt compelled to step into the other woman's embrace.

After a few minutes, Hannah managed to pull herself together, and noticed a wet patch on the silky fabric of Geeta's sari. "I'm so sorry. I'll pay for the cleaning costs."

"Nonsense, there'll be no cleaning costs. Believe me, this outfit has dealt with much more than a few tears. Now, are you going to tell me what's upset you so?"

The concern in the woman's voice almost caused another meltdown.

"You mean, you haven't heard the gossip?"

"I never listen to gossip, my dear."

Hannah walked to the sink, splashing her face. When she turned, Geeta was waiting patiently.

"I've been seeing somebody—somebody in management, and I'm worried I won't be able to keep my job here."

"There's no law in who you can and can't see, my dear."

"I know, but we were meant to be keeping it a secret, and now, everybody knows."

"I didn't know, and frankly, I don't care. Why should it matter to anybody else?"

"Kate Darling seems to think it matters."

Geeta inhaled deeply, and nodded her head. "Kate Darling never has a nice word to say about anybody."

"I know, but—"

Geeta wagged a finger in front of Hannah's face. "Trust me. It doesn't matter. Good for you, if you've found yourself a partner. Do you love him? It is *a him*, isn't it?"

Hannah gave a short laugh, as she tried to tidy her eye makeup in the mirror. "Yes, it is. And yes—I think I do."

"Well, then. That's all that matters. Who cares what Kate Darling thinks?"

"You're right. I haven't done anything wrong. She's got no right to make me feel guilty for falling for my boss."

"That's better, my dear. Now, you need to hold your head high, and get back to your desk. And if you ever need to talk, come and find me." Geeta placed a reassuring hand on Hannah's arm before turning to leave.

Hannah looked back in the mirror. Geeta was correct—she had nothing to feel guilty about. She gasped, as she remembered hanging up on Max.

Taking a deep, bracing breath, she pulled the hem of her blouse down, and smoothed her palms over the fine fabric, then left the room.

The first person she spotted was Max, whose face was drained of all colour. In two strides, he was beside her. "There you are. Are you okay?"

"Max! You shouldn't have come. It'll just make things worse."

He put his arm around her shoulder, and led her to one of the sofas. "What are you talking about? Is that why you were upset? Has somebody said something to you?"

She hesitated. "I don't want to cause any more trouble." She glanced around, and spotted Kate standing in the doorway, her face and neck had coloured nicely.

"I panicked when you hung up," Max continued. "I could tell you were upset, and I convinced myself Angela was here."

She shook her head, confused. "No, it was nothing to do with Angela. Although everyone seems to know about us, and she's the only person who could have blabbed."

"Can't say I'm surprised, really. Do you fancy a coffee?" he asked, looking at the half-full coffee pot.

"I don't know. Maybe I should get to work, before I'm accused of slacking. Can we meet up at lunchtime instead?"

"I can make the canteen at twelve-thirty, if that suits you?"

"Perfect." She got to her feet, and scurried away, in case he tried to kiss her.

She knew how it must look to the rest of her team, but it really wasn't like that. She wouldn't use her relationship to better her position. As the new girl, she still had a lot to learn, and she was in awe of each of her teammates. She marvelled at how they all specialised in different areas within the marketing team. Before now, they'd all been willing to share what they knew with her, and she'd hate for that to change, just because her love life was looking up.

She turned on her computer, and began sorting through a pile of paperwork while it loaded.

Dawn appeared at her side, handing her one of two plastic cups of water she'd fetched from the water cooler.

"Oh, thanks." Hannah nervously took it from her.

"Sorry about before, Hannah. I should know better than to listen to idle gossip. I hope we can still be friends."

Hannah pursed her lips to one side and eyeballed the other woman. "That depends."

"On what?"

"On whether or not you tell me what's being said."

Dawn shrugged. "That you got Angela Beanie fired because you want her job. And that you're thick as thieves with Mr Myers."

Hannah placed the cup down on the desk, and sighed. "I am seeing Max, I won't lie to you. But, I had nothing to do with Angela losing her job. She did that all by herself, and I definitely don't want it."

"Good for you," Dawn said. "He's quite a catch, that one. And I know for a fact nobody would blame you. In fact, plenty of them have tried to get him to notice them in the past, and failed miserably."

"Thanks, Dawn. But, I want it to be known I won't be getting any special treatment. I'm here to do my job, just like you. Max and I are still early days, and chances are we might not see the week out, so I'd prefer it if things could stay as normal as possible."

"Fair enough, and speaking of work, we'd best get to it."

When he got back to his office, Max angrily called a meeting with all the department managers for that afternoon. There was no way he'd allow anybody else to interfere in his private life, and if it meant he had to fire the fucking lot of them, then that was what he'd do.

CHAPTER 32

Engrossed in a backlog of paperwork, Hannah was surprised to find it was almost twenty to one.

"Shit, shit, shit!" She grabbed her handbag, and rushed to the canteen.

Max got to his feet to greet her when she entered. "I thought you'd got a better offer."

Hannah grinned, and slipped into the seat opposite him. "Better than you? Impossible."

A smile played at the corner of his delicious lips. "I hope you don't mind, but I ordered for you. I figured you'd be on a tight schedule."

"Yeah. It's my boss's fault—he's a slave driver. What did you order?"

He slid a paper menu over the table to her. "What would *you* have ordered?"

She glanced over the menu, but only one item stood out. "Macaroni cheese," she said, crossing her fingers.

Max smiled and raised his eyebrows, then focussed on a point just over her shoulder.

Startled, Hannah spun around as a member of the canteen

staff reached them, and placed two generous servings of macaroni cheese before them.

Thrilled, Hannah waited until the waitress turned, and was out of earshot. "You remembered."

"Of course I remembered, you told me only yesterday it was your favourite."

She picked up a fork, and tucked in—her eyes rolling.

He was clearly amused. His phone vibrated beside his plate, and the smile dropped from his face, as he quickly rejected the call.

"Something wrong?" she asked, another forkful of stodgy pasta paused halfway to her mouth.

He shook his head, and shrugged. "It's Angela. She's been calling all morning."

"What does she want?"

"I don't know. I haven't accepted her call."

No longer hungry, she dropped her fork, and shoved her plate back a few inches. "You should call the police. She's been told not to contact you."

"I know, but she'll soon get the message when I don't respond."

His phone beeped.

"She's left a message, hasn't she?"

He nodded, digging into his food.

"Aren't you going to listen to it?"

He wiped his mouth on a napkin. "I wasn't going to, no."

She glanced at his phone again.

"*You* want to listen to it, don't you?"

"I'm just curious to know why she did it."

"Oh, that reminds me. Don left your gym bag in my office."

"My gym bag? You mean my missing gym clothes?"

He shook his head. "No. I mean bag, clothes, and sports shoes, too."

"Can we go and see it? Maybe it's not even mine. I'm only

missing a few items of clothing." She got to her feet, and downed a glass of water in one.

"What about your food?"

"I'm not hungry anymore."

He took another couple of mouthfuls, and threw his napkin down on top of his plate. He picked up his phone, and followed her from the canteen.

They travelled up to the top floor in silence.

In his office, he reached down the side of his desk, and withdrew her Adidas gym bag.

Hannah gasped.

"What? Is it not yours?"

She shook her head. "No, that's not it. I'm shocked, because it *is* mine. But, why?" She opened the zipper of the bag and took out the contents. "You see, I only suspected some of my clothing had been replaced, not everything." She shook her head confused, as she inspected one of the Reeboks. "But, these are definitely mine."

Max sat on his leather office chair. "Maybe Angela was telling the truth about having a crush on me. I think it's more likely she has a crush on you. Why else would she go to such trouble? Not to mention the expense."

"Can we listen to the message, Max?"

He dug his phone out of his trouser pocket. After pressing a few buttons, Angela's no-nonsense tones filled the room.

"Max, this is ridiculous. You know I'd never do anything to hurt you. I admit to warning Hannah off, and it was wrong of me, but I honestly had your best interests at heart, you've got to believe me. However, that's all I'm guilty of. The bag in my locker had been planted there. I'd never seen it before yesterday. I want to help sort all this craziness out, but how can I, if I'm banned from entering the building? Please call."

He turned the phone off, and placed it face down on his desk. "So, what do you think of that?"

Hannah shrugged. "She sounded genuine. But, she's hardly going to admit it, is she?"

He glanced at his watch and sighed. "Listen, sausage, I've got a meeting I need to get to. Shall I come around to your flat tonight? I could bring Thai food."

Hannah didn't want to offend him, but she just wanted to go home, fall into bed, and sleep. "Would you mind if we give it a miss tonight? I'm shattered."

His forehead furrowed for a second, and then he smiled. "Of course I don't mind. I could do with a good night's sleep myself. But what about your weekend case? It's still in my car."

"I've got everything I need at home. Maybe you could bring it over tomorrow night, instead. We could order Thai then, if you like?"

"If I'm back early enough. I've got a meeting in Portland tomorrow afternoon, so it will depend on how soon I can get away."

"No worries. We can play it by ear. But, can I leave this here, for now? I really don't know what I want to do with it."

He took the bag from her, dropped it to the carpet, then reached for her hand, taking her into his arms.

Hannah gasped, and turned to look out of the window into the corridor.

"Nobody can see us," he said. "I need a kiss, if I'm not going to see you until tomorrow night."

His luscious lips silenced any protests she might have.

CHAPTER 33

Hannah arrived home to a ringing phone. She knew it would be her mother—nobody else called her on the landline.

She dropped her things in the hall, and reached for the phone. "Hello?" she panted into the handset.

"I was about to hang up, sweetheart. Are you alright?"

"I've just walked through the door. Are you and Daddy okay?"

"You know us, same old, same old."

A feeling of homesickness washed over her. "Oh, Mammy. I miss you both so much."

"I knew it. Something's wrong. What's happened, sweetheart? You know you can tell me."

Tears sprang to her eyes and rolled down her cheeks, as she looked around the cold grey flat. She realised she hadn't been back since hearing about poor Diane's death, and she couldn't stop her tears now they were already flowing.

"You're worrying me. What is it?"

After a few moments, Hannah regained a little control. "I'm just being silly, Mammy, that's all. I've had a full-on weekend, and I need an early night."

"There's something you're not telling me. I've seen you dead on your feet before now, but you wouldn't cry. You've never been a crier."

"Okay. I'll tell you, but I don't want you worrying about me."

"I'm always going to worry about you, sweetheart. So you may as well tell me."

"My friend, Diane, was killed last week."

"Hannah! That's awful. What happened?"

"I'm not really sure. She lived next door, and worked as a doctor at the local hospital. Apparently, some young thug attacked her, while she was trying to save his life. She died on the spot."

"Oh, my poor, poor girl. When is the funeral?"

"On Thursday. I'm dreading it, if I'm honest. I don't know any of her other friends or family."

"What about your other neighbour? The man?"

"Simon? He's left for Seattle, and won't be back for ages. I haven't even managed to get hold of him."

"I'll call you back in five minutes." The phone went dead.

Hannah shrugged, and replaced the handset.

In the lounge, she opened the curtains, and picked up a couple of cushions from the carpet. They had been there since Max had been cooking a meal for her on Friday. It seemed crazy to think that was only a few days ago. So much had happened since then.

She warmed a cup of milk in the microwave, and carried it through to the bedroom, where she stripped down to her undies and threw her clothes in the laundry basket.

The phone rang again, and, grabbing her robe from the back of the door, she ran out to the hall.

"Hi, Mammy."

"Hannah, I need you to meet me at Piccadilly bus station at six-forty tomorrow evening."

"I can't ask you to do that. What about Daddy?"

"Your father can manage without me for a couple of days. I need to be with you."

"Oh, Mammy. You're going to set me off crying again."

"Don't you dare. My beautiful daughter isn't a cry-baby."

"I won't. I promise. I'm so excited. I can't wait to see you."

"Me too. I'll get off now, sweetheart. See you tomorrow."

"Gosh. Are you sure you want to come, Mammy? It's a long way."

"Four hours, that's all. I'll enjoy the peace and quiet. And besides, I'll be able to catch up on some reading."

Hannah hung up and ran to her bedroom. Bouncing up and down on the bed, she squealed like a pre-schooler.

Climbing under the sheets, she plumped up her pillow, and sat up against the headboard to drink the milk. Her phone buzzed beside her on the bedside table.

7.48pm - *Goodnight, sausage. I wish you were here.*

She smiled, and held the phone to her chest for a moment. Her feelings were so strong for him after such a brief amount of time, it made her feel dizzy.

7.48pm - *Stop calling me that!*

7.48pm - *Okay, sausage.*

Hannah barked out a laugh.

7.49pm - *Ring.*

. . .

Moments later, her phone vibrated on her chest. "Hello," she whispered.

"Were you asleep?"

"Not really. Although I *am* in bed."

Max groaned.

She heard nothing but wanton mischief in her own giggle. "Come on over, if you like?"

"What? Now? I thought you were too tired."

"Oh, don't bother then, if you've got something better to be doing."

"You're joking, aren't you? I'll be there in twenty."

The phone went dead in her ear, and she chuckled.

True to his word, Max tapped on her bedroom window twenty minutes later.

Wearing nothing but a skimpy black lace bra and a pair of almost matching undies, she crawled out of bed, and opened the door, before rushing back to the warmth of her duvet.

He was behind her in a flash and, kneeling on the mattress, she helped him tear off his shirt, throwing it in a heap on the bedroom floor. Then, he tantalised her by slowly removing the stonewashed jeans, which had an obscene bulge in the front of them.

"Hurry up," she cried, trying to paw at him.

He batted her hand away. "Hold your horses, woman. I'm not a piece of meat."

She chuckled at his mock offended expression, and held her hands up as a sign she was backing off.

Max continued to tease her, opening the button of his waistband, and slowly undoing the zip.

She gasped, as he quickly turned his back, and she watched as his jeans dropped like a denim curtain around his ankles.

Unable to control herself for a second longer, she jumped off the bed, spun him around, and pushed him backwards on top of the duvet. Then, straddling him, she took his wrists in her hands, and raised them above his head.

He groaned, his eyes fixed firmly on her heaving breasts.

Hannah had never felt so powerful and in control, as she took the lead, and showed him exactly what she had been planning for the evening.

Afterwards, they lay in each other's arms. She told him of her mother's imminent visit.

"So, will she go with you to the funeral?"

She nodded. "Is that alright?"

"Of course it is. I just didn't want you to have to go alone."

"But, with her being here a couple of days, you won't be able to stay over. I've only got this one bedroom, and I can't see Mammy being okay with you snuggling up to us."

"Oh, you never know—and it could be an opportunity to cross another thing off my bucket list."

Hannah squealed, and pinched his nipple.

"I'm joking! I'm joking," he cried, pulling her hand away. "But, seriously, I would like to meet her while she's here, if that's okay?"

"I'd love that."

They spent the rest of the night sleeping in each other's arms, and Hannah vaguely remembered him kissing her goodbye at the crack of dawn.

Enraged, Don watched every movement and listened to every sound coming from Hannah's bed—the bed he'd slept in so peacefully just a few hours before.

He waited until they were both asleep, before venturing out of the hub. A sound from behind him made his feet leave the floor.

"Oh, there you are, Don," Ken said. "I was coming to find you—thought you must've got lost."

Don turned on the younger man, rushing towards him, and he

body-slammed him into the wall. Then, he gripped the shocked man's face, squeezing his cheeks so hard he could feel the outline of Ken's teeth through the skin. The terror in Ken's eyes spurred him on all the more. Although they were of similar build, Don was in no doubt he'd be able to drop the younger man on the spot. "I don't answer to you—you understand?" he growled.

Ken nodded, clearly petrified.

"Never question me, or my whereabouts, again. You get me? Or you'll wonder what the fuck's just fucking hit you." With a grunt, he shoved Ken away, and turned in the direction of the lifts. "Now, should you need to question where I am, I'm going outside for a bit of fresh air and to cool myself down. Is that alright with you?" he yelled over his shoulder.

"N-no problem, Don."

Outside, he headed down the service alley, and walked along a short way, trying to calm himself down. As he passed a large green dumpster, a man cried out, and launched himself towards Don, an almost empty bottle of booze in his hand.

Don quickly stepped back, and shoved the drunk away from him.

The man fell sideways, landing on several overflowing rubbish bags, and closed his eyes—completely gone.

With a sneer, Don kicked the drunk repeatedly, feeling his frustrations flow out of him each time his foot connected with the prostrate man's midriff.

Standing upright, Don steadied himself on the wheelie bin, and breathed out through pursed lips forcing his heart rate to calm down.

Snap-snap-snap.

The band disintegrated once again in his fingers. Irritated, he threw it to the ground. Then, he brushed a fleck of dust off his shoulder, tugged down the hem of his jacket, and walked back towards the front of the building—a renewed spring in his step.

CHAPTER 34

Hannah's alarm sounded just before eight. After taking a few minutes to gather her thoughts, she flew out of bed, and began tidying the flat.

The plan had been to get up earlier, considering her mother was coming for her first visit. She couldn't allow her to see the place in a less than perfect state, yet twenty minutes wasn't enough time to give it an overhaul, so it would just have to do.

On the train, her phone buzzed.

8.43am - *Good morning, beautiful*

8.43am - *Hi*

8.44am - *I'm having breakfast with two business bores, and can't drag my mind away from you*

. . .

She laughed, and looked up self-consciously. A pretty, dark-skinned woman, with huge black eyes, smiled at her warmly. Hannah smiled back, and returned her attention to her phone.

8.45am - *I missed you when I woke to an empty bed*

8.45am - *Yeah, sorry about that. You looked so peaceful, I didn't want to wake you. What time does your mother arrive?*

8.45am - *Not until this evening. Maybe we could meet for dinner, if you're back early enough*

8.47am - *Sounds wonderful. I'll message you later xx*

The day flew by.

She considered racing home after work to put some finishing touches to the flat, but she had a mountain of paperwork to get through, so she decided to stay behind and wait, instead.

At 6.15pm, she packed up her desk, turned off the computer, and headed from the building.

"Hello, Ms McLaughlin. You're here late," the security guard said, as she stepped into the lift beside him.

"I've been catching up on some paperwork while waiting for my mammy to arrive."

"Oh, that's nice. Will she be staying long?"

"Just a day or two. But, yes, I can hardly wait to see her."

"Treasure the time you have with her, dear. You only get one mother."

The lift door opened on the ground floor. Hannah nodded. "This is me. And thanks for the advice. I intend to spoil her rotten while she's here." She smiled at him, and headed for the sliding glass doors.

Her phone buzzed in her pocket.

6.19pm - *Where shall we meet? I'm almost back*

6.19pm - *I'm heading to Piccadilly bus station now. Shall we meet you there?*

6.20pm - *Okay, see you soon*

Hannah waved down a taxi. Less than ten minutes later, she was standing at the outdoor bus station, waiting for her mother to arrive.

She felt nervous butterflies fluttering in her stomach, and more than a little light-headed.

She glanced around for a seat, and spotted an elderly man gathering his shopping bags together. When he vacated his seat, Hannah gratefully claimed it, her heart hammering in her chest.

The stench of the fumes coming from the buses made her feel woozy and suddenly claustrophobic. She'd love nothing more than to be able to strip her clothes off, and lie down on the cold concrete.

Just then, another bus arrived. She forced herself to her feet. She wanted this moment to be perfect.

Her mother appeared. Her striking red hair was now slightly more muted than Hannah's, but still the first thing you noticed. Instead of coming down the steps, her mother escorted a young woman off the bus with a stroller and several bags.

Hannah waited patiently for her to turn around, and then, she was pounced on and dragged into a bear hug.

"Oh, I've missed you. I've missed you. I've missed you," her mother squealed into her ear, before planting a huge kiss on her cheek.

Hannah laughed, and hugged her back. "I'm so glad you're here, Mammy."

Suddenly, her mother stepped backwards, a strange expression on her face.

"What is it?"

Her mother nodded at something which had caught her eye over Hannah's shoulder.

Hannah spun around, her eyes resting on Max, who was dressed to kill in a navy pinstriped suit. His white shirt was open at the neck and a few wispy dark hairs poked out of the top. She smiled, turning back to her mother.

"Mammy, I'd like you to meet someone. This is Max. Max meet my mammy, Agnes."

Max stepped forward, and kissed her surprised mother's cheek. "It's lovely to meet you, Mrs McLaughlin. I can see where Hannah gets her looks from, you're both so alike!"

"Only in looks—not everything," her mother said, stiffly.

Max's face had flushed deep red, and Hannah couldn't help but smile at the hardened businessman's sudden embarrassment.

"I hope you're hungry, Mammy. Max is going to take us out to dinner."

"A little, but I have my suitcase."

Hannah noticed how her mother's Irish accent came to the fore, once she became flustered.

"Here, allow me." Max picked up the suitcase, and set off walking towards the car.

Hannah could sense her mother's disapproval, without even looking at her face. She tucked her mother's hand through her arm. "You ready?"

Her mother nodded, and gave a tight-lipped smile.

They fell into step, as they followed Max and the suitcase.

However, once seated in a booth of a popular steakhouse, it didn't take long before her mother made her disapproval known.

"So, Max. Am I right in thinking you're Hannah's new boss."

Max gulped, his Adam's apple bobbing up and down nervously, before nodding. "Yes. That's correct."

"How did you know that, Mammy?" Hannah asked.

"I'm not as green as I'm cabbage-looking, sweetheart."

"I never said you were. I just wondered how you knew."

Her mother sighed, and made a play of moving a fork to one side, clasping her hands on top of the table instead. "I remember you had an interview with Max before you left home. There can't be many people around here with that name, so I put two and two together."

"I can see where Hannah gets her sharp mind." Max grinned.

"Yes. But, what I want to know is, do you always take your employees and their families for dinner, or do you have an ulterior motive?"

"Mammy!" Hannah cried, mortified her normally placid mother would be so outspoken.

"No, that's a fair question, Mrs McLaughlin. The truth is, Hannah and I have been seeing each other for a little while. And I know what you must be thinking, but I have the utmost respect for your daughter. I swear I don't make a habit of dating my staff. This is the first time, in fact."

"Really?" Her mother arched one eyebrow, as she continued peering at the menu, her lips pursed to the side of her face.

"Yes. Really," Hannah said. "Now, can we change the subject, please?"

They ordered their food, and Max excused himself when his phone rang.

Hannah and her mother watched him in silence, as he headed to the exit.

"Mammy, why did you say all that? I could've died!" she hissed, as the door swung closed behind him.

"He's your boss, Hannah."

"Do you think I don't know that? But, I like him. Please keep your nose out of it."

"I hope you know what you're letting yourself in for, young lady. I see nothing but heartbreak coming from this."

"I don't see why. So what if he's my boss. That doesn't make a blind bit of difference to the way I feel. The way we *both* feel. I really like him, Mammy. He might just be the one."

Max cleared his throat, clearly embarrassed. "Sorry about that. I've switched it off now." He placed his phone on the table, and slid into the booth beside her.

Hannah smiled at him nervously. It was obvious he'd heard her confession, loud and clear.

The awkward moment was broken, as the waitress appeared with a tray of drinks.

CHAPTER 35

After dinner, Max dropped them off at the flat. He carried the suitcase up the stairs, then said his goodbyes.

Hannah walked him back to the stairs. Checking the coast was clear behind them, she turned to face him. "I'm so sorry about tonight. I was mortified."

He pulled her into his arms, and kissed the tip of her nose. "Hey, don't worry about it. She cares for you. That's all."

"I know she does, but I honestly didn't think she'd be like that, or I wouldn't have put you through it."

"I didn't expect her to be such a fiery redhead. But, at least we've met now. Next time shouldn't be so bad. I hope." He grinned.

"Next time? You mean you haven't been put off me for life?"

"It would take more than a bit of a grilling to put me off you. Although, I haven't met your dad yet."

Hannah groaned. "Oh, don't even joke about it."

He belly-laughed, and cupped her buttocks in both hands, pressing her into his groin. "Go on. You'd better go in before she comes looking for you. I'll see you after the funeral tomorrow."

"I was going to come in to the office for a couple of hours in the morning."

"Don't be silly. Take the day off. Just call me, and I'll meet up with you afterwards. If you want to, that is?"

"Of course I'll want to. I wish you didn't have to go now."

"Go and catch up with your lovely mother. You don't know how lucky you are to be able to do that. I'd move heaven and earth to be able to spend ten minutes with my mother. You only get one."

"That's the second time today somebody's said that to me."

"Really? Who else said it?"

"That security guard at AdCor."

"Who? Don?"

"I think so, yes."

Surprised, Max nodded. "Maybe he has a human streak in him after all."

"He's always very pleasant to me."

"I'm pleased to hear it. Listen, I'll get going. Call me tomorrow." He kissed her, before heading down the stairs. "Sleep well, my sausage," he called over his shoulder.

"I wish you'd stop calling me that," she hissed.

He laughed all the way to his car.

Don was thrilled to discover Hannah's mother would be around for a few days. At least that would keep Maxwell-fucking-Myers at a distance.

He'd really felt a connection with Hannah today. It was clear she was as interested in him as he was in her, but he wouldn't be able to make his move until he'd got their sleazy boss out of the picture.

After doing his rounds, he sought out Ken, who had been very cool with him since their run-in last night. He found him in the staff kitchen, making himself a hot drink.

"Hey, Ken. How's things?"

The younger man's face dropped, and his posture stiffened. "F-fine. I've done my rounds and was just making some coffee."

"No problem, mate." He slapped Ken on the back, as though they were best buddies. So what if they'd had a disagreement. They were adults, and had no choice but to work together. Don had no time for pettiness in the workplace. When he officially took over from Steve, he'd make a number of changes to ensure the team developed tougher methods and practices, just like he'd learned in the army.

He left Ken to it, and took the lift down to the basement. As the door swished open, he crashed into Max, who was heading into the lift.

"Ah, Don. I'm glad I bumped into you. Can you spare a minute, and travel up with me?"

"Certainly, sir."

His boss pressed the top floor button, and Don swiped his security pass for him.

"What can I do for you, sir?" Don reached for the band at his wrist, remembering he needed to replace it, when his agitated fingers found a patch of bare skin.

"Just a catch up, really. Things have been hectic around here for a little while, and you've been left to keep all the plates spinning single-handedly."

"No problem, sir. I've enjoyed the extra responsibility, if the truth be known."

"Well, I want you to know how much I appreciate your hard work. I promise it won't be for much longer. I've contacted the employment agency, and hopefully, we should have some suitable candidates soon. Cheryl will probably be in touch for a job description at some point, if you don't mind helping out?"

"Not at all, sir. Would you like me to be on the interview panel too?"

"The interview panel? No, I don't think so. But, if I need you, I'll let you know."

The lift door opened. Max stepped forward, placing his foot on the door track.

"We are also interviewing for Angela's position. How did the staff react to her shock departure?"

"Oh, so-so. There were Chinese whispers spreading from floor to floor, but nobody seemed too bothered. Angela wasn't that popular, frankly."

"Good. Hopefully, it will have blown over by next week," Max said, stepping into the corridor.

"I'd put money on it, sir." Don's fake smile dropped, as the doors closed between them. He shook his head, exhaling noisily, and pressed the button for the basement.

Although he couldn't stand the bloke, Don had to admit Max was being good about getting him a new member of staff. He'd even asked him to liaise with the agent to give her a job description and possibly sit in on the interview.

It *was* only fair, though. Steve used to have a lot of input into the hiring and firing, as well as the staff rosters. And, now Don was Head of Security, of course the responsibility would fall at his feet. But, he was a little concerned they hadn't renegotiated his salary or senior staff benefits. If he was expected to work extra hours, then they could damn well pay him for them. He'd mention it to the agent, when she called.

CHAPTER 36

Hannah's mother was waiting, hands on hips, when she returned to the flat.

"Just spit it out, Mammy."

"Don't be like that, Hannah. It doesn't become you."

Hannah shook her head. "I don't even know what that's supposed to mean."

"Well, you can't blame me for being worried. You left home just a few weeks ago, and I've been worrying you're probably homesick and lonely. But, no—not you. You're already shacked up with some sleazy man. And not just any sleazy man. Only your bloomin' boss. So, when it all turns to custard—and it will, you know—not only will you lose your job, but you'll have thrown away everything you've worked for these past years."

She caught hold of her mother's hands mid-flap. "Mammy. Calm down. Maybe I should have warned you, but I honestly thought you'd be cool with it. If Daddy was with you, I would've been worrying, but not you."

Her mother pulled her hands free, and sat down on the sofa. "It was a shock, that's all."

"I'm a big girl now, you know."

"I know you are, but that doesn't stop me being concerned if I think you're making a mistake."

"Do you think I haven't thought about all the points you've made?"

Her mother shrugged.

Hannah shook her head, and rolled her eyes. "Of course I have. There are no guarantees with any relationship. All we really have to go on is our instincts. And my instinct tells me Max isn't a mistake. If you just give him a chance, I know you'll love him, too."

"You can be the one to explain it to your father. He'll only chew my ear off when I get home."

"I'd actually thought about bringing Max home to meet you both."

"Don't just arrive with him. Your father would have a fit!"

"I won't. I'll call Daddy, and tell him everything soon. Now, will you stop going on, and tell me all the gossip. I need a dose of normality—these past weeks have been chaotic, compared to my normally boring life."

"Your life was never boring, sweetheart."

"Well, you know what I mean." Hannah settled on the sofa beside her mother, and curled her legs underneath her.

"Oh, okay, then."

The sound of her mother's tinkling laughter filled Hannah's heart with joy. She didn't realise how much she'd missed her family and the steadiness of her old life.

They spent hours talking. By 2.00am, Hannah yawned, and sent her mother to bed.

"Why don't you get in with me, sweetheart? There's plenty of room."

Hannah usually wouldn't have worried about it, but having spent the last few nights in Max's passionate embrace, she worried once asleep, she might begin groping her mother. She shuddered at the thought.

"No. The sofa's really comfy, and I'll only keep you awake with my tossing and turning."

"Okay, then, if you're sure. Goodnight, sweetheart."

Once alone, Hannah checked her phone. It had been vibrating in her pocket all night. Seven messages from Max.

9.20pm - *Hope you're having a nice time with your mother.*

10.34pm - *My ears are burning-she hates me, doesn't she?*

11.02pm - *Miss you*

11.39pm - *Going to bed now – goodnight sausage, lol*

12.15am - *Can't sleep. Watching a movie, a chick flick. Must be getting soppy in my old age*

1.42am - *OMG! I'm crying! Bloody stupid film.*

1.58am - *Has your mother whisked you off to Shropshire? She hates me, doesn't she?*

Hannah was belly laughing by the time she'd read them all. She hit reply.

2.22am - *I'm still here, and no, she doesn't hate you. Mammy's only just gone to bed, and yes, we had a lovely evening, but I miss you now. Have you stopped crying yet? What was the movie, by the way? Cry-baby.*

2.22am - *Cry-baby? I'll give you cry-baby when I see you!*

2.23am - *Oh, so you're a tough guy now? Too late, I know you're a cry baby – ah, diddums...*

"I thought you needed to get some sleep?" her mother said from the living room doorway. She had changed into a white cotton, calf-length nightie.

"I do. Sorry. Did I disturb you?"

"Not really. I just need a glass of water."

Hannah made as to get up off the sofa.

"I'll get it. Don't get up." She trudged past her to the kitchen.

"The glasses are in the cupboard above the coffee machine," Hannah called.

2.24am - *If you don't watch out, I'll come over there, and show you what a man I am.*

Hannah chuckled, and glanced up to make sure her mother wasn't watching, before tapping in a swift reply.

2.24am - *Mammy's up again, and wants to know why you're keeping me awake! She's not happy. Still fancy your chances?"*

2.25am - *Perhaps I'll leave it until tomorrow night.*

2.25am - *Thought you might say that, lol. Goodnight, my lovely xxx*

Her mother reappeared carrying a glass of water. "Come on now, sweetheart. Try to get some sleep. You know how tetchy you can be when you're tired."

"Okay, Mammy. Goodnight." Her phone vibrated, but she didn't look at it until her mother was out of sight.

2.25am - *Goodnight, sausage. X*

Hannah grinned, and held the phone to her chest, as she snuggled down on the sofa.

Don decided he liked Hannah's no-nonsense mother. There was no way Maxwell-fucking-Myers would get a look-in with her daughter while she was around.

He'd spent the evening listening to all sorts of things about people from Hannah's hometown. Somebody called Betsy was pregnant to Carole's husband. Stephanie from Perth had lost her job for being rude to the customers. Hannah's brother and his family were settling in nicely in Ireland—he loved his new job, and was thrilled he'd taken the chance.

Of course, Don wasn't interested in any of it, but he couldn't take his eyes off Hannah, and the way her face lit up, as she listened to all the updates.

He'd never been to Shropshire. It had never appealed to him, until now.

Once Hannah had drifted off to sleep on the sofa, and her mother snuggled in Hannah's bed, reading in the dim light with her metal-framed glasses perched on her nose, he turned off the monitors. He needed to make an appearance, or Ken would be wondering where he was, again.

CHAPTER 37

Hannah groaned, as she tried to straighten herself up on the sofa.

"See! You should've shared with me."

Hannah glanced around to see her mother sitting in the armchair, a steaming mug in her hands. "Oh, hey! I didn't hear you get up." She shuffled to a sitting position.

Her mother nodded at another cup on the carpet beside the sofa. "I made you a cuppa."

"Thanks. I need that. I feel as though I've spent the night out on the tiles."

"Drink up, and then, I'll run you a nice hot bath. What time do we have to be ready by? Did you organise flowers?"

"The funeral isn't until two. The family don't want flowers. They've requested donations to Diane's favourite charity."

"That's nice. Flowers are such a waste of money."

Hannah nodded. "I'm dreading today. It's hard to believe Diane is dead. She was such a bright and bubbly person. I liked her a lot."

Her mother wandered over, and sat beside her on the sofa. "I know, sweetheart. I'm dreading it myself. I saw your neighbour this morning. Won't he be going?"

"My neighbour? Who are you talking about?" Hannah's stomach twirled.

Her mother pointed towards Simon's flat. "He rushed past the window at the crack of dawn. I wouldn't have seen him, had I not been tidying the pleat on your pelmet."

Hannah leapt to her feet, and ran outside barefoot. She wore only a thin nightie.

"What is it?" Her mother followed close behind.

Hannah banged the flat of her hand on Simon's front door. "He's been away in Seattle. I've left him lots of messages telling him about Diane, but he's not replied."

"Maybe he came home, as soon as he heard."

"He must have."

She knocked a couple more times, but there was no answer.

"Are you sure it was him?" Hannah shaded her eyes and tried to peer in Simon's bedroom window.

"How can I be sure? I've never seen him before."

"What did he look like?"

Her mother shrugged. "Tall. Short hair. Stocky build."

"Sounds like him. Then, why won't he answer?"

"He could've gone out again."

"Yeah, I guess so."

Deflated, Hannah linked her arm through her mother's. They headed back inside.

After his shift had ended, Don considered going to his own flat until later, but he'd checked the monitor, and both women were sleeping soundly, so he headed to Simon's.

Once inside, he'd showered, and changed into T-shirt and sweatpants, before dragging his weary body to bed. He was used to everyday noises when trying to sleep. He'd lived above a fast-food shop for years whilst working nights. He had a knack of deciphering the different sounds. In a semi-conscious state, he registered Hannah's front door opening. But, he hadn't imagined she'd be heading his way.

After the initial series of bangs, he slid to the floor, and pinned himself flat to the carpet on the far side of the bed. Then, he heard the women discussing Simon directly outside the window. The interfering old bat had seen him.

His sloppy, blasé attitude had almost blown his cover. He would need to be more careful. He wasn't ready to make a move towards Hannah, just yet. Then, he heard the woman describing him in detail. How would he be able to introduce himself as Hannah's boyfriend in the future if there was a chance she could recognise him?

Yet another fucking problem he would need to fix, before too long.

He spent the rest of the morning on tenterhooks, in case they returned, and he didn't manage a wink of sleep until he heard them leave a little after one. Then, he threw together his belongings, and scarpered back to his own flat.

Hannah was surprised at the huge crowd of mourners gathered together outside the main doors of the Bramhall Inn Function Rooms. Several members of the group held onto large bunches of pink and white balloons.

"Seems a strange venue for a funeral," her mother hissed, as they approached the crowd.

Hannah nodded.

The first thing she noticed was nobody had dressed in black. Instead, it seemed they'd chosen the brightest clothing possible, making Hannah and her mother stand out in their dark colours.

Hannah glanced at her mother, feeling suddenly self-conscious. But, her mother just nodded in silent encouragement.

Moments later, the doors opened, and two formally dressed men invited them inside.

Upbeat music reached Hannah's ears, as they approached the doors. This was unlike any funeral she'd ever attended before, not that she'd been to many back in Shropshire, but still.

A short, rotund man appeared in front of them. He was dressed in a multi-coloured shirt and bright orange trousers. "Welcome. I don't think we've met," he said.

Hannah gasped when she looked into his face. His resemblance to Diane was striking. "I'm Hannah. I live in the flat next door to Diane, and this is my mother, Agnes."

"Ah, Hannah." He took Hannah's hand and shook it warmly. "I did call around a couple of times, but you weren't home. I'm pleased you could make it. I'm Edward, Diane's brother."

Edward escorted them inside, and was distracted by an elderly man, who was bent double, silent tears rolling down his face. "Uncle Ernie. We're not supposed to be crying today." Edward glanced at Hannah, and shrugged an apology.

She smiled, and made her escape to the back row of seats, dragging her mother by the hand.

"I feel as though I've landed in an alternate universe," Hannah whispered.

Her mother nodded towards two women, who were tying the balloons all around the room. "They certainly do things different in the city."

Once everyone was inside and seated, the surprisingly upbeat music died down. A gaunt-looking woman with a severe haircut introduced herself as the funeral director. She welcomed everyone to the celebration of Diane's life.

At that point, Hannah noticed the enamelled yellow casket at the side of the stage area. She was relieved the lid was fitted firmly. The thought of her friend being *inside* the box was enough to make Hannah feel nauseous.

After a number of heartfelt and surprisingly amusing eulogies, the music started up again. Several boxes were passed from person to person, up and down the rows. Hannah presumed they were collection boxes, and took a twenty from her purse. But, when theirs got closer, she realised everyone was taking something from it, not putting money in. When the young, yellow-shirted man beside her handed it over, she was shocked to see the box contained brightly coloured, felt-tip marker pens.

Hannah took a purple one, and handed the box to her mother, who chose an orange marker, before passing it on.

The front row of mourners, Hannah presumed were Diane's family, including grandparents, got to their feet, and approached the casket.

From their position at the back, Hannah couldn't see what they were doing. But, they surrounded Diane's casket, each of them spending a minute or two before making way for the next in line. It appeared everybody knew what was happening, except for them. Not wanting to appear stupid, she got in line, along with the rest of her row, and slowly made her way to the front.

Several upbeat songs played, some of which Hannah hadn't heard before, but one of them, *Don't Worry Be Happy*, made Hannah chuckle – this was Diane all over.

As she approached, there was a brief gap beside the casket, and Hannah whispered, "They're writing on the coffin!"

"I guessed as much," her mother said.

"But, what will I write?" Her mind was suddenly blank.

"Just write what she meant to you. Or how you're feeling now she's gone."

Her stomach began tightening. She'd never been very good at expressing her feelings—especially in front of others. "I can't do it, Mammy." She grabbed her mother's arm.

Her mother gripped her by the upper arms, and looked directly into her eyes. "Yes, you can. I'll be right beside you, so don't worry."

She allowed herself to be propelled forwards. Then, before she knew it, she was beside the casket.

"Come on, sweetheart." Her mother smiled, and nodded, as she pulled the top off her pen, then she found a gap between all the scribbled messages and drawings, and scrawled, *Taken too soon – AJM.*

Tears poured down Hannah's face, as she read some of the messages. She backed away from the casket, handed her pen to her mother, and headed for the bathroom.

CHAPTER 38

Hannah splashed her face with cold water, and leaned against the sink, forcing herself to calm down.

Somebody farted in one of the cubicles, followed by a mouthful of expletives.

Hannah snorted, and tried to stifle a chuckle.

Moments later, a woman who Hannah guessed was in her sixties shuffled from the cubicle, pulling on her pink, flouncy, layered skirt. "Look what they've dressed me in. Diane would be killing herself laughing."

Hannah wiped her nose on a hand towel. "Maybe that was the point." She smiled.

"Don't let Edward see you blubbering—we've all been read the riot act this morning."

"I know. I let the side down, I'm sorry."

"Don't be. In my day, funerals were all about saying goodbye and mourning the passing. The wake is for sharing funny anecdotes and reminiscing. People do everything upside down nowadays."

"I must admit, it was different."

The older woman put her pudgy arm around Hannah. "Was she a good friend of yours?"

"My neighbour, but yes, we were good friends."

"She was my niece. My brother was her dad. And, for once, I'm pleased he met his maker before his time—this would've killed him. He idolised his little girl."

Hannah nodded. The tightness in her chest made it difficult to say anything. She blinked a few times. "I'm sorry," she eventually managed.

"Let the tears flow. They're better off out than in. Just like my windy problem."

Hannah burst out laughing, snot mixing with her tears. "You're a scream."

"Always was the laughing stock—that's why they dressed me in this awful lot." She swished the skirt comically.

Hannah wiped her eyes, still chuckling. "I feel such a fool. I don't usually blub, but it has been a terrible week."

The woman nodded. "Yes, it has. Come on. Escort a poor old duck out. Apparently, they've organised refreshments." She held her arm out for Hannah to take. "I don't even know your name."

"I'm Hannah."

"Pleased to meet you, Hannah. Now, come on, take Auntie Ethel for a glass of sherry."

The mourners had moved through a set of sliding doors to a room beyond. They were standing in small clusters, chatting quite happily.

Hannah escorted Ethel through to the far side of the room, where a man was waving at them frantically. "Is that your husband?" Hannah asked.

"Lord, no. He's just a friend. I think he has designs on me, though."

Hannah sniggered. "Really?"

"Don't know what's so funny. I'm still a catch—got all my own teeth and a full set of marbles."

Hannah shook her head, her eyes wide. "I'm not laughing at you. I promise."

After making sure Ethel was safely seated with her cheeky old admirer, Alfred, Hannah scanned the room for her mother. She spotted her deep in conversation with Diane's brother.

She made her way over to them.

"Ah, there you are, sweetheart. Are you feeling better now?"

"I am, thanks. I don't know what's got into me lately. My emotions are all up in the air."

Her mother patted her shoulder. "Totally understandable. I was just telling Edward how upset you've been."

Hannah smiled apologetically. "No more upset than he must've been, Mammy." She shook her head, and eyeballed her mother.

Edward smiled. "Don't worry, Hannah. We all grieve differently—take your other neighbour, for instance—Diane had a lot of time for him, but he didn't turn up today."

"Simon? Oh, he's in Seattle. I've been trying to contact him all week."

"He didn't say he was leaving for America."

"Why would he? When did you speak to him?"

"Earlier in the week—Monday, I think it was. When Trish and I cleared out Diane's flat."

Her mother gripped Hannah's arm. "See, I told you. I wasn't seeing things. Your friend's back, after all."

"But, it doesn't make sense. Why didn't he let me know? Or come today, for that matter?"

They stayed a little longer to have a few nibbles and a glass of fruit juice.

But, Hannah couldn't get Simon out of her head. *Had he even gone to the States, after all?* Thinking about it, it seemed funny how he'd left right after they'd spent the night together. It wasn't as if she'd come over all heavy—declaring her true love. In fact, the opposite was true. So why would he avoid her?

"Penny for them?" Her mother startled her from her trance, and she realised she'd driven halfway across town on automatic pilot.

"Oh, sorry. I was miles away."

"That's okay. Are we heading home?"

"Oh, I didn't even think, to be honest. What do you want to do?"

"Well, if we're not far from home, I could do with putting my feet up for an hour or two."

"Of course. I told Max we'd catch up with him later. He was going to bring Thai food."

Her mother's lip curled.

"Don't you like Thai?"

"Not really. It's much too spicy for me. Listen, swing by the store, and we can pick up some groceries. I'll cook dinner."

"Are you sure? We can just get a different takeout. Save you cooking."

She shrugged. "You know I don't like fast food, sweetheart. It's overpriced and full of salt. If we grab a few steaks and some salad it won't take much effort to throw together."

"Well, if you're sure. But, I'll drop you off, so you can have a rest, and *I'll* go to the supermarket on my way back from the office."

"I didn't realise you had to go back to work. I thought you had the day off."

"Well, I do, but I told Max we'd call in after the funeral. You can come, too, if you want to see where I work."

"Maybe tomorrow, sweetheart. I'm shattered. So, yeah, drop me home, if you don't mind."

Don finally got a couple of hours' sleep. When he woke, he was startled to see he was in his own flat—he hadn't slept there in quite a while.

It wasn't long before he was logging in to the cameras again.

He had installed three cameras in Hannah's flat, but only two were showing—the bedroom and the lounge. The one in the bathroom had been flickering for a little while. He'd been meaning to fix it.

As far as he could tell, Hannah's mother was home alone. She pottered around in the kitchen for a time, before returning to the living room. Sitting on the sofa, she began to unpin her hair. And then, she brushed the rich red waves until it shone.

Don presumed she got the colour from a bottle, as most women were predominantly grey at her age.

After a few minutes, she placed the brush on the coffee table, lifted her feet up onto the sofa, and closed her eyes.

A thought struck him. This might be the only chance he got to iron out his little wrinkle.

He quickly dressed in casual black trousers, grey T-shirt, and black trainers. Then, he shrugged into his charcoal-coloured jacket, grabbed his keys, and left.

His only problem was finding out where Hannah was. He presumed she'd gone back to the office after the funeral, but he couldn't be certain—she could be in the bath.

When he parked on the street opposite the flats, he searched around for Hannah's car. It wasn't anywhere to be seen, which was a good sign.

He swiftly exited the car, and ran for the staircase. He knew what he was about to do could prove foolish, but he had no real choice. He marched past Hannah's front door and straight inside Simon's, where he once again checked if the coast was clear on the cameras.

Taking a few deep breaths, he began to psych himself up for what he planned to do. As before, the older woman was sound asleep, sprawled out on the sofa. He could make out her gentle snores.

There was still no sign of Hannah. She could possibly be in the bathroom, but she didn't usually spend this much time in there.

If he was going to do this, it had to be now.

CHAPTER 39

As a soldier going into battle, he would mentally and physically prepare himself for conflict. He rechecked the monitor, because preparation was essential. No soldier should enter a battle zone without first accessing three essential pieces of information—terrain, people, and potential hazards.

In this case, the coast was clear. He knew exactly where his target was. He could be at her side in less than sixty seconds. His only hazard would be if Hannah returned, or her mother woke before he could get to her. Dropping to the carpet, he did ten push-ups, before jumping to his feet, flapping his arms about himself to warm his muscles.

Pumped up and in the zone, he took several self-assured steps towards Hannah's front door. He paused, listening for any sound.

Nothing.

Taking great care to make no noise, he placed the key in the lock, and turned it. Once inside, he left the door ajar, for fear of alerting the target of his presence.

The woman's soft snores could be heard from the hallway. He scanned the bathroom and kitchen first.

All clear.

Standing beside her, he leaned forward, holding his breath while his face was inches from hers. She had no idea he was there. He smiled, as he noticed the opening at the front of her black blouse. The crossover fabric had parted giving him a good view of her lacy pink bra.

His cock twitched.

Surprised by his body's reaction to this rather attractive pensioner, he wondered how it would feel to fuck her pretty, little mouth while she was dead. Or to bend her over the back of the sofa and fill both holes in turn, ramming his now fully engorged cock in as far as he could.

He stepped away, and lifted a cushion from the chair. Then, bending towards her again, he held it in front of her, ready to pounce as soon as she stirred.

With a finger and thumb, he gently pulled the fabric of her blouse wider apart giving a much better view of her generous tits. The desire to fuck her stupid was almost taking over the logical part of his mind. He'd never been in a position like this before. Normally he couldn't perform with fully conscious, consenting women, but to be this close to a woman, without her knowledge, stirred feelings in him he'd never experienced before.

He began to lift her skirt, wishing he had brought a condom from the packet next door. He had to remind himself without one, any physical contact would leave behind far too much evidence.

Once the tops of her milky white thighs were exposed, Don rubbed his free hand along the length of his cock, through the fabric. The excitement was overwhelming, and he longed to undo his trousers. The pain in his crotch was almost too much to bear.

"What the heck?"

Her voice startled him—he'd allowed himself to be distracted. In a split second, he fell forward, covering her face with the cushion.

Pinned on her back, with his knee on her chest, she was no

match for him. She struggled, but not for long. He released his hold on her.

The further excitement had caused him to ejaculate inside his trousers. He wouldn't be able to fuck her after all.

Standing upright, he placed the cushion back in place, pulled her clothes straight again, and headed for the door.

As an afterthought, he entered the kitchen, and turned on the faulty knob of the gas cooker.

That would confuse everybody for a while.

Hannah was disappointed to find Max in the middle of a meeting when she arrived at the office. She checked a few emails, and wasted half an hour in the hopes he'd be finished, but he wasn't.

Gathering her things together, she sent him a message to let him know her mother was cooking dinner, and to come over after work.

She called into the supermarket on the way home, and was surprised how busy it was. She glanced at her watch. 5.23pm. She hadn't realised it was rush-hour.

Grabbing the last basket, she almost came to blows with a hefty woman, who had a baby wrapped in a sling and a toddler on a lead.

"That's mine!" the woman screeched, yanking at the basket handle.

Not wanting to get into a slanging match, Hannah handed it over.

After wasting even more time searching for another, she began to collect the items she needed for dinner, holding them in her arms. She could've cried when she reached the checkouts to see four massive queues.

It was almost six o'clock, before Hannah eased into a parking spot outside her flat.

She'd just opened the boot, when someone came up behind her and tickled her ribs.

She squealed and spun around. "Oh, Max. I almost socked you one then."

"I'm sorry. I couldn't resist. Here, let me help."

She loaded him up with grocery bags, and together, they headed to the stairs.

"How was your day?" he asked.

"Sad. But, really strange. Everybody was dressed in bright colours, and nobody was allowed to cry—although I failed miserably at that one. Diane's casket was painted bright yellow, and everybody wrote a message on it in bright-coloured marker pens —I failed at that, too. Although, I did pop back and sign it quickly before we left."

"Hadn't the casket been removed after the service?"

"No. Apparently, the close family plan to have their own burial service tomorrow."

"Burial? I didn't think anybody did that these days."

"Clearly some still do. I don't want to be buried though." She shuddered. "The thought of wiggly worms slithering through my empty eye sockets and bugs munching their way through my innards—no way."

"I'll remember that." He smirked.

They reached the front door, and Max hung back to allow Hannah to open it.

"We're here, Mammy," she called, as they entered.

"Can I smell gas?" Max said.

"Oh, no!" Hannah ran to the kitchen, and saw the faulty knob was turned all the way around, and gas was pouring out. She switched it off, opened the window, and began waving her hands to remove as much of the awful stuff as possible.

"Hannah," Max said quietly.

Alarmed, she followed his voice into the lounge. Max held his phone, and headed back out the front door. But then she noticed her mother, unconscious on the sofa.

"Ambulance, please!" Max's voice carried through.

"Oh, no!" Hannah screamed, and fell to her knees beside her. "Mammy! Wake up!" She shook and shook her mother. It was no use.

She was vaguely aware of Max returning. "Hannah," he snapped. "Hannah, listen to me. We've got to get outside. The gas is toxic and highly flammable—this whole place could blow."

He put his arms underneath her mother, and lifted. "Come on. Hurry."

Hannah numbly followed him out of the flat, and down onto the street, where he lay her mother on a small strip of grass.

"Is she dead?" she whispered.

"I don't know." Max felt her mother's wrist. "I'm sure I can feel a faint pulse."

"She can't die, Max. She can't die. Please, don't let her die." Suddenly light-headed, she sat down on the footpath.

They heard the ambulance minutes before they saw it.

Hannah climbed back to her feet, and stood in the middle of the road, waving, when they arrived.

CHAPTER 40

After confirming her mother did indeed have a slight pulse, the paramedics transferred her to a stretcher, and into the back of the ambulance.

"Can I come?" she asked the middle-aged male driver.

"Best not to, Hannah," Max said. "We'll follow behind in the car."

"But…"

He gently took her aside. "There's hardly any room in there. Let them do their job, and we'll meet them at the hospital. I promise."

The driver nodded his agreement, and closed the door.

She sobbed as the ambulance sped away, the sirens wailing again.

"Come on." He guided her to his car, and fastened her seatbelt. "I won't be a minute. I'll just lock up your flat."

She watched, as he ran towards the stairs. He was back moments later, carrying her handbag, jacket, and keys.

"The gas seems to have dissipated. Did you manage to turn something off?"

She nodded. "It's all my fault. I meant to call the rental agency about the faulty knob, but I forgot."

"It's nobody's fault. Just an accident. That's all."

"But, what if she dies, Max? I'll never forgive myself."

"She isn't going to die." He reached for her hand, and stroked her fingers.

Hannah could tell by his expression he wasn't certain.

"I need to call Daddy." Shoving his hand away, she began rummaging in her bag for her phone.

"It may be a good idea to wait until we find out a little more. It's pointless stressing him out unnecessarily."

Hannah nodded. Max was right, of course.

They found a car park close to the emergency entrance of Cheadle Royal Infirmary. Hannah's thoughts went to memories of Diane, when she saw the uniforms. A member of staff took down her mother's details, and then showed them to a smaller waiting room, where she explained the doctor would inform them as soon as they had any news.

Max sat beside Hannah, placing his arm around her shoulder. She jumped to her feet. "Don't! I feel claustrophobic."

He held his hands up, then placed them in his lap.

The silence was deafening.

A while later, the door swung open. Hannah's breath hitched. Another staff member showed an elderly man in, and escorted him to a chair.

"Now, the doctor will come and find you once your wife is settled, Mr Christiansen. Will you be okay?"

The dear old man nodded, his lips and hands trembling.

Hannah glanced at Max. "I'm sorry for snapping," she whispered. She sat beside him, and reached for his hand.

"I know."

"I just wish somebody would tell us what's happening."

"Shall I go for some coffee?" he asked.

"It's up to you. I don't want one."

"Water?"

She nodded, just to shut him up.

"Can I get you a cup of water, buddy?" Max asked the man.

The man turned to them, the pain in his watery blue eyes breaking Hannah's heart.

"That's very kind of you, son. Thanks." He nodded.

Max went off in search of refreshments.

"Are you waiting for your wife?" Hannah asked.

He nodded. "Angina. She's had it for a while, but this time was different."

"I'm sorry."

"You?"

"My mammy. We found her unconscious in my flat—gas leak."

He reached to pat her hand. The fingers of his wrinkled and liver-spotted hand were twisted. Hannah recognised it as arthritis. Her friend's grandmother had suffered with it.

She smiled, and looked back down at her feet.

"We've been together for sixty-three years. I always thought I would be the one to go first."

Hannah nodded. "I've never thought of it, to be honest. You just expect your parents to be around forever, don't you?"

"Yes. Although, I don't remember my father. He was killed in the war, but my mother died quite young. I was only seventeen."

"That's terrible!" Hannah moved over one seat to sit beside him. She linked her arm through his. "You were still a child."

"Grew up pretty quick after that, let me tell you."

"Do you have children?"

"Two. Julia and James. But, they both have families of their own."

"Have you called them?"

He shook his head. "I'll ask the nurse to do it for me later."

"Do you want to use my phone? They probably should be here."

"Could I?"

Hannah reached for her purse, and pulled out her phone. "Here you go."

He took it, and turned it around several times in his hand, his eyebrows furrowed.

"I can call them, if you like?"

"Yes, please." He handed the phone back, and recited a phone number for her.

Hannah dialled, and waited for it to ring, before handing it back to him.

His entire body shook as he put the phone to his ear. "Julia. It's Dad." He almost shouted. "I'm at the hospital again." He nodded a couple of times, before handing the phone back to Hannah. Then, he wiped his eyes on his shirtsleeve.

"What did she say?" Hannah asked.

"She's on her way."

She sighed. "Good. You shouldn't be alone at a time like this."

Max returned carrying two plastic cups filled with water. He handed one to each of them. "You won't believe it, but I had to go all the way back to the entrance for these."

The door opened and a tall, blonde nurse appeared. She smiled at Hannah. "Ms McLaughlin?"

Hannah nodded.

"Can we have a little chat?"

Hannah handed the cup back to Max, as she picked up her purse and jacket. "Can my friend come, too?"

"Of course he can." Her smile caused dimples in her pretty face.

They followed her out.

"Good luck," the old man said.

"Thanks. Same to you." Hannah waved, and then ran back to give him a hug. "Will you be alright until your daughter arrives?"

"Don't worry about me, pet. I'll be fine."

They followed the nurse around a series of corridors, and through to a busy open area.

Hannah wanted to scream at her to stop walking and just fucking tell her—was her mother dead? But, she was terrified of hearing the actual words. She wanted to put it off for as long as she could.

The nurse paused beside a curtain. "Your mother is stable. We will be transferring her to a ward shortly, but I'm sure you're keen to see her."

"Yes, please." Tears spilled down Hannah's cheeks at the welcome news. "Will she be alright?"

"We hope so. She's still unconscious, but that's quite normal. We've run a series of tests, and we should get the results back in a few hours."

"Thank you." Hannah gripped Max's hand.

"Ready?" the nurse asked.

They nodded, and she pulled the curtain open.

Hannah ran to her mother's side, and kissed her beautiful face. "Oh, Mammy. You gave us such a fright."

CHAPTER 41

Don headed back to his own flat to get ready for his shift. He checked the cameras as he arrived. In the time it took for him to drive across town from Hannah's, he missed them finding Hannah's mother. He did, however, see Max return, to grab a few items, before rushing off again.

Don had been surprised the place wasn't swarming with police and specialists, as was usual in a case like this. The body had also been moved. He figured it was probably down to Maxwell-fuck-ing-Myers acting all macho-like. He could imagine him running in like Rambo, and after detecting gas, evacuating the building, and rescuing Hannah's mother's body for a few fucking brownie points.

That man needed dealing with—and fast.

He tuned into the local radio for the news updates, but nothing was said about a death. If it was accepted as a tragic accident, it may not be considered juicy enough for the news bulletin, and he'd need to watch the evening news instead.

He was in a great mood, no doubt due to his sexual encounter with the older woman. He knew he would have felt better had he managed to do what he'd wanted. This opened up a lot of new possibilities for him. He'd finally discovered something which turned him on enough to ejaculate, without thinking about his own mother. His cock twitched again just thinking about it.

At work, a short time later, he busied himself with his rounds, and planned the following fortnight's roster. When he checked the cameras a while later, he was surprised Hannah hadn't returned home. Maybe she couldn't face it, considering that was where her mother had died. He hadn't considered that.

With a few taps of the keyboard, images of the car park filled the screen. He scanned Max's reserved space—it was empty. They weren't up in his apartment, either. *Where the fuck could they be?*

He felt his earlier good mood slip away.

They moved her mother to a ward a couple of hours later.

In the corridor, on the way to the lift, Hannah spotted the old man from earlier. She was about to call over to him when she noticed his distraught face. A man and woman came from the bathrooms. It was clear they'd been crying. They each took one of his arms, and slowly led him towards the exit.

Hannah's eyes filled for the hundredth time that day.

"Hey, sausage. What is it?" Max asked, putting his hand on her arm.

She couldn't speak. Instead, she shook her head, closed her eyes, and let the tears fall.

He embraced her, and she buried her head in his chest. "She's going to be alright. Are you worried about calling your dad?"

"A little," she managed.

"Well, don't. What happened is in no way down to you. That knob didn't turn itself on, so your mother must have done it."

"I think that old man's wife has died."

Max hugged her tighter. "That's sad, but inevitable, at their time of life. Your mum has years in her yet."

He called the lift, and they travelled up to Ward 8 in silence.

Hannah was relieved to find they'd placed her mother in a room of her own. She knew the hospital had a strict visitor policy, but one of the nurses had told her they overlook a lot, if the patient was in a private room. Hannah had decided she wasn't going anywhere until her mother woke up.

"I need to call Daddy," she said, standing at the foot of her mother's bed.

"What will you tell him?"

"The truth. I thought some of the test results would have been back by now—but I can't wait much longer."

"I noticed a family room at the end of the corridor. Why don't you go in there?" Max suggested.

"Yeah, I will. I won't be long."

He hugged her as she walked past and kissed the top of her head.

Just then, a man they hadn't seen before, dressed in a blue, linen shirt and navy trousers, entered. He had a file in his hands. "Ms McLaughlin?"

Hannah nodded, backing up beside Max again, and reached for his hand.

"I'm Sebastian Roberts, the consultant in charge of your mother."

"Do you have the test results?" Hannah asked.

"Some of them. There were high levels of carbon dioxide in her system."

"What are you saying? I don't understand."

"Well, there are several types of asphyxiation. Natural gas isn't toxic in itself, but inhaling it in large amounts, enough to render your mother unconscious, would dilute her oxygen intake substantially. Asphyxiation without the painful and traumatic feeling of suffocation."

"I'm confused."

"I'm a little confused myself, to be honest. There is no doubt her body's been deprived of oxygen. She's displaying the symptoms of asphyxia, but at this stage, I don't think it had anything to do with gas inhalation."

"What else could it be, then?" Hannah knew her voice sounded screechy and irrational, but she couldn't help it.

"Some other forms of asphyxiation include drowning, smothering, or suffocation. Drowning is easy to diagnose, water floods the lungs, of course."

"Are you saying she drowned?" Hannah shook her head, impatience getting the better of her.

"Of course not. I'm not explaining myself very well, am I? Please bear with me. If a person is suffocated, having the airways obstructed, they can't breathe, but more importantly, they can't breathe out, which causes a build-up of carbon dioxide. Add this to the marks around your mother's nose and mouth, the discolouration of her tongue, and bloodshot eyes, I'd say your mother was suffocated."

"That's crazy. She was fine a couple of hours earlier. We found her unconscious, and the flat was filled with fumes."

"I'll reorder the tests to be sure. But, if the findings are the same, I'll have no choice but to inform the authorities."

"Is she going to be alright? Why hasn't she woken up yet?"

"We're hopeful. The initial prognosis appears favourable. As with any asphyxiation, permanent damage can occur, depending on how long your mother was deprived of oxygen. But, her pupils are reactive, which is a good sign, and the MRI scan showed up nothing untoward. However, high levels of carbon dioxide can harm your body's organs. She's already on a ventilator, which is blowing increased amounts of oxygen into her lungs, so hopefully, we'll see an improvement by the morning."

"Is she in a coma?"

"No. She's in a state we call wakeful unresponsiveness. She suffered a massive trauma, and her body needs a little time to heal itself. As I said, by tomorrow, we should see signs of improvement. Now, if you don't have any more questions, I need to be on my way."

Hannah stepped forward, and shook his hand. "Thanks so much for taking the time to explain. I do appreciate it."

"You're welcome."

She waited until he'd left before turning to Max. "So, what did you think about that?"

"It must be a mistake. She was taking a nap on the sofa, and the gas was on."

"I know, but I did wonder what those marks were on her face. They weren't there earlier."

"With a bit of luck, she'll remember what happened. Now, you'd best go and call your dad."

She headed to the other end of the corridor to find the family room Max had told her about.

Hannah scrolled through her contacts, and inhaled deeply before tapping the call button. Her father answered on the second ring.

"Hi, Daddy. It's me."

"Hello, sweetheart. How did the funeral go?"

"Oh, err... fine, thanks. But, listen, Daddy, I need to tell you something."

"What is it?" The smile in his voice had gone.

"It's Mammy. She's in hospital."

"What the hell!"

"Don't panic. The specialists think she should make a full recovery."

"Just tell me what happened," he snapped.

Hannah thought of the old man from earlier, and could hear the same desperation in her father's voice.

Hannah told him everything.

"I'm on my way."

"No, Daddy. There's no point. If she's no better tomorrow,

then, yes. But, chances are, she'll be okay. If she is, then I'll drive her home for the weekend myself."

"It's not up for discussion, Hannah. She's my wife. Who's responsible for your stove, by the way?"

"The owners, I guess, although the tenancy's being managed by an agent."

"Get me the agent's details first thing. This needs fixing immediately."

CHAPTER 42

When there was still nothing on the evening news, Don began to panic. Hannah hadn't returned home, and neither had Maxwell-fucking-Myers. He desperately needed to know where they were.

Snap-snap-snap.

He hacked into the company's alarm system, and set off the alarm on the emergency exit on the fifteenth floor.

A deafening siren sounded.

Moments later, his earpiece crackled to life. "Don—an alarm has been activated on the top floor. It appears to be the emergency exit."

"I'm heading up there now. I'll check it out," Don replied.

He reset the alarm, and then triggered it again a minute later.

"You still up there, Don?"

"Yeah, Ken. I think we have a technical fault. Could you go to the hub, and deactivate all the sensors for the top floor?"

"Will do, boss."

Don left the hub, and headed up to the next floor via the stairs.

The alarm sounded for a further few minutes, and then nothing, although Don's ears were still ringing.

He reached for his phone, and dialled Max's number.

"Max Myers," his boss said, in a quiet voice.

"Sorry to disturb you, sir. But, there seems to be a security fault on the top floor. Do you happen to be in the building?"

"No, I'm not. What's happening?"

"The emergency exit is triggering the alarm. I checked the door and the sensors, and then reset it, but it happened again moments later. I was standing beside it the second time, so I know there was nobody tampering with it. I made the call to disarm the floor, but I thought I'd check with you—just in case."

"Good call, Don. Can you contact the relevant department tomorrow? Steve will have left a list of numbers somewhere."

While Max was talking, Don tried to listen for any tell-tale sounds in the background, but there was nothing. "Will do, sir. Also, I was wondering if I could have a chat with you later."

"Is it important? The thing is, I probably won't be back tonight. I'm at the hospital."

"Nothing bad, I hope? No, not important."

"I'm here with a friend. I'll catch up with you tomorrow at the start of your shift."

Don hung up and rubbed his temples. So, they were at the hospital. Max said he was with a friend, but he must mean Hannah. *Had she had an accident? Could finding her dead mother have caused her to have some kind of breakdown?* Surely not.

He reached the lift, suddenly feeling drained and confused. Maybe he shouldn't have acted on impulse today. Just because his own mother's death hadn't affected him, didn't mean everyone would feel the same. In fact, he witnessed the closeness between them both the other night.

For the first time in a long time, he felt a twinge of guilt. And he didn't like it. He didn't like it one bit.

Hannah was startled from a daydream, as Max returned. "You get going, Max. You must be exhausted."

"Not on your life. I'm staying." He moved the chair up beside her armchair.

"It's seems silly us both getting no sleep." She knew the sensible thing to do would be for them both to go home for a few hours, but she refused to leave her mother's side. However, she didn't expect *him* to stay, too.

"Who says we'll get no sleep? I made a deal with the night nurse. She said she'll bring us an extra armchair, once the place settles down for the night."

"Oh, good. I was feeling a little guilty sitting here, while you were on that hard thing."

"We could always swap."

"I don't feel *that* guilty." She gave him a wide, exaggerated grin.

"I didn't think so."

"Who was on the phone?"

"Security. An issue with the alarms, or something. Nothing to worry about. Are you hungry?"

"A little. There won't be anywhere open now, though."

"I could pick up a couple of burgers. There's a twenty-four-hour place not far from here."

Her stomach growled loudly, which made them both laugh.

"I'll take that as a *yes,* then." He grabbed his jacket from the end of the bed. "I shouldn't be too long."

While he was gone, she went into the small adjoining bathroom, where she rinsed her face and ran her fingers through her hair. The end result wasn't much better. Her eyes were still red and swollen from crying on and off all day.

The thought of red eyes brought to mind what the consultant had said—her mother had bloodshot eyes, and some chemical, which only builds up if she was unable to breathe out. When he'd first said it, she thought it sounded stupid. If she'd been struggling to breathe in, then *surely* she'd struggle to breathe out, too.

Hannah left the bathroom, and located her phone. After a few minutes on the internet, she'd found the explanation. Suddenly, the penny dropped.

With gas inhalation, a person doesn't struggle to breathe, as such. Instead, the available oxygen is diluted with the gas, and their system will slowly shut down. But, with suffocation, a person will be fighting to breathe. However, all the time they are being suffocated, they can't breathe out the harmful carbon dioxide.

So, if the initial tests *were* correct, it's likely her mother *had* been suffocated. *But, how could that be?*

By the time Max returned, Hannah had worked herself into a frenzy. Her words poured from her mouth like Alphabetti Spaghetti.

"Whoa, slow down." He caught both of her hands in his, and looked into her eyes. "Now, tell me again. What happened?"

Hannah went over the information she'd found, stressing the point about carbon dioxide.

"What are you trying to say? Somebody entered your flat, and attacked your mother?" He shook his head. "It doesn't make sense, though. You saw her—she looked as though she'd just gone to sleep. There were no signs of a break in, or a struggle."

"I know, but if the tests results are the same tomorrow, the police will be informed. The specialist must be pretty certain, if he contacts the police."

"Let's wait for the results before we jump to any conclusions. I mean, who else knew the cooker was faulty?"

"Nobody. Well, Diane did, but…" She shrugged.

"Could she have told anybody?"

"I don't see why she would. But, it's possible, I guess."

"There are just too many coincidences for me. I'm sure it will all be cleared up by tomorrow."

"I hope so, Max. Because, if not, it means somebody attempted to murder Mammy!"

CHAPTER 43

Hannah hardly slept. The armchair proved to be terribly uncomfortable, with the wooden arms digging in her ribs every time she changed position.

When she eventually got up to use the bathroom, she realised Max had gone. He must've changed his mind, and headed home after all.

She leaned over her mother, and kissed her cheek. "Wake up, Mammy. I need you to wake up."

Nothing. Not a flicker.

While she was in the bathroom, she heard the outer door opening. A few minutes later, she emerged from the bathroom. "Did you go home for a decent sleep?"

She froze. Her father was standing beside the bed, stroking her mother's face.

"Daddy!" Tears streamed from her eyes and down off her chin, before she reached him.

He held his arms open, and she launched herself into them.

"Oh, Daddy. I'm so relieved to see you."

The door opened, and Max appeared holding two coffee cups and a paper bag.

"You're awake," he said, before his eyes settled on her father.

"Max, this is my daddy, Liam. Daddy, meet Max. He's my..." she paused, her eyes fixed on Max's, and she cringed. "...boyfriend."

Max passed her a cup, then, with his free hand outstretched, said, "Pleased to meet you, sir."

Her dad bristled slightly, and glanced at her, before accepting Max's handshake.

"Max was with me when I found Mammy," she explained, suddenly aware of the frost in the room.

Her dad cocked his head backward in acknowledgement.

"He also stayed with me last night. Neither of us has left the hospital since we arrived."

"Has there been any change with your mother?" he asked, ignoring her waffling.

"No. Apparently, the doctors do the rounds just after eight." She glanced at her watch. "So, they should be here within the hour."

"Can I get you a coffee, Mr McLaughlin? There's a cafeteria on the floor below," Max said.

"I'm fine, thank you. I stopped for petrol a little while ago, and bought something then."

"Daddy. There's something I need to tell you."

His eyes narrowed, making her squirm.

She told him all about the consultant's comments and explained the carbon dioxide information.

"I agree with Max—too many coincidences," he said.

"I hope so," Hannah said. "The thought of anybody intentionally hurting Mammy blows my mind."

"When the doctors have been, you and the lad should go home for a rest."

Hannah glanced at Max, embarrassed by her father's words.

Max gave two quick lifts of his eyebrows, then winked.

"Are you sure? I would like to have a shower and a change of clothes, and then, I'll come straight back."

Her father shrugged, his eyes fixed on his wife's face.

Several doctors arrived a few minutes later. They mainly spoke amongst themselves, and had no updates for them, except to say they hoped her mother would wake up soon, but she could remain in this state for several days.

"The consultant said she was to have more tests," Hannah said, as the doctors turned to leave.

"More tests have been ordered, yes," a stony-faced charge-nurse said. "We're still awaiting the results."

And then, with a whoosh of white coats, they were gone.

"It could be days," her father repeated, returning to her mother's side.

"The consultant was quite certain she should start showing some improvement by today."

Her father scowled at her. "You kids get off now. And Hannah, get some sleep. I'll call you, if there's any change."

"I'm sorry my father was rude to you," she said, once they were in the corridor heading for the exit.

"He wasn't. Was he?"

"Calling you *the lad!* Didn't it bother you?"

"Not at all. I am a lad, to him, I guess. I bet he thinks I'm some little punk, sniffing around his daughter. There *is* a protocol every man goes through when he meets his girlfriend's father for the first time."

"Is there?"

"Of course. It's a well-known fact dads and daughters have a close bond. You would have idolised your father all your life. For him, you are still that tiny baby he brought home from the hospital. And then, some punk makes an appearance, and thinks he's going to take his place in your heart. Your dad will feel undermined, territorial, ready to fight to the death, if need be. He needs to establish the relationship from the word go, and make it clear the punk isn't worthy of his daughter, and if he dared to hurt her, then—" He made a throat slitting movement with his finger.

She laughed.

Opening the external door open for her, she ducked under his arm, and out to the dreary, drizzly day.

"I see. You've really studied it, haven't you?"

"Not at all. I just know how I'd feel if it was my daughter. There would be pistols at dawn."

"Rather excessive, don't you think?"

"Nowhere near excessive enough!"

"You do realise we're having another argument about children, don't you?" She grinned.

"Not an argument, as such, just a little discussion."

They reached Max's car. "Okay, shall we go to mine, or yours?" he said.

"Do you still have my overnight bag?"

He nodded. "Yes, it's in the boot—I brought it back with me yesterday."

"Then, yours—if that's okay? I can't face my place, yet."

Once at his apartment, they showered, and fell into bed, totally exhausted.

Hannah was asleep, almost immediately, cradled in Max's strong arms. They woke to a phone ringing a couple of hours later.

Max answered.

From what she could make out, she knew there was a problem.

He slammed down the phone, and turned to her. "We've got an issue with the Sullivan account. The main server crashed, and seems to have lost the entire campaign."

Hannah gasped. "Oh, no! What will you do?"

"Fuck only knows." He rubbed his face angrily. "If I organise you a ride to pick up your car, will you be okay to go back to the hospital without me?"

"I'll get a cab. Don't worry about me. And Daddy's here now, anyway."

"Are you sure?"

She nodded. "Just go."

"I'll call you as soon as I get a spare moment." He hurriedly dressed in slacks and a short-sleeved, checked shirt. Grabbing his jacket off the sofa, he bent to kiss her, before rushing out the door.

Hannah took another quick shower, dressed, and left.

She waved a cab down outside, and headed to her flat to collect her car.

Standing at her car, she rummaged in her bag, but couldn't find her keys. Max had picked up her door key, but must've left the car key behind.

The flat seemed eerie after the chaos of the previous day. She found her keys on the benchtop beside the cooker. Instead of heading out, she stepped into the living room. Everything appeared normal, not as you'd expect if somebody *had* attacked her mother.

She flopped down on the chair, moving the cushion onto the arm. What a mess. She prayed her mother would be showing some signs of recovery when she got back there. Losing her wasn't an option.

She needed to head back. Climbing to her feet, she plumped up the cushion, and placed it back on the chair.

She froze.

The centre of the beige cushion was covered in make-up. Lipstick and foundation. At the top of the large smudge was the same shade of her mother's powder-blue eyeshadow.

It was true! Somebody *had* tried to kill her mother!

Running on shock and adrenalin, she raced back to the hospital. She tried Max's number on the way, but it went straight to voicemail.

Up on the eighth floor, things were the same as she'd left them. Her father was dozing in the armchair. Her mother was still unconscious.

"Daddy, it's true! I found the cushion covered in Mammy's make-up. Somebody did this to her."

CHAPTER 44

Once the doctors were informed of Hannah's discovery, they all rallied around, and the police were called.

Her father was angrier than she'd ever seen him before, and kept snapping at her, as though he blamed her. But, she knew he didn't mean it.

The specialists told them her mother seemed to be responding, and, although Hannah couldn't see it, she figured *they* were the experts, after all.

Max's phone was still going to voicemail.

She didn't know how he'd react when she told him of her theory. The more she thought about it, the more she believed Angela could be responsible. *If not her, then who?* Angela clearly blamed Hannah for everything. *But, could she be angry enough to actually kill her mother?* It didn't seem likely, but she would need to tell the police, and let them check it out.

It was almost 7pm, before the police arrived. The senior officer introduced himself as Detective Rudy Owens. He had a pockmarked complexion and fine, wispy blond hair. A younger, geeky-looking detective was with him

Hannah got the impression they thought they were wasting their time. However, the more they heard, the more excited they appeared.

Before they left, they asked for Hannah's key to arrange for the flat to be searched. They said they didn't think it would be until the next day, but advised her to stay away, until they contacted her.

Max still hadn't called. She presumed they hadn't managed to restore the campaign. The same thing happened to her once when she was still at the *Daily Post*. The entire team had to work all hours to redo it from scratch, and that wasn't anywhere near the scale of the Sullivan account. He'd no doubt be tied up all weekend.

Her father was still very cool towards her. She'd tried to talk to him several times, but he cut her dead. She knew he was heartbroken. Her parents had been together since they were teenagers, and the only time she stayed away from home without him, her mother ended up in hospital fighting for her life.

They shared a pizza for dinner in silence.

Before they settled down for the evening, she strolled to the family room, and tried Max one last time.

Voicemail.

Don's phone rang as he headed in for the nightshift. He pulled the car over before answering.

"Don Henry."

"Good evening, Don. Cheryl Thompson, from Asset Recruitment."

"Yes. What can I do for you?"

"I'm working on the advertisement for the security position. Max told me to liaise with you regarding the job description."

"Ah, yes. He did mention it. I told him I'd be available to sit in on the interviews—the way Steve did."

"Really? Okay, that won't be necessary, but thank you."

"I'm heading into the office now. I'll get the information together this evening, if you like?"

"No hurry. I won't be back at my desk until Monday morning."

"Could I ask you something?"

"Fire away."

"Do you organise all the employment contracts, or is that down to Mr Myers?"

"I do. Why?"

"I haven't received my new contract yet. I wanted to renegotiate a pay increase in accordance with the increased responsibility."

"I don't negotiate the salary of existing staff, I'm afraid. Just new contracts."

"Yes. But, mine *is* a new contract. I've been doing the job since Steve died. I'm not saying I want it backdated. But, I would like to get it all signed and sealed, as soon as possible."

"There must have been some confusion, Don. The position I'm advertising for is Steve's—Head of Security. But, you could always apply, like anybody else."

A sharp pop went off inside Don's mind.

Max had been snowed under all day. It turned out the loss of the campaign file was down to human error, and nothing to do with a server crash. It seemed that Francine Powers, the campaign manager, had actually deleted the wrong file, and then, to top it all, she'd emptied the deleted items folder, too. Once she realised what she'd done, Francine tried to blame everyone and everything, rather than make the admission herself, but the evidence spoke for itself. Max hadn't been too hard on her. Mistakes are made all the time. But, it was going to take days to fix. He missed Angela more than ever.

He couldn't persuade the team to stay late, so they called it a day, just after 6pm.

On the way to the lift, he tried to call Hannah, but his phone had died.

Don Henry appeared in front of him. His face looked greasy and red.

"Ah, Don. I almost forgot. Come up to my office, and we can have that chat you wanted."

The lift door opened, and Max indicated Don should enter first. It was clear something was terribly wrong with him. In fact, Don's cold, protruding glare was unnerving Max a little.

"I've had a hard day," Max said, trying to fill the silence, as they travelled up to the top floor. "Some idiot deleted a whole campaign, and we've had to start again from the beginning."

Don said nothing. His jaw muscles flexed, as he stared at the numbers of the console.

"Are you alright, Don? You don't seem to be yourself. Has something happened?"

Don slowly turned his head to face Max. "I'll tell you in your office."

"Okay." Max's mouth had dried up. He'd never really liked this man; he'd always felt there was more to him than he let on. However, he'd always been polite and respectful.

They stepped from the lift, and walked the rest of the way in silence. Max suddenly felt very vulnerable, as he glanced around the deserted floor.

Once inside his office, Max flicked on the light, and rounded his desk trying to put some space between them. "Take a seat, Don."

Don snatched up the chair, and threw it aside. It slammed off the filing cabinet and settled on two legs, leaning against the wall.

"What the...?" The contents of Max's stomach turned to molten lava, and he thought he might shit himself right there.

Don leaned forwards, his knuckles on the desk, and his face twisted in an uglier, scarier version of himself. "Look at you. Sitting there, all business-like, pretending to care," he growled.

Max licked his lips nervously. "I do care, Don. If you have any problems, just tell me, and I'll see what I can do to help you."

"You don't fucking get it, do you?" Don roared. "You're my problem." He swiped a pile of papers off the desk onto the plush brown carpet.

Max jumped backwards, chair and all, and slammed into the wall behind him. "Calm down, Don. This isn't the way to behave. Think of your job."

"That's a joke." Don's nostrils flared, and his lips were drawn back, showing a full set of uneven teeth. "What job?"

Completely shocked, Max didn't know how the hell to deal with a situation like this. In the past, if something seemed to be getting out of his control, he'd call security. But, this *was* security!

"Don," he said, trying to make his voice remain even. "Whatever it is, we can sort it out. Just calm down, take a seat, and let's discuss it properly."

"It's gone too far for that! I don't want to talk to you—I want to rip your scraggly fucking head off your neck, and stick it up your arse."

"What? I don't understand."

"*I don't understand.*" Don mimicked in a whiny voice. "I had a call from Cheryl Thompson. She wants me to send her the job description for the security vacancy. I thought she wanted the description of *my* old position—but no! She said you're advertising for the Head of Security."

"I—I..." Max shook his head.

"Oh, don't worry. She said I was welcome to apply. Wasn't that kind of her?"

"Don. I promise you, she's mistaken. I told her we had a vacancy, and she obviously heard about Steve, and just presumed." He could tell he was getting through, as Don's hands dropped to his sides. His face smoothed over, and he stepped back, as his anger dissipated.

"So, you didn't tell her to advertise Steve's job?"

"Not at all. Now, if that's all, Don—I've had a shitty day, and could do with getting in the shower."

"Of course." Don bent and picked up the pile of papers from the carpet, and returned them to the table. Then, he righted the chair, and muttered his apologies before leaving.

Max released the breath he wasn't aware he was holding. *What the fuck?* He didn't know how he was going to get out of *this* situation, without feeling the wrath of that head case. But, that was a problem for a later date—he'd had all he could stomach for one day.

CHAPTER 45

Back at the hub, Don wiped some of the earlier footage, and replaced it with footage from the day before—Max walking from the lift, and into his office—alone.

Then, he radioed down to Ken. He knew exactly where the lazy bastard would be—on the front desk, playing some kind of stupid war game on the computer. The dumb fuck thought Don didn't know what he got up to, but nothing much escaped Don's attention.

"Ken? I've just had a call from Mr Myers. He wants me to collect a bag belonging to Ms McLaughlin, and leave it at the front desk. He's going to swing by later and pick it up."

"Okay..."

"I'm sat on the shitter—dodgy curry. Could you go and get it for me? It's a gym bag down the side of his desk."

"Yeah, of course, boss. I'll go now."

"Good man."

Don watched on the monitor, as Ken ambled over to the lift. He wished he could put a rocket up the idle bastard's arse—it drove him wild how lazy the younger generation was.

Ken arrived on the top floor, and, as he passed the last camera

Don quickly pasted an hour's worth of empty corridors onto the tape, waiting for Ken to return, carrying Hannah's bag.

Don smiled. He was just too fucking smart for this lot.

Once Ken had arrived back down on the ground floor, Don tampered with the alarm again on the top floor.

"The alarms are at it again, boss. You still in the bathroom?" Ken said.

"I am. Just disarm the whole floor again, Ken. We need to get it checked out next week." Just like last night, Don ran up one flight of stairs, while Ken headed to the hub to disarm the alarms.

Moments later, the racket stopped.

Now, there had been two separate nights where Ken had switched off all alarms and footage for the top floor. Ken would be the one to record it in the day book, and fill out the incident reports.

Things were working out perfectly.

He headed back up to the top floor, making sure the sensor lights were not flashing on the cameras. They were all off. It was a design flaw the security staff were aware of. To disarm one area on a level would disarm everything.

Don headed to the caretaker's room, where he found most of what he needed—cable ties, tape, a multi-knife tool, rubber gloves, and a large tube of expanding foam, which he thought might come in handy. As he was leaving, his eyes lit up, as he spotted a container of lighter fuel beside a box of matches. He slid them into his jacket pocket.

In Max's office, he approached the door which led into the flat. Max and Steve had the only two security passes for the flat. Don grinned, as he pulled out Steve's pass, and silently opened the door. There was no sign of Max in the room.

Don felt suddenly sick. *Had he missed Max leaving the building?*

A sound from the bathroom allayed his fears. Max was still in the shower.

Don was blinded by steam, as he opened the bathroom door.

The terrible singing coming from the cubicle assured Don he hadn't been heard.

Poised, ready to strike, he grinned again. He'd been waiting for this moment for so long. He intended to savour every exhilarating second.

Max switched the jets off. Nothing could beat a long, hot shower after the kind of day he'd had. The massaging shower head was so powerful, the water had numbed his skin, and pummelled his aches away.

He needed to call Hannah. His phone was charging, but took a while to restart after being totally drained. Then, he was going to get an early night—he was shattered.

The sudden whoosh of the shower door opening startled him. He whirled around expecting to see Hannah, not the sturdy metal torch aiming for his head. He deflected the first blow with lightning speed. The torch glanced off his shoulder. The sudden pain was excruciating, but Max was used to pain. His years playing football had seen to that. He reacted to the assault by punching out wildly. His fist connected. His assailant staggered backwards, dropping the torch. Wiping the shower water from his eyes, Max focussed on his attacker.

"Don! What the fuck's got into you, man?" he yelled.

Don lunged forward with a roar, wrapping his arms around Max's waist. Max fell backwards, and crashed into the shower screen.

With a deafening crack, the glass shattered into a million tiny pieces, covering the floor. Max landed heavily on the bed of glass, with Don still on top of him.

Max was too stunned to move for a second. This gave Don the chance to get to his feet, and grab his torch.

When Don pounced, Max saw the murderous look in his eyes

and he knew there was only one possible outcome—one of them would die. Determined it wouldn't be him, Max raised his feet, and rammed them into Don's midriff, flinging him backwards.

Max rolled towards the rear wall, startled by the sight of blood covering the tiles. He was oblivious to the pain, as he scrambled to his feet.

Suddenly in front of him, Don kicked out, catching Max square in his naked balls with his leather combat boot. Then, he brought his knee up. It connected with Max's chin.

Max crumpled back to the tiles. As he landed, sharp pain made him examine his legs. Lumps of glass had torn into the flesh of his knees and shins. When he looked up, it was too late to react. The torch smashed into his skull.

Don dropped the torch, and his body sagged in relief. He staggered backwards to the wall, sliding down into a squat.

That had been a fight and a half. He had new respect for Maxwell-fucking-Myers, who now lay unconscious, covered in blood and glass, on the tiles. He'd expected the Nancy-boy to crumple after the first whack, but he hadn't—he'd put up a fucking good battle.

Don hadn't felt this exhilarated since Afghanistan.

Forcing himself to move, Don hurried back to the office and wheeled the chair through to the bathroom. He lifted the naked man onto it, and used the cable ties to secure the bloodied ankles and wrists. He smiled at all the cubes of glass protruding from Max's skin. Don knew when Max came around, the pain would be unbearable. He looked forward to that.

Max opened his eyes to a spinning room. Eventually, his feet came into focus. They were a mess—sliced, cut, and bloody. He tried to move his head, but the pain was too intense. "Fuck!" he cried out in agony.

When he attempted to lift his hand to block out some of the bright light, he couldn't move. He realised he was fastened to a chair.

He squinted, and spotted Don leaning against the wall opposite. "You crazy bastard. What the fuck's wrong with you?" Max couldn't bear the excruciating pain a moment longer. His head flopped forwards once more.

After a short while, he roused himself again.

Don hadn't moved. He just sat staring at him, showing no emotion.

"You're not gonna get away with this, you know—you sick fuck!"

Don stood up, raising his torch high above his head.

"No! No, don't, Don. Please. No more." He closed his eyes tight, and braced himself for the impact.

CHAPTER 46

Max had no idea how long he'd been out. Don was gone. The pain in his head throbbed like a bitch. He was certain that last whack had done permanent damage.

He scanned the room for something to help get him out of the chair. He kept a pair of scissors in the drawer, but there was no way he'd be able to make it over there.

The sound of whistling alerted Max that Don was on his way back. Max recognised the tune—he'd heard it many times as a child. *The Teddy Bears' Picnic*. The crazy bastard had totally lost his marbles.

Don appeared in the doorway. "Ah, so you're awake—I was looking for something which might get you to open your eyes— it's no fun torturing an unconscious person."

"Why are you doing this, Don? Please—just tell me."

"Because you think you can do what the fuck you like, with no comeback."

"I told you. Cheryl was mistaken. The job was yours."

"Do you really think I believed any of that fucking bullshit? You were just trying to shut me up—get me out of your face."

"Honestly, Don. The job was yours. Could still be yours, if you just let me go."

Don chuckled, shaking his head. "And what? You'd forget all about this, would you? Greet me in the corridor tomorrow morning, and bid me good day?"

"It may be strained at first, but yes. I'd be willing to try, if you stop this right now." He wanted to scream, *YOU FUCKING MANIAC,* but he couldn't. His only hope was to convince the crazy son-of-a-bitch to let him go!

"But, what about the others? Are you willing to forgive what I did to them?"

Max's stomach dropped. Visions of Hannah immediately sprang to mind. "What others?"

He grinned. "Ah, well, let me see. Now, first there was Steve. The stupid bastard thought he could get one over on me. Sneaking around and creeping up on me, as though I didn't know he was there! Me! I'm a trained soldier, for fuck's sake. But, I waited, let him think he'd caught me red-handed, and then, boom!"

Max winced. He'd never suspected someone else might be responsible for Steve's death.

"Oh, the sound he made when he splattered at the bottom of that lift shaft was harmonic."

Tears streamed down Max's face, he couldn't stop them.

"And who was next? Ah, yes, Simon Fowler. Hannah's next door neighbour."

"What? I don't…"

"You ought to be thanking me for him. Did you know he fucked our lovely Hannah every which way possible? For hours, they were at it. Like dirty fucking rabbits." Don's eyes lit up, and he laughed. "Fucking rabbits…do you get it?"

Max closed his eyes, everything suddenly making sense. "You planted that stuff in Angela's locker, didn't you?"

"Sheer stroke of genius, that. Your lake house is nice, by the way. I thought yours was the front cottage at first, but no—I should've known Maxwell-fucking-Myers only has the biggest and best of everything. Sorry about the bed—it looked like it would've been a comfy mattress."

The intense fury Max felt was dampened by the need to close his eyes. He'd lost a lot of blood, but it was the head injury he was worried about.

"Don't go to sleep, Max. I'm getting to the best bit." Don shoved Max's forehead, making his head flop backwards.

Max winced.

"You're pretty tough for a Nancy-boy, aren't you? Anyway, where was I? Ah, yes. The doctor."

Max opened one eye. He stared at Don.

Don nodded. "Yeah. That was me. She seemed nice. Pity, but the silly bitch spotted me coming out of Hannah's flat, and so she had to go. I made it quick. She didn't suffer."

"How? Why were you not seen on the hospital cameras?"

"I went in the back way, stayed far to the left of the corridors, and walked around every area. A man in a security uniform is rarely spotted, or questioned. You're forgetting—I'm an expert at this. My training was intense and complete. Mostly, I was chosen to infiltrate gangs and gather intelligence, because of the way I look. I'm so ordinary in appearance people rarely remember my face unless they've seen me several times. She did though. Diane. She remembered my face."

Max's head lolled forwards again. There was a strange buzzing sound in one of his ears. "You're completely loopy," he slurred.

"When Hannah's sweet, and very fucking sexy…" Don nodded incredulously. "…mother saw me. I knew she had to be next. I regret that one, because, as I've just said, the odds on her recognising me were negligible."

"She's not dead," Max said. But, it sounded more like, 'Seeznotdead.'

"She's not dead? Open your eyes, you fuckwit." Don prodded at him again. "Did you say she's not dead?"

Max nodded slightly, his eyes still shut.

"That's great news. I wanted to fuck that woman so badly, I've regretted killing her ever since."

Max tried to lift his head. Only one eye would open fully, but he wanted to smash Don's face right in. Totally destroy the sanctimonious murdering bastard. "*Leaveherlone,*" he growled.

The phone rang on the other side of the door. Don pushed himself from his leaning position against the bathroom wall, and went in search of the sound. He appeared moments later, with the phone in his hand.

"Ah, it's Hannah."

The ringing stopped.

"Ooops. We missed it. Never mind. I'll send her a message." He began tapping at the phone. "Kinda tied up right now, sausage. Call you later," he said. "You do call her *sausage*, don't you? How sweet. There you go. Send." Don wiggled the phone in front of Max showing him the words, *MESSAGE SENT*, on the screen.

The phone buzzed.

Don glanced at it. "She says she's going to sleep, and she'll call you in the morning. Ahh, she sent you three kisses. Never mind, Max. I'll collect those kisses for you later."

Finding another surge of energy, Max lifted his one good eye, and fixed it on Don. "I'm bored of this, you sick fuck. Just get it over with, why don't you?"

"Bored? Oh, no, that won't do. Now, what else do I have up my sleeve? Ah, yes." Don pulled a yellow container from his pocket.

Max had neither the strength nor the inclination to read the label. He allowed his eyes to close once more. He needed sleep. A strange sensation at his bare pubic area startled him, and a fumy smell he recognised assaulted his nose. Lighter fluid.

Don laughed hysterically as Max tried to look at him.

The sight of Don holding a match against the strike area of the matchbox caused tremors to flow through Max. "Don't," was all he could manage.

"Not bored anymore! Are you?" He struck the match, and launched it to Max's crotch.

The pain was extraordinary. But, the stench of burning skin and hair caused Max to puke. A steady stream of yellow-tinged bile spewed from his lips, on to his knee, and ran down his leg.

"If your plan was to put the fire out, your aim was off by a couple of inches."

Max passed out.

Don had had enough. Max's pain threshold had been exceeded, and now, his body had gone into shock. He knew Max would feel nothing more tonight. His entertainment was at an end. He fitted the applicator onto the tube of gap filler. Then he prodded Max with the pointy end.

Max didn't react at first. He'd been unconscious for several minutes. Thick blood was oozing from his head, and his legs were dotted with cuts and lumps of glass. Yet it was the little blackened cock that thrilled Don the most.

With a shove in the shoulder, Max finally opened one eye.

"Open wide, Maxwell. Say, ahhhhh."

Max just groaned.

Don shoved the point of the tube in between Max's lips and pushed. The plastic felt resistance from the teeth, but with a further shove, it entered his mouth.

"Shame you're not more *compos mentis*, Maxie-boy. I'd have loved to watch you struggle with this." He pressed the clip of the applicator. The hissing sound reminded Don of squirty cream. He knew the foam started out liquid, and would only thicken and expand as it came into contact with air. Each attempted breath would assist the gap filler to live up to its name.

Apart from a few body tremors, Max didn't move, or make another sound.

Once his mouth and throat were filled to capacity, the foam began to exit from his nostrils.

Maxwell-fucking-Myers was dead.

CHAPTER 47

Wasting no time, Don wiped all his fingerprints down. He had a bruise on his cheek, where Max had punched him earlier, which might cause a problem later on.

He headed for the stairs. On the tenth floor, he took the lift down to the ground floor.

After ducking into the bathroom to double-check his appearance, he approached Ken on the desk.

Ken jumped to his feet. "Oh, there you are, boss. I was just about to make a coffee. Can I get you one?"

Don shook his head. "Had another call from Mr Myers."

"Yeah? I thought he was coming in for the bag?"

"Seems he got held up, but it's important the bag is dropped off at Ms McLaughlin's flat tonight."

"Tonight?"

"Yeah—fucking pain in the arse. Anyway, he asked if you'd do it for him. He told me where to find the key. He said you can go home after, and he'll pay you for the full shift."

"Really?" The stupid man's eyes lit up.

"Yeah. So, go and get out of your uniform, and I'll find the key and the address for you."

"You don't mind? This would mean you being here the rest of the night alone."

"Doesn't take two of us, really, does it? What's the likelihood of something happening? I've been here years, and the only thing that's happened was when Steve fell down the lift shaft. And we weren't even aware of that."

"Okay, then. If you're sure. Thanks, boss. I'll get changed now."

Don pulled Simon's key off his key ring, and wrote the address down on a scrap of paper. He gave them to Ken when he reappeared a few minutes later, dressed in jeans and an old Status Quo T-shirt.

"So, Max said let yourself in, and wait for him, if he's not already there."

"Are you sure? This seems odd to me, Don."

"So... what? You think I'm making all this up?"

"No, but..."

Don pulled his phone from his pocket, and dialled Max's number. He turned the phone to Ken, as it began ringing. "Ask him yourself, if you like." The voicemail kicked in.

"Leave him a message, Ken. Tell him what you just told me."

Ken shoved the phone away. "No. Turn it off."

Don ended the call.

"Alright, I believe you. So, tell me again—what does he want me to do?"

"Let yourself in. If he's not there, wait a few minutes. Then, you can get yourself off home."

Ken nodded. "Okay."

Don escorted him to his car, and, once out of sight, he raced up to the staff lockers, opened Ken's with his lock pick tool, and swapped uniforms and torches. Although there was nothing on Don's uniform which could be detected with the naked eye, he had no doubt it would be covered in fibres placing him at the murder scene.

Then, he left the building. He knew he was taking a chance, but he had no choice.

He parked on the deserted road, and spotted Ken's dilapidated white Ford parked opposite. He took a length of rope from the car-boot, and stealthily headed up the stairs. Outside Simon's front door, Don arranged the rope. He knocked.

Ken opened the door seconds later, the broad grin on his face was replaced with confusion. "Boss?"

Don stepped forwards pushing Ken inside and up the hallway. "Been a change of plan, apparently, mate."

Ken had his back to Don, as he entered the kitchen. He didn't see the sucker punch coming. With a groan, Ken dropped to the floor.

"Lights out," Don said. He knew dealing with Ken would be easy, but not *that* easy.

Putting the makeshift noose over Ken's head, he dragged him by the arm to the balcony, where he tied the other end of the rope to the railing.

Ken was heavier than Don expected. Getting him up and over the railing proved difficult. But, not impossible. When he let go, Ken dropped rapidly. Once the rope reached its limit, the sickening crack of Ken's neck bones could be heard from where Don stood looking down.

Almost done.

He swept through the flat, wiping and clearing anything he may have touched or could be traced back to him. Then, he switched on Simon's computer, opening the live feeds from Hannah's flat and Max's lake house, and left them running for someone to find.

He raced back to AdCor.

When he arrived, he was relieved nothing seemed untoward. He headed for the hub, where he rewound the camera footage for the entire building back to the exact point Ken turned off the fifteenth floor.

Then, Don called Max. It went straight to voicemail.

"Sorry to call so late, Mr Myers. It's Don Henry here. I tried to call earlier, too, but there was no answer. I've had no choice but to make a decision alone. Earlier this evening, we had the same problem as last night on the fifteenth floor. Ken closed off the alarms up there, but in the process, he somehow managed to shut off all surveillance cameras in the entire building. When I confronted him, he was standoffish, and actually punched me in the face. I had no option but to stand him down. I'll write it in the day book, and fill out an incident report. If you need me to do anything else, please give me a call back. Goodnight, sir."

Don hung up, and grinned. Then, heading down to the front desk, he sat, put his feet up, and waited for his shift to end.

CHAPTER 48

Hannah was thrilled to wake up, and find her mother's eyes open.

She gently hugged her. "Oh, Mammy, you don't know how happy I am you're alright."

"Come on, let go of her now, sweetheart," her father said.

Hannah glanced at him, relieved he, too, seemed to be back to his usual self.

Her mother couldn't remember much of what happened. She said she woke to someone holding a cushion over her face, and then blackness. But, that was enough of a description to confirm to the police what Hannah already knew—it was no accident.

Her mother couldn't talk properly. Her throat was sore and scratchy, and although she'd done nothing but sleep for days, she was still exhausted. But, the specialists were confident she'd make a full recovery, in time.

Hannah tried Max's phone, but there was still no answer. She thought it strange he hadn't called her back this morning after his message last night.

She called Detective Owens, and left a message to say her mother had woken, and confirmed somebody had put a cushion over her face.

Hannah was fidgety. Now her mother was awake, she wanted to scream it from the rooftops. Or, at the very least, let Max know.

"I might go home for a shower, Daddy. Do you want to come?" she said.

"No, I'm fine. I had a stand-up wash at the sink earlier. I'll be okay. You go, though."

"Okay, can I get you anything?"

Her mother lifted her fingers, and Hannah took her hand.

"What can I get you, Mammy?"

"*Polo mints*," her mother whispered.

Her mother always had a packet of mints on the go, either in her purse or her pocket.

"Of course. Anything else?"

The minimal effort of shaking her head seemed to take it out of her.

"You rest now, Mammy. I'll be back soon." Hannah kissed her mother's cool cheek, and hugged her father before leaving.

As she got into her car, she realised she wasn't permitted to go back to the flat, until she got the all clear from the detective. She tried his number again, but there was no answer. After leaving a message, she headed to AdCor. At least there she'd be able to kill two birds with one stone—take a shower, and catch up with Max.

When she arrived, emergency vehicles surrounded the front and side of the building.

Hannah entered via the car park entrance. It was just as chaotic inside. A police cordon was in effect, and nobody was permitted to enter the building.

"What's happened?" she said to a woman she recognised from her floor.

"Apparently, they've found a body."

"What? Another one?"

The woman's eyebrows raised in confirmation.

"Who is it this time? Do you know?"

"Not really. I've heard a few whispers, but nothing has been confirmed."

Hannah called Max again. When there was still no answer, she left a voicemail message. "Max, I'm downstairs. What the hell's happened? Call me."

Her phone rang, and Max's name flashed on the screen.

"Max! Thank God. I'm downstairs. Nobody's allowed in. What's happened?"

"Who am I speaking to, please?" a woman said. Hannah's heartbeat thudded in her ears. "Hannah-Hannah McLaughlin. Who are you? Where's Max?"

"Hannah, are you a relation of Mr Myers?"

"I'm his girlfriend. Why? Would you please tell me what's going on?"

"Where are you? I'll send an officer down to escort you inside."

Not five minutes later, the geeky detective she'd met at the hospital appeared at her side. "Can you come with me, miss?"

On the ground floor, dozens of detectives, uniformed cops, and scene of crime officers were milling about. The young detective led her to a staff room off the main area.

"Take a seat. Someone will be with you shortly."

A woman with shaggy dark hair and kind eyes appeared, wearing tight black trousers and a fitted blue shirt. "Ms. McLaughlin, I'm Lucy Ward. Take a seat, please."

Hannah did as she was asked. "Where's Max?"

"You're his girlfriend? Right?"

Hannah nodded.

"Can you tell me who Mr Myers' next of kin would be?"

"Er, possibly his best friend, Lenny. Has something happened to Max?"

"I'm sorry." The detective reached for Hannah's hand, and held it tight. "Maxwell Myers was found dead this morning."

The screams escaping Hannah made her feel woozy and light-headed. She vaguely remembered the woman helping her down to the carpet. She lay curled in a foetal position for what seemed like ages.

The detective left at one point, but returned soon after, with a blanket and pillow that had the ambulance logo on them.

A younger woman brought in a tray bearing two cups of coffee.

"Do you think you could answer a couple of questions now, Hannah?"

She nodded. Feeling spaced out, she shuffled to her feet, and returned to the chair. "How can he be dead? I only spoke to him last night."

"I know. It's a lot to take in, Hannah. But, it appears a man called Ken Barber has been behind all the recent occurrences."

"You mean the break in at the lake?"

She nodded. "Everything, including the attack on your mother."

"Oh my fucking God! Why?"

"We're still looking into it, but up to now, it appears he was infatuated with you."

"Me? I don't even know him."

"He worked here as a security guard."

"I only know Don."

"It's not surprising. Most stalkers worship their subject from afar. Nine times out of ten the object of their affections will never lay eyes on them."

Hannah buried her head in her hands, and tore at her hair. "It doesn't make sense," she shrieked, jumping to her feet. "Why the fuck would he *do* this?"

"That's also unclear, sorry. But, he left a list of names in the day book."

"Names?" Hannah paced backwards and forwards in the tiny room.

The detective checked her notes. "Steven Miller, who I believe was Head of Security."

Hannah nodded.

"Simon Fowler."

"He's my neighbour. He went back to America."

"Did he? Was it sudden?"

"Very."

"And did you see him before he left?"

"I saw him the night before, but he left in the early hours of the next day. Apparently, he got some bad news about his grandmother."

The detective nodded at the geeky man, who Hannah hadn't noticed was still standing by the door.

"How about Diane Nagel?"

Hannah gasped. "She was my other neighbour. Someone murdered her at Cheadle Royal Infirmary. She was a doctor."

"Agnes McLaughlin is your mother, I believe?"

Hannah nodded, more tears streamed down her face.

"And Maxwell Myers."

Hannah couldn't speak.

"It appears to be a list of deceased people, excluding Simon Fowler, at this stage. And each one is closely connected to you."

"H-how did Max die?" she asked quietly, not even sure she wanted to know.

The detective looked down at her hands for a moment and then took a deep breath. "It appears he had been tortured over several hours, but he ultimately died of suffocation."

"Oh, no!" she cried. "My poor, poor Max. I should have allowed him to call me back last night. I said I was going to bed. Now, I'll never get to speak to him." She wiped her face with her sleeve and sobbed.

"When did you last speak to Max?" The detective asked softly when Hannah finally looked up again.

"Yesterday morning. We came here from the hospital to get some sleep, and then, he got a call just after eleven. Something to do with a campaign. He rushed off saying he'd call me later." Hannah rubbed her face again. "I tried to call him several times throughout the day, but last night, I tried again, just before Daddy and I settled down for the night. Max didn't answer, but I got a text right after, saying he was busy, and he'd call me back."

"What time was that?"

Hannah couldn't think. "Hang on." She checked her phone. "Ten thirty-two."

The detective's head shot up. "Are you sure?"

"Yeah. It's right there, if you don't believe me." She handed over the phone.

The detective frowned, as she read the message.

"What? What's wrong?"

"I think this message was sent by the killer. We know Max's ordeal began around seven, and continued for several hours."

"But..." Hannah shook her head. "But, he called me 'sausage.'"

"I'm afraid he was probably making a joke. Possibly taunting Max, at the time. You see, he says, *'I'm tied up right now.'* Max had been tied to a chair for hours."

"No!" Hannah cried. "I went to sleep, content I'd got hold of him, and all the while, poor Max was being..." She couldn't continue. Deep, racking sobs shook her to the core.

The detective put her arm around Hannah, and allowed her to cry.

A sudden thought struck Hannah. "Do you know where this man is? I need to get back to the hospital. Mammy isn't safe. What if he tries again?"

"Ken Barber took his own life last night. He hung himself from your neighbour's balcony. We found a number of surveillance cameras in your flat, and, we believe, at a lake house owned by Mr Myers."

"So, he's dead?"

The detective nodded.

With a sigh, Hannah sat back down on the chair.

"We also need someone to formally identify Mr Myers' body. I don't suppose you..."

Hannah shuddered. "No. Not me. But, I know someone who will." She took her phone off the detective, and located the number.

The ringing tone was halted by a surprised female voice. "Hannah?"

"Angela? I'm so sorry to tell you this, but Max is dead." Hannah didn't mean for her words to sound so brutal.

Angela was devastated. She hung up soon after, saying she was on her way.

It seemed only minutes later, Angela rushed in.

Hannah jumped to her feet at the sight of her. "I'm so sorry, Angela. We blamed you, but Max was always certain you'd never do anything to harm him."

Angela's face was wet with tears. She held her arms out, and Hannah stepped forward, hugging the older woman.

As Hannah expected, Angela organised everything. She identified Max's body, and contacted Lenny and Charmaine. Then she assisted the police with the security footage.

Apparently, the night before, Don had reported Ken for switching off all the cameras, but Ken had made a huge error. The final images on the tapes showed him heading towards Max's flat, and coming out over an hour later carrying Hannah's gym bag. Then, he headed into the security hub, and turned off all the cameras.

"Never was the sharpest tool in the shed," Angela said. "But, I wouldn't have thought he was capable of this."

"I've honestly never set eyes on this man before," Hannah said, shaking her head. "And to think he's been in my flat—in my bed—through all of my things. I just feel so dirty."

Angela comforted her, never once leaving her side.

Later that afternoon, it was confirmed Simon's body had been found in the chest freezer of his flat.

EPILOGUE

Hannah couldn't face staying at her flat. Instead, Angela helped her clear out all her belongings. Then, Hannah handed the keys back to the agent. She wasn't sad to leave. She left flowers on Diane and Simon's doorsteps.

Hannah knew if she hadn't moved to the city, all these people would still be going about their day-to-day lives. She wasn't responsible, but that didn't make the guilt go away.

She spent a couple of nights with Angela, and they'd grown close in that short time. But, Hannah would never forgive herself for falsely accusing her, although Angela didn't seem to hold a grudge.

Once her mother was discharged, they spent a night in a hotel, awaiting Max's funeral. She intended to go home with her parents afterward.

On the day of the funeral, it broke her heart to see Lenny and Charmaine. They hugged and sobbed for what seemed like hours. None of them could speak.

Thanks to Angela, the funeral was lovely. She chose a classic, ornate white casket, with not a marker pen in sight.

It tore her heart out to say goodbye to her beautiful, funny man—her soulmate, of that she had no doubt.

After the service, she mingled for a while, but she felt out of place. Max would understand. He knew how much she hated that kind of thing.

After saying her goodbyes to Angela, Lenny, and Charmaine, she signalled to her parents it was time to leave.

Outside the front of the building, she saw a man she recognised but couldn't place, leaning against the wall, smoking a cigarette.

"Hello, Hannah," he said.

"Don! I barely recognised you out of your uniform."

He smiled sadly. "That happens a lot."

"How are you?"

"Not coping very well, to be honest. I feel responsible."

"Oh, you silly thing. Come here." She wrapped her arms around his neck, and hugged him tight. Then, kissing his cheek, she pulled away. "It was no more your fault than mine. And believe me, I've blamed myself enough. But, the truth is, Ken was crazy."

"You ready, Hannah?" her dad called.

"I have to go. I'm glad I got to see you before I left."

"Are you going home?"

She nodded. "Back to my parents'. I'm looking forward to boring, for a while." She waved. "Take care, Don."

The following weeks and months passed in a flash. Anybody who knew Hannah would say she was just the same as before. But, she wasn't—it was just easier to go along with things. All her old friends rallied around her, and tried to include her in activities whenever they could. She helped her mother make her preserves and sold them on the weekend. But, a part of her had died along with Max that night. The worst part was none of her friends or family had known him. Her parents had met him, but discouraged any mention of his name. She knew, in their hearts, they were looking out for her, but that wasn't what she needed.

Her closest friend turned out to be Angela. Hannah called her every night from her bedroom. They would talk for hours, telling funny stories, mostly about Max. Hannah found that therapeutic.

Six months later, she was offered her old job back. She knew Angela had been behind it, but she snatched the opportunity with both hands.

And, on her first day at work, she finally felt she did indeed have a future. Maybe not with Max, although she knew he'd never be far from her thoughts. But, she did have a future,

Old Mr Turnbull's eyes sparkled when he welcomed her back, and she felt genuine affection for the team. Like a well-worn sweater, she fit just right.

"Okay, that'll be all," Mr Turnbull said, after everyone had settled down. "She's back for good now, and we're expecting her to have picked up some magic tips from the city. Hannah, you know where your office is."

She smiled. "I do. Thanks, everyone."

In her office, she set about putting everything in its place. Someone tapped on her door, and she smiled and turned. "No need to kn…" Her words caught in her throat. "Don!" she gasped.

"Hello, stranger."

She rushed into his arms. "I'm so pleased to see you. Angela told me you'd gone travelling."

He nodded. "I breezed into Shropshire a couple of weeks ago, and heard about the vacancy."

"You work here?"

"Don't sound so surprised." He laughed.

"No, I'm not. I'm thrilled. You must come to dinner, sometime."

The End

Find out what happens next in *The Lodger*.
Grab your copy NOW!

ACKNOWLEDGMENTS

As always, I need to mention Paul, my long suffering husband. Your support means the world to me.

To my wonderful critique partners Susan, Marco, Jay, Sandra & Serena—you're the best.

To Mel, Ross, and all my friends and fellow authors—thanks so much for letting me bend your ear.

The wonderful ARC group – you're awesome.

To all the team at Junction Publishing - you are amazing!

And finally. To my wonderful family, especially Joshua, David, AJ, and Marley, my lovely grandsons, who give me immense joy. I am truly blessed.

ABOUT THE AUTHOR

 My name's Netta Newbound. I write thrillers in many different styles — some grittier than others. The Cold Case Files have a slightly lighter tone. I also write a series set in London, which features one of my favourite characters, Detective Adam Stanley. My standalone books, The Watcher, Maggie, My Sister's Daughter and An Impossible Dilemma, are not for the faint hearted, and it seems you either love them or hate them—I'd love to know what you think.

If you would like to be informed when my new books are released, visit my website: www.nettanewbound.com and sign up for the newsletter.

This is a PRIVATE list and I promise you I will only send emails when a new book is released or a book goes on sale.

If you would like to get in touch, you can contact me via Facebook or Twitter. I'd love to hear from you and try to respond to everyone.

f 🐦

ALSO BY NETTA NEWBOUND

Behind Shadows

Amanda Flynn's life is falling apart. Her spineless cheating husband has taken her beloved children. Her paedophile father, who went to prison vowing revenge, has been abruptly released. And now someone in the shadows is watching her every move.

When one by one her father and his cohorts turn up dead, Amanda finds herself at the centre of several murder investigations—with no alibi and a diagnosis of Multiple Personality Disorder. Abandoned, scared and fighting to clear her name as more and more damning evidence comes to light, Amanda begins to doubt her own sanity.

Could she really be a brutal killer?

A gripping psychological thriller not to be missed...

Positively Murder

An Edge of your Seat Psychological Thriller Novel

For Melissa May, happily married to Gavin for the best part of thirty years, life couldn't get much better. Her world is ripped apart when she discovers Gavin is HIV positive. The shock of his duplicity and irresponsible behaviour re-awakens a psychiatric condition Melissa has battled since childhood. Fuelled by rage and a heightened sense of right and wrong, Melissa takes matters into her own hands.

Homicide detective Adam Stanley is investigating what appear to be several random murders. When evidence comes to light, linking the victims, the case seems cut and dried and an arrest is made. However, despite all the damning evidence, including a detailed confession, Adam s certain the killer is still out there. Now all he has to do is prove it.

Mind Bender

An Edge of your Seat Psychological Thriller Novel

Detective Inspector Adam Stanley returns to face his most challenging case yet. Someone is randomly killing ordinary Pinevale citizens. Each time DI Stanley gets close to the killer, the killer turns up dead—the next victim in someone's crazy game.

Meanwhile, his girlfriend's brother, Andrew, currently on remand for murder, escapes and kidnaps his own 11-year-old daughter. However, tragedy strikes, leaving the girl in grave danger.

Suffering a potentially fatal blow himself, how can DI Stanley possibly save anyone?

Prima Facie

A Compelling Psychological Thriller Novel.

In this fast-moving suspense novel, Detective Adam Stanley searches for Miles Muldoon, a hardworking, career-minded businessman, and Pinevale's latest serial killer.

Evidence puts Muldoon at each scene giving the police a prima facie case against him.

But as the body count rises, and their suspect begins taunting them, this seemingly simple case develops into something far more personal when Muldoon turns his attention to Adam and his family.

Ghost Writer is a 24,000 word novella.

Bestselling thriller author Natalie Cooper has a crippling case of writer's block. With her deadline looming, she finds the only way she can write is by ditching her laptop and reverting back to pen and paper. But the story which flows from the pen is not just another work of fiction.

Unbeknown to her, a gang of powerful and deadly criminals will stop at nothing to prevent the book being written.

Will Natalie manage to finish the story and expose the truth before it's too late? Or could the only final chapter she faces be her own?

Embellished Deception

A Gripping and Incredibly Moving Psychological Suspense Novel

When Geraldine MacIntyre's marriage falls apart, she returns to her childhood home expecting her mother to welcome her with open arms. Instead, she finds all is not as it should be with her parents.

James Dunn, a successful private investigator and crime writer, is also back in his hometown, to help solve a recent spate of vicious rapes. He is thrilled to discover his ex-classmate, and love of his life, Geraldine, is back, minus the hubby, and sets out to get the girl. However, he isn't the only interested bachelor in the quaint, country village. Has he left it too late?

Embellished Deception is a thrilling, heart-wrenching and thought provoking story of love, loss and deceit.

Conflicted Innocence

An Edge of your Seat Psychological Thriller Novel

Geraldine and baby Grace arrive in Nottingham to begin their new life with author James Dunn.

Lee Barnes, James' best friend and neighbour, is awaiting the imminent release of his wife, Lydia, who has served six years for infanticide. But he's not as prepared as he thought. In a last ditch effort to make things as perfect as possible his already troubled life takes a nose dive.

Geraldine and James combine their wits to investigate several historical, unsolved murders for James' latest book. James is impressed by her keen eye and instincts. However, because of her inability to keep her mouth shut, Geri, once again, finds herself the target of a crazed and vengeful killer.

Grave Injustice

A Gripping Psychological Suspense Novel.

Geri and James return in their most explosive adventure to date.

When next door neighbour, Lydia, gives birth to her second healthy baby boy, James and Geri pray their friend can finally be happy and at peace. But, little do they know Lydia's troubles are far from over.

Meanwhile, Geri is researching several historic, unsolved murders for

James' new book. She discovers one of the prime suspects now resides in Spring Pines Retirement Village, the scene of not one, but two recent killings.

Although the police reject the theory, Geri is convinced the cold case they're researching is linked to the recent murders. But how? Will she regret delving so deeply into the past?

Maggie

Do you love **gripping psychological thrillers** full of twists and turns? If so you'll love **best-selling** author Netta Newbound's stunning new *Maggie*.

When sixteen-year-old Maggie Simms' mum loses her battle with cancer, the only family she has left is her **abusive stepfather**, Kenny.

Horrified to discover he intends to continue his nightly abuse, Maggie is **driven to put a stop to him once and for all**.

However, she **finds her troubles are only just beginning** when several of her closest allies are killed.

Although nothing seems to be linking the deaths, Maggie believes she is jinxed.

Why are the people she cares about being targeted?

And who is really behind the murders?

Sometimes the truth is closer than you think.

An Impossible Dilemma

Would you choose to save your child if it meant someone else had to die?

Victoria and Jonathan Lyons seem to have everything—a perfect marriage, a beautiful daughter, Emily, and a successful business. Until they discover Emily, aged five, has a rare and fatal illness.

Medical trials show that a temporary fix would be to transplant a hormone from a living donor. However in the trials the donors die within twenty four hours. Victoria and Jonathan are forced to accept that their daughter is going to die.

In an unfortunate twist of fate Jonathan is suddenly killed in a farming accident and Victoria turns to her sick father-in-law, Frank, for help. Then a series of events present Victoria and Frank with a situation that, although illegal, could save Emily.

Will they take their one chance and should they?

Mother Knows Best

An Edge of your Seat Psychological Thriller Novella

All her life twenty-two-year-old Ruby Fitzroy's annoyingly over protective mother has believed the worst will befall one of her two daughters. Sick and tired of living in fear, Ruby arranges a date without her mother's knowledge.

On first impressions, charming and sensitive Cody Strong seems perfect. When they visit his home overlooking the Welsh coast, she meets his delightful father Steve and brother Kyle. But it isn't long before she discovers all is not as it seems.

After a shocking turn of events, Ruby's world is blown apart. Terrified and desperate, she prepares to face her darkest hour yet.

Will she ever escape this nightmare?

Made in the USA
Las Vegas, NV
13 June 2023

73386569R00182